OUR MARRIAGE IS MURDER

ALSO BY CAROL GOODMAN

The Lake of Dead Languages
The Seduction of Water
The Drowning Tree
The Ghost Orchid
The Sonnet Lover
The Night Villa
Arcadia Falls
River Road
The Widow's House
The Other Mother
The Night Visitors
The Sea of Lost Girls
The Stranger Behind You
The Disinvited Guest
The Bones of the Story
Return to Wyldcliffe Heights
Writers and Liars

CHILDREN'S AND YOUNG ADULT

Blythewood
Ravencliffe
Hawthorn
The Metropolitans

AS JULIET DARK

The Demon Lover
The Water Witch
The Angel Stone

AS LEE CARROLL (WITH LEE SLONIMSKY)

Black Swan Rising
The Watchtower
The Shape Shifter

OUR MARRIAGE IS MURDER

A Novel

CAROL GOODMAN

WILLIAM MORROW
An Imprint of HarperCollins*Publishers*

HarperCollins books may be purchased for educational, business, or sales promotional use. For information, please email the Special Markets Department at SPsales@harpercollins.com.

hc.com

FIRST EDITION

Interior text design by Diahann Sturge-Campbell

Castle image © stefanotermanini/Stock.Adobe.com

Library of Congress Cataloging-in-Publication Data has been applied for.

ISBN 978-0-06-339878-8

ISBN 978-0-06-339882-5 (simultaneous hardcover edition)

Printed in the United States of America

26 27 28 29 30 LBC 5 4 3 2 1

To Lee,
Partner in Crime,
ita scribendo atque vivendo

OUR MARRIAGE IS MURDER

CHAPTER ONE

We are 36,000 feet above the Atlantic Ocean when my husband asks me to plan a murder.

"How about defenestration from the top of the bell tower?"

"Didn't we do that already in *Death Takes the Castle*?" I counter.

He rolls his eyes and I notice that he looks tired. Usually by this point in the flight he'd have his footrest up, his eye mask on, and be out until landing, but something has him on edge. Hence the murder plotting, an activity that has always soothed him. "We'll be hard-pressed to find a murder method we haven't used. We've littered the globe with our victims."

"The tour of the bell tower isn't on the itinerary until the second day and that's a bit long to wait for the first murder," I point out, which only causes more eye rolling. He's always made fun of my itineraries along with my outlines. Fred is the original pantser, while I am the die-hard plotter, in writing as in life, which might as well be the motto for our mystery series, Death Takes a Holiday. We should have it translated into Latin and use it for the epigraph of our next book. I open my notebook and scribble down a note: *Translate into Latin: "In Writing as in Life." What's the Latin word for writing? In scriptis?* My college Latin professor would be appalled at how much I've forgotten.

"Plotting a murder, Thea?" Fred asks hopefully.

"Yes," I lie, shutting my notebook before he can see anything else. "I think the first murder should be poison by Aperol Spritz at the reception."

"Let me guess, in a drink meant for someone else?"

"Of course—or at least that's what's assumed—"

"Like in *Triangle at Rhodes*," he says.

"Yes," I agree warily. Fred always cites Agatha Christie when he wants something from me. "That was a Pink Gin."

"Isn't that how the first victim dies in *Death Takes the Castle*?" he asks.

"Oh," I say, abashed that I'd forgotten. Usually, I'm the one who keeps track of our past books and maintains the series "bible." I eye his leather satchel, tucked into the seat back pouch, suspiciously. "Is that a copy of *Death Takes the Castle*?" I ask. "Have you been rereading it?"

"Guilty," he says, blushing as if he really had committed a crime. He once told me he couldn't bear to reread our books. "Deb asked me to help her with the treasure hunt for the conference. She's basing it on clues in *Death Takes the Castle*."

"Really?" I ask, surprised and a little hurt. Deb Andersen, retired librarian and executive director of International Murder Writers, is an old friend and one of my favorite people in the industry. "Why didn't she ask me?"

"You mean because you're the official historian and I'm so unreliable?"

"I didn't mean—"

He holds up a hand to halt my clarification. "She asked me because she didn't want to bother you. She figured you were too busy working on the last novel's revision with *Aleister.*"

Fred pronounces the name of our editor with his usual note of disdain. He's never made a secret of his feelings about him, which is why I've been the point person on editorial communications, making me the middleman, the bearer of bad news, apologist, and peacemaker. It's also why I talked to Aleister about my decision before talking to Fred, which I feel guilty about. But Fred has been unusually unavailable, almost as if he's been avoiding me all summer, and yes, I had been busy getting ready for this trip and editing our last novel and finishing the outline for the next book, but it still stings a little that Deb asked Fred instead of me. Now we're on a plane headed to Italy for this year's MurderCon, where we have been nominated for the prestigious Poirot Prize for Best Mystery Series. Aleister will be at the conference (he and our agent, Penelope, are behind us in business class) and I can't risk Fred finding out I told Aleister about my decision first. Besides, Fred will know as soon as I show him the outline for the next book.

"Look," I begin, turning to my writing partner and husband of twenty years. "There's something I have to tell you—"

The plane lurches as if the pilot, too, were wary of Fred's reaction to my news. Does he think Fred will respond by hijacking the plane and demanding we fly back to New York? It's what Rick Charles, Fred's alter ego in the Death Takes a Holiday series, does in *Death Takes a Spin*, but that was only a little Cessna. Even Rick Charles, former Navy SEAL, kung fu black belt, and—let's face it—*fictional* hero, would have second thoughts about taking over a Boeing 767 jet.

"Are you okay?" he asks with a solicitude I haven't heard from him in a while. "Do you need a Xanax? I know flying makes you anxious."

"It's not the flight," I say truthfully, although now that he mentions it, a Xanax would not go amiss. "It's the announcement at the reception. I told PR that I didn't like the idea of doing it on our first day—"

"And?" he interrupts. "Why is it still in the schedule? If I'd known how you felt about it, I'd have talked to Ava and insisted we reschedule."

And, of course, Ava, the head of publicity, would have listened to him because she has a soft spot for Fred and also because when a man asks for something, he gets it, while a woman just gets a reputation for being difficult. Fred has long maintained that I'm a pushover, but what he doesn't understand is how often I have greased the wheels behind the scenes—soothed bruised egos, explained away Fred's snits—to get what we needed from our publishing company.

"*And* she explained that the first day at the conference would be our best opportunity for press coverage. Announcing that we're returning to Castellarosa for our"—I stop myself before saying *last*—"*next* book will garner a lot of goodwill in the Italian press."

"I don't understand why we need it," he says, downing the last of his (second? third?) scotch. "The books sell. Why else would we have gotten this nomination?"

I could show him our declining sales on BookScan (I have a spreadsheet) and explain that we've gotten the award not just because the books are good (*most of them*), but because of all the years we've put in at this conference and others, all the hours we've spent (or rather, *I* have spent while Fred hangs out at the bar) arranging panels, mentoring newbies, judging contests, blurbing up-and-coming authors (some of whom have done so well that we've had to beg blurbs off them in turn), tweeting, retweeting, posting, reposting, and generally being attentive to our readers and supporting our fellow mystery writers. This is how the industry rewards its team players.

Not that the Death Takes a Holiday books aren't good. At least the first twelve were. Book #13, *Death Takes a Siesta,* nearly tanked our career. It was, according to a *Publishers Weekly* review burned into my amygdala, *as if we'd written it while asleep after a few too many shots of tequila*. Which was, to be fair, kind of true considering that one of us was asleep while the other was drinking a lot of tequila during the writing of that one. It had been an uphill climb after that disaster to reclaim our reputation and readership but we (meaning I) had done it through hard work and the goodwill of our editor, Aleister Crown. No series lasts forever, though, and the reviews and sales for the last book had been cautionary.

I don't say any of that because I know Fred will counter with competing statistics and a lecture on how statistics can be manipulated and how no one knows what they're doing in publishing anyway and didn't that reviewer at *PW* have it in for us? Besides, Agatha Christie wrote far more books than we have and no one complained when *she* was repetitive. All forms of magical thinking, but Fred is a persuasive debater and can argue me stupid. Instead, I remind him that we're contractually obligated to assist in publicizing the series.

"Besides," I say, "we might as well get the most we can out of this nomination. I—I've been thinking . . ." I pause, waiting for another altitude drop to interrupt me, but the plane glides smoothly through the upper atmosphere. *Damn.* "I've been thinking that this would be a good time to end things."

"What do you mean?" he asks, staring at me with those gray-blue eyes that show up so nicely in author photos. I realize that the way I've put it makes it sound like I'm talking about *ending myself*—that's the problem with writing about murder for twenty years; everything ends up being about death—and I start to clarify but the next thing out of his mouth tells me that my individual welfare and mental health are not his primary concern. "Are you talking about ending the series?"

"Well," I say, piqued into honesty at last, "Rick and Dora are getting a bit long in the tooth for the kind of hijinks we put them through. I'm afraid the series is getting a bit . . . *stale.*"

"Poirot lasted for thirty-three novels and over fifty short stories—"

"And poor Agatha Christie was so sick to death of him she killed him off in *Curtain* thirty-five years before the world let her get rid of him."

"She put the manuscript in a vault to be published after her death. Are you talking about killing off Rick and Dora? If you really want to do that, I'll be happy to hold on to the manuscript until after your death."

I raise an eyebrow, tempted to point out that women live longer and I'm a year younger than him, but instead opt for something less contentious. "We don't have to kill them. We could give them a happy retirement."

"You mean like a condo in Boca?" he shouts so loudly that the dozing passengers in the Delta One cabin stir beneath their puffy blankets and sleep masks.

"You're right," I say, "it might be more romantic if they go out in a blaze of glory." More romantic *and* more final, I think, leery that if we leave Rick and Dora alive our fans—and Fred—will plead for a sequel. "Think of how satisfying that would be to write. Rick could make a grand gesture to sacrifice himself for Dora. It could be like the end of *Butch Cassidy and the Sundance Kid*—"

"You want Rick and Dora to get shot to pieces at the end?"

"Well, maybe not anything that bloody; our readers don't go for gruesome. I just think it would be better to write them a great ending while they're at the top of their game—"

"You just said that sales were declining," he says in a warning voice that makes the hairs at the back of my neck prickle.

"Declining but not at rock bottom yet," I say. "If we write a great finale now with all the publicity from the nomination, the book will be a bestseller. We can bank the royalties—maybe even get a streaming deal out of it. You've always wanted to write for television. Or you could do something different—write that literary novel you were working on when we met—"

"I wrote *Death Takes the Castle* instead," he says.

"*We* wrote *Death Takes the Castle,*" I amend, bristling.

"I wrote the first draft," he counters.

"From my outline," I say, "and I did all the edits."

He shrugs. He's never thought much of my outlines or of the editing process. "You did make it more commercially viable," he concedes. "It could have been a great literary novel."

"Instead, it launched a twenty-book series and made us pretty comfortable financially," I point out, the last salvo in an argument we've had so many times that we could each recite our lines in our sleep. "But now you can go back to the kind of book you always wanted to write."

He stares at me, his eyes moving back and forth the way they do when he's calculating. I've reached him, I think. This won't be as hard as I feared. But instead of embracing the opportunity—*the freedom!*—I've offered him, he narrows his eyes and asks in a dangerously low growl, "Where is this coming from?"

"What do you mean?" I ask, feigning innocence.

"It's Aleister, isn't it," he accuses.

"No," I say truthfully. "Aleister doesn't want to end the series. Even if the sales are flagging, the new books sell the backlist—"

"You've discussed this with Aleister already?" he asks in a cold, flat voice. Mixed with the usual disdain is a note of jealousy I thought he had gotten past.

"Only because you haven't been available—Look," I say, laying my hand on his arm. His warm flesh sparks a memory of a shuttered room in San Miguel—the scent of mimosa, the coo of mourning doves, slatted light on bare flesh—that softens something in me. *Maybe this is a mistake,* a voice whispers in my ear, but then I recall what came after those magical nights in San Miguel and harden my resolve. "This isn't coming from Aleister or the publisher. It's coming from *me*. I can't keep on writing the series and pretending we have a real marriage. I want to end the series—and the ruse of our marriage."

MAYBE YOU'VE HEARD of us? Fred and Thea Morgan-Lane (it was Fred's idea to hyphenate our last names because he thought it made us sound like posh Brits, while I thought it made us sound like a law firm). Or maybe you know our alter egos, Rick and Dora Charles, the detective duo in the Death Takes a Holiday series. Our first novel, *Death Takes the Castle,* set in the Italian medieval walled village of Castellarosa, introduced Rick and Dora to each other and to the world. It won Best First Novel at the Edgars and Agathas that year and got us a lucrative five-book deal.

Castellarosa is also where Fred and I met. I was doing research for my doctoral dissertation on twelfth-century female scribes and medieval love poetry. I'd gone there because there was a legend attached to the castle that I thought might have inspired a poem by an anonymous twelfth-century poet. I'd been spending my days exploring the walled city, hiking in the surrounding forest of holm oaks and myrtle and hawthorn, picking violets and cyclamen and hellebore and pressing them into my notebook.

After having spent the last three years cloistered in a library researching my dissertation, I felt like I had been let loose into a living medieval millefleur tapestry. In the evenings I sat at an old taverna built into the city walls filling my notebooks—only not with the scholarly work I was meant to be writing. Instead, I began a story about a young medieval girl named Bianca Rosa who had fallen in love with a knight on his way to the Crusades and the modern woman who discovers her secret and sets her ghost free. A fairy tale. An indulgence, I thought. A warm-up for the academic book I was meant to be writing.

One night I realized I wasn't the only one writing at the taverna. There was a young man about my age, in jeans and a tattered denim shirt that perfectly matched his eyes, sitting at a little table in the corner, with his own notebook spread out in front of him. Only instead of writing he seemed to be spending most of his time staring into space—or, I realized when I lifted my gaze from my story to meet his denim-colored eyes, staring at me.

"*Mi dispiace*," he said in American-accented Italian, "I didn't mean to stare. It's just that I've never seen anyone so lost in their work. You must be writing a masterpiece."

"I have no idea what I'm writing," I admitted, "but it's certainly not the book I'm *supposed* to be writing."

"Ah," he said, tapping his forehead as if he saw deep into my head, "that's your secret. You're cheating on one book with another. No greater pleasure than the illicit."

I felt my face flame in the candlelight and thought about my dissertation adviser, Fraser Halliday, with whom I'd been having an illicit affair. I wasn't blushing because of the shame of that affair, though, but because I suddenly knew, looking into those deep blue eyes, that it was over. And then, because I was such a nerd that I always resorted to other sources when rattled, I quoted (from Proverbs, no less): "*Stolen water is sweeter and food eaten in secret tastes better.*"

He grinned back at me (he had one lopsided dimple, I noticed, and a slight gap between his front teeth). "Maybe that's what I need, too, to cheat on this book with another"—he raised his hand to one side of his mouth as if shielding his notebook from what he was saying—"because this one seems to be dead in the water."

"Ouch," I said, side-eyeing his notebook. "What did it die of? I think my dissertation has died of exposure to the sunlight like the bloodsucking vampire it is."

He laughed so hard he spit out his wine and thumped his hand on his notebook. "I wish someone would drive a stake through this monster's heart and put us both out of our misery."

He was writing a novel, I soon learned, and had been since dropping out of his MFA program (*Iowa, no less!*) three years before and taking to the road to write the great ex-pat bildungsroman. His models were Hemingway and Cervantes. He'd written some 200,000 words but still didn't have a plot.

"What you need," I told him, realizing over our second bottle of wine that it was what I needed, too, "is a murder."

CHAPTER TWO

I expect Fred to put up a fight when I mention ending our marriage but instead he holds out his hand. For mine? Is this a gesture of peace and reconciliation? Maybe he's as tired of Rick and Dora as I am and is ready to call it quits, too. But then he wiggles his fingers and says, "Hand it over," like he's Sam Spade ordering Brigid O'Shaughnessy to give up her gun. "The outline," he adds. "I know you've got one."

He's right, of course. Even that time I promised to go freestyle—"pantsing it"—for *Death Takes a Siesta* I secretly wrote an outline. I dig into my carry-on and retrieve a portfolio—robin's-egg-blue cardstock embossed with my initials and lined with hand-marbled paper that Fred bought at a Florentine *cartoleria* for our first anniversary (*the paper anniversary,* he'd said as he gave it to me, *which should be all our anniversaries*)—and hand it to him. He opens it up and rifles through the thirty-six single-spaced, color-coded typed pages with Roman numeral headings, footnotes, and citations, and takes out his reading glasses and red fountain pen (my fourth-anniversary present to him, the red rose etched on the cap qualifying it for the fruit and flower anniversary) and gets to work. I put on noise-canceling headphones, a sleeping mask, and take that Xanax. Once that red ink starts to flow, it's best to stay out of Fred's way.

WHEN I COME to, the cabin lights are back on and coffee is being served. My clothes are rumpled, my bra's come undone, and my mouth tastes literally like sour grapes from the Brunello I drank with the in-flight meal. I feel like I've been ravished but remember it's only my outline that's being plundered. Fred is sitting upright, clean-shaven in a crisp white button-down and the blue Italian merino-wool sweater I gave him for our seventh anniversary that year we stayed in Milan and wrote *Death Takes a Spin*. He smells like toothpaste and aftershave. *If you were a murderer,* I told him on our last day in San Miguel de Allende, *you'd be the cold-blooded sociopath type.* (*And you'd be Lizzie Borden with an ax,* he'd snarled back.) Right now, the only sign of the carnage that has taken place during the flight is a trace of red ink on his fingertips.

"Well?" I ask, despite my resolution not to this time.

"I have some notes," he says, handing me back my portfolio. At least it's in one piece. At least the red ink hasn't leaked out onto the surface. But when I open it up, I see that the pages are so crimson soaked it looks like they have been savaged by wild animals. Like the first murder victim in *Death Takes a Safari*.

I snort. "Was there anything you liked?"

"I decided you were right about the first murder," he concedes. "Death by Aperol Spritz it is."

"But, as you pointed out, that's how the first victim dies in *Death Takes the Castle.*"

"Exactly! It will be a nostalgic callback—in fact, what if *all* the murders are based on the ones in *Death Takes the Castle* because the murderer is deliberately baiting Rick and Dora? I've been thinking about it while working on the treasure map with Deb." He takes out his copy of *Death Takes the Castle,* which I see now is well thumbed and bristling with multicolored Post-it notes, and a folded map. It's a map of Castellarosa with *X*'s and scribbled notes all over it.

"Are those the clues to the treasure hunt?" I ask.

"Just notes," he says. "Deb wouldn't tell me where she was planting the clues, but she had some questions because she couldn't find all the places and objects that are in the book."

"Because we made them up," I say. "Deb realizes that, right? And she knows there's no real treasure?"

"I did try to explain that," he says, with that crooked smile that once made me weak in the knees. "But you know Deb; she takes her fiction pretty seriously."

I return Fred's smile, reminding myself that I'm now immune to his charms. Over the years we've shared more than a few laughs over how seriously our readers take their fiction—as if our entire lives haven't been ruled by the biggest fiction of them all. Maybe Fred is as tired of the fiction of our marriage as I am. Maybe this won't be so bad, I allow myself to think. Once we're back in Castellarosa he'll remember who he was before we met. Maybe he'll want a second chance.

Not for us, of course. That boat sailed a long time ago (long before he rewrote the ending for *Death Takes a Cruise*), but maybe it's not too late for each of us to have a chance on our own. He can write the literary novel he was always meant to write and I . . . I can be *free*.

"Thanks for the notes, Fred," I say. "I appreciate you giving this book a chance. All I've ever wanted was for you to be happy."

"And that's all I've ever wanted for you," he says with a tight-lipped smile. "So, what do you say? Drinks Roulette at the reception?"

Despite our temporary truce I can't shake the feeling that Fred is up to something. Drinks Roulette is a game we invented one year at Bouchercon after we failed to win the Anthony Award and, to add insult to injury, Buck Orson, an international espionage writer whom Fred despises, had. The Anthony is voted on by conference attendees so it was hard not to eye our peers with suspicion.

"I could poison each and every one of them," Fred had announced, surveying the crowd at the after-party.

"Let's," I'd proposed, plucking a glass of champagne from a tray. I got out my lipstick and marked the bottom of the glass and then placed it back on another passing tray. "Marked for death," I'd said. "Let's see who gets it."

We'd spent the rest of the night watching our colleagues fictively expire from our marked glasses. It was somehow wildly satisfying, but perhaps not *us* at our best. Since then, we've resorted to the game when feeling low or invidious. I can't help but think that Fred suggesting it now indicates a less-than-generous mindset.

That feeling stays with me through Passport Control and out to the passenger pickup area of the Rome airport. I get into the first limo with Aleister and Penelope, while Fred manages to slip into the second one, which is for the PR and marketing teams—including Ava, who I'm pretty sure has a big crush on Fred. Fred gallantly holds the door for her and then turns to greet a tall slim young woman in a tight-fitting white T-shirt, skinny black jeans, and aerodynamic black running shoes who steers a cream-colored Louis Vuitton suitcase toward the limo and steps straight into Fred's open arms.

"Is that—" I squint through the tinted windows at the familiar-looking woman who is wearing huge sunglasses, her long blond hair tucked in a baseball cap, as if she is trying to avoid paparazzi.

"Nadine St. George," Aleister says. "We coordinated transportation since she was flying in at the same time from the UK. She had some sort of teaching fellowship at Oxford this spring."

"*Oxford,*" I echo, feeling a pang of longing and envy. Back when I was planning an academic career my dream was an Oxford postdoc. *How did Nadine St. George get that?*

"I didn't think they gave out Oxford teaching gigs to mystery writers," Penelope remarks from behind dark sunglasses. Her habitual uniform of white linen blouse and slim black trousers looks miraculously unrumpled after our eight-hour flight.

"Her series has gotten a lot of academic attention with her use of a metafictional antihero narrator," Aleister says, looking rather professorial himself in a Harris tweed jacket and loose oxford-cloth button-down. "How did things go with Fred?" he asks, smoothly changing the subject away from the success of the younger author. "Did you tell him?"

"I told him," I confirm, "and he seemed a little surprised about how the books have been doing. You know he doesn't really concern himself with the business end of things."

"He hasn't had to," Penelope murmurs. "You've done that for him. And did he, um, mention anything about the termination clause?"

"Termination clause?" I dimly recall that when we'd drawn up our collaboration agreement there was a clause that specified that if one of us wanted to leave the series the other had an option to continue on their own with the approval of the other. "And have to come up with the ideas and outlines on his own *and* still hand over fifty percent of the royalties to me? Please, I don't think so. Besides, I'd never give my approval."

Aleister and Penelope exchange a veiled glance and then Aleister asks, "And he didn't convince you to change your mind about ending the series? Because, you know, you still can. This Poirot nomination will boost sales and if it wins—"

"Which it will," Penelope adds loyally. "Your series is by far the best of the five."

Even better than Nadine's sociopath serial killer thrillers? I wonder meanly. *She must be sleeping with one of the judges,* my friend Joan had immediately texted me when the nominations were announced. *I didn't even think three books constituted a series.*

"Definitely," Aleister seconds. "You could still set the next book at Castellarosa and we could tie it in with the anniversary edition of *Death Takes the Castle*—"

"No," I say, reaching for a bottle of chilled water from the limo's bar—and grabbing a mini prosecco along with it, "I can't do it anymore. *Death Takes a Bow* will be the last Rick and Dora Charles book. And I want to announce it at the reception."

AS WE HEAD north along the main highway to Florence beneath umbrella pines and tall cypresses, Aleister goes over the conference schedule. "I know you've been busy with the revisions," he says diplomatically, handing me the schedule with all my events highlighted in Day-Glo tangerine, "so you might not remember it all. You and Fred will be on the dais at the opening reception this afternoon with all the other Poirot nominees, and then there's an evening panel, and a guided hike in the morning . . ."

As his melodious mid-Atlantic voice purrs on (*Why does someone born and raised in Scarsdale sound so British?* Fred has often carped) I feel my eyes growing heavy and I drift off for the rest of the drive, overcome by jet lag and that ill-advised prosecco. When I come to, we're passing through a fairy-tale landscape of vineyards, olive groves, and sunflower fields cradled by hills topped by turreted castles and walled medieval villages. We pass a sign with a figure of a pilgrim walking with a staff indicating that we're on the legendary Via Francigena, the ancient road that led from Canterbury to Rome and then on to the port of Apulia, where pilgrims and Crusaders embarked for the Holy Land. Even though we're in a limo, not walking barefoot along the sacred way, I feel that old familiar thrill of being on the track of adventure, the way I'd always feel when Fred and I embarked on a new book. When I make out the outline of Castellarosa perched on top of its own steep mountain I feel a strange pang in my chest. We turn onto a narrow twisting road lined with tall cypress trees and begin the climb, my ears popping with the altitude change. I roll down the window and inhale the heady scent of roses and jasmine, bringing me instantly back twenty years to the first time I approached Castellarosa.

I'd been on an overcrowded bus then, with a backpack stuffed with books, craning my head out the window to get my first glimpse of the castle. I'd read about the sublime in Romantic fiction but I'd never really felt the peculiar combination of dread and beauty that came over me on the vertiginous approach to Castellarosa or the pure physical rush when the ramparts of the medieval village appeared across a deep gorge, wreathed in clouds as if it were floating in the sky. Gazing into the abyss and then up to the heights, I felt as if I had been splayed open, exposed and made vulnerable to whatever came next. A shiver had passed through me but it hadn't felt like fear; it had felt like excitement. Like I couldn't wait to rush over a cliff and meet my fate.

Now the narrow switchbacks are twisting my guts, each turn pulling the knot tighter.

"Dear Lord," Penelope exclaims, pointing out the window to the rose-colored fortress towering above the gorge. "Is that where we're going, Salvatore?"

"*Si, signora,*" the driver—*Salvatore; of course Penelope has learned his name*—replies. "Castellarosa. There is nothing else on this road."

"Who in the world, other than a mountain goat, would choose to live at the top of a road like this?" asks Penelope, who lives on the twenty-eighth floor of a Sutton Place co-op.

"Someone who wants to keep out marauders and pillagers," Aleister replies, without looking up from the manuscript he's reading on his iPad. I can tell it's a manuscript—probably one of the submissions for the discovery contest for unpublished authors he's reluctantly volunteered to judge—by the critical scoff painted across his face.

"It was built in the tenth century by a duke and then turned into a monastery in the twelfth century," I say. "There's a legend—" I begin.

"And now it's a five-star hotel," our driver interjects, cutting short my history lesson and skipping over a couple of centuries. "It has been made famous by Rick and Dora Charles."

"Hear that, Thea?" Penelope crows, nudging me. "Think of how many locals you've given jobs. Publicity should be all over that angle, Aleister."

"I'm sure Ava has it covered," Aleister replies, taking out his phone, "but I'll send her a text . . . Uh-oh, no service."

"Not on mine either," Penelope says. "I assume there will be wi-fi at the hotel?"

"For what we're paying there should be high-speed fiber optic," Aleister says. "And if not, get ready to watch a hundred bookstagrammers and influencers lose their minds."

"There was nothing when I was here twenty years ago," I

say wistfully. "Not even phones in the rooms, only a little public phone booth behind the refectory. It felt like going back in time." I'm having a hard time imagining the Castellarosa I remember with twenty-first-century connectivity and five-star amenities. I'd stayed in a cell in the old monastery and lived on bread and goat cheese and the local wine. "Does the hotel really make a go of it all the way up here?" I ask the driver. "I'd think the location would make it inconvenient."

The driver gives one of those characteristic full-body shrugs that could mean almost anything as we cross over a rushing stream on a narrow stone bridge. I'm surprised the bridge hasn't been modernized since I was here. Built on the back of a Roman aqueduct, the bridge has been washed away many times, but the aqueduct always remains. "The American couple who bought the old monastery have spent a fortune on the renovation and are counting on the fame of your book to bring in guests," the driver says.

"I read about them on the conference website," Penelope says. "The couple, Greg and Sonia Wilson, said they bought the monastery because they were fans of *Death Takes the Castle* and they wanted a partnership as fruitful as the one you and Fred have. Isn't that romantic?"

"Sure," I say, wondering if they, too, have a termination clause in their partnership.

"Ecco! Siamo qui!" The driver interrupts my cynical thoughts. *"La Porta Rosa."*

We have come to the towering city gates, built out of local pink limestone, the massive arch carved with all the fantastical creatures of the medieval bestiary to ward off invading armies. The driver pulls the car into a narrow parking area beside a low stone building that I recall the nuns referring to as the Granaio because it once served as the monastery's grain storehouse. There are several low buildings here—the gatekeeper's cottage, the olive press, the winery, and sheep barns from when a village ringed the monastery. Here, too, was the taverna where Fred and I had met, but it appears to have been turned into meeting and function rooms and something that looks like a water purifying plant for the new hotel. I remember that the bus had let me out here, the driver unceremoniously ousting me without answering any of my questions about how I was supposed to get to the monastery from the gate. I'd felt then as if I'd come to the edge of the known world, the view of the valley below and the castle above both as unreal as an illustration in a fairy tale. After all, I'd come looking for a ghost—the legendary Bianca Rosa. What should I have expected but a portal to the unknown?

"We're getting out here?" Penelope squawks, as outraged as I'd been twenty years ago. At least Salvatore is more courteous than my long-ago bus driver.

"*Certo, signora,* the hotel porters will take your luggage up to the hotel and there is a funicular to the hotel entrance. You can walk up but it is a hundred steps—"

I get out and walk toward the steps while Penelope and Aleister negotiate transportation. I stand for a moment in the shadow of the gate, staring out at the view, trying to grasp what it is about this place that has haunted my dreams all these years. It's the quiet, I realize, that feels not like an absence but a palpable quality—an elixir distilled over the centuries, as rare and precious as the olive oil and wine the valley is famous for. I see the second limousine pulling in and smirk a little at the high heels that Ava is wearing. No doubt Nadine in her running shoes will sprint up the stairs, but I see her going over to embrace Aleister instead.

Et tu, Aleister? I think, shouldering my backpack—a lighter, more fashionable one than I'd carried twenty years ago—and starting up the stairs. I have no intention of taking a funicular—not with the curse.

According to the legend of Castellarosa the castle is guarded not just by the griffins, manticores, and dragons carved above the gates, but also by the ghost of Bianca Rosa, the daughter of the duke who built the castle. Shortly after building the castle, the duke hosted a party of knights on their way to the Crusades and Bianca fell in love with the poor squire of one of them. Her father, of course, forbade their marriage. She vowed, though, to wait for her beloved and remain faithful to him and he in turn promised that he would return from the Crusades a knight and with a fortune so they could marry. While he was gone, though, her father tried to force Bianca into an arranged marriage with another nobleman. When she refused, he walled her up in the crypt. Years later, the squire returned, true to his word, knighted and with a large fortune, and heard about the fate of his beloved. Breaking into the sealed crypt, he discovered her veiled lifeless form laid out on a stone bier, her faithful dog curled at her feet, and a white rose—still fresh and sweet-smelling as Bianca herself—clutched in her hands. He laid the red rose he had brought from the Holy Land beside the white one in her hand and buried his treasure in the crypt. Then he walled himself back in and lay down beside her to await death. With his dying breath he cursed the castle and all those in it who were not true of heart to be trapped within its walls for eternity. The only way to prove that you are true of heart, and avoid the curse, is to climb the one hundred steps from the Porta Rosa to the monastery door, confessing your sins as you go.

You don't believe all that about Bianca Rosa's curse? Fred had asked me that first night at the taverna when I told him the story.

Of course not, I'd replied, laughing, but because I was drunk, I'd added, *But why take a chance?*

In our book *Death Takes the Castle*, Rick and Dora find the sealed tomb of Bianca Rosa and her knight but they don't take the treasure because the legend has it that you can either have the treasure or you can have true love. You can't have both—

I pause to catch my breath and inhale the sweet, rose-scented air. On either side of me are the terraced rose gardens where the nuns of Castellarosa cultivated a white and red rose, which, according to the legend, had miraculously sprouted from the red and white roses laid on Bianca's tomb. The nuns had distilled the rose into a perfume that was popular with royalty throughout Europe. They had also, according to legend, concocted a poison that was popular with Catherine de' Médici.

"You're walking up?"

I recognize Fred's voice but I don't turn around.

"I need to stretch my legs after the long flight," I say. "I'm surprised your new bestie Nadine isn't jogging up—isn't she a triathlete or something?"

"She had something she wanted to discuss with Aleister," Fred says. "Are you sure you're not walking up because of the legend?"

"Why would it have anything to do with the legend?" I snap, wondering what Nadine wants with Aleister. He's not her editor. Her books are published by a whole other—*lesser*—division of the publisher.

"Wasn't there something about having to do penance by walking up the hundred steps on your knees repeating some mea culpa crap?"

"Only if you've broken faith with your true love and, as I recall, I'm not the one who did that."

"Ouch," Fred says. "Is that why you're pulling the plug on the series? Because of what happened in San Miguel?"

"You think I've waited six years to get back at you for San Miguel, Fred? I'm not the procrastinator in this partnership."

He doesn't say anything for several steps and I wonder if he's decided to go back down and take the funicular with Nadine and Aleister, but then I hear his voice again, this time so close his breath is cool on my sweat-soaked neck and I remember—*goddamn it*—the way he used to blow his breath in a trail down the back of my spine—

"It hasn't really been a partnership for some time now," is what he says.

Not since San Miguel de Allende and *Death Takes a Siesta*. For the last six years we have been married in name only, a ruse to keep the series going. Some couples stay together for the kids; we stayed together for the series. *Frederick and Dorothea Morgan-Lane divide their time between New York City and the Hudson Valley,* our bio reads, not spelling out that Fred lives in the Washington Heights apartment while I live in the Rhinebeck house. Instead of a divorce (*Too easy to find in the public records,* Penelope, anxious to protect our brand, had pointed out) we'd spent a few hours in a lawyer's office hammering out a "division of financial assets" settlement. It was the sensible thing to do. Why throw away a lucrative writing career just because we weren't in love anymore?

"No," I say, turning around and facing him. *How is he not sweaty? How is he not even breathing hard?* "It hasn't. Don't you think it's time we made it official?"

He holds my gaze for a few seconds and then he says, "I'm not giving up Rick and Dora without a fight." Then he passes me, easily sprinting up the last few steps—*has he been working out?*—while I trudge behind him, repeating in my head a mea culpa for every step. No, I'm not the one who betrayed the marriage six years ago in San Miguel de Allende. I betrayed it much earlier than that when I turned our marriage into a business partnership and sacrificed our love for money. Which in the long run was the same as choosing the treasure over love.

CHAPTER THREE

I'm breathless and soaked in sweat by the time I get to the top, grateful for the sparkling red juice the doorman offers at the entrance to the castle. *"Benevenuti a Castellarosa,"* he says, *"e Il Convenzione di Omicidio."*

I nearly spit out my drink, which I discover is a Pomegranate Spritz garnished with a sprinkling of pomegranate seeds. Like most mystery conventions, MurderCon revels in the macabre. There's a blood-splattered banner with the words *MurderCon* written in dripping red letters. The lobby is full of authors, publishers, and fans wearing blood-splattered T-shirts and sporting totes adorned with gory daggers and fountain pens dripping blood. There's something about the Italian translation—*Il Convenzione di Omicidio*—though, that turns my blood to ice. Or maybe it's just the realization that I'm not going to have time to go to my room and change before the opening reception because it's happening *now.*

I'm wondering if I can make a dash to my room when a woman in a floor-length sparkly red gown bears down on me.

She embraces me, kissing one cheek, then the other, so effusively that I feel sure I must have met her before, but my mind is drawing a blank. Then Fred appears at my side and embraces the woman as if they're old friends. Luckily, he speaks her name loudly and clearly enough that I realize the woman is Sonia Wilson, co-owner of this magnificent hotel.

"Look, Greg," she says, beckoning to her side a tall, tanned man in an impeccable tux whom she introduces as her husband and business partner, Greg Wilson. "Aren't they just as we imagined them—the famous Rick and Dora! You know it was you two who inspired us to buy Castellarosa and turn it into a romantic retreat. Isn't that so, darling?" She turns her adoring gaze onto her husband and he returns a 1,000-watt smile to his wife. They practically glow in the aura of marital bliss, bathed in light like a quattrocento Madonna and Child.

"Your story of Bianca Rosa and her beloved knight inspired us to re-create the perfect atmosphere for lovers," Sonia purrs, nestling into the crook of her husband's arm. "And your example of working together inspired us to do it together."

I could point out that Bianca Rosa and her knight did not have a happy ending—nor have Fred and I—but Greg interrupts the thought. "And what do you make of Hotel Castellarosa? You must find it quite changed from the last time you were here."

I look around at the hotel lobby and recognize—just barely—the vestibule of the old monastery, which had been the great hall of the original castle. It had been lofty, gray, and cold, I recall. Now the old marble floors have been polished to a reflective gleam and richly hued tapestries and gilt-framed mirrors hang from what had been bare stone walls. Plush red couches are fitted into the alcoves where stark crucifixes had once hung. The left-hand side of the room is lined with glass doors opening to a terrace where ancient urns and statues frame a view of the valley and the hilltops and mountains to the west. There's still an ecclesiastical, medieval feel to the space, but as imagined by the directors of *White Lotus*. I wonder what the nuns would make of the naked statuary, copious alcohol, and faux blood–splattered guests.

"It's certainly . . . different," I manage. "I imagine the nuns who lived here would be quite shocked to see it now . . . What happened to them, by the way?" I add, suddenly remembering Sister Beatrice, a tiny, sharp-eyed nun who'd pushed wheels of cheese and bowls of porridge on me each morning to make sure I was eating enough. "Do you remember if there was a nun named Beatrice?" I ask.

Greg makes a face. "Hm . . . yes, I think there was a nun by that name but I'm afraid she was losing her faculties."

"Oh yes," Sonia chimes in, "that was the nun who kept asking us so many questions about what would happen to this little painting and that piece of bric-a-brac and making such a fuss about it all. It was really kind of sweet but sad, too."

"Are you sure that was Beatrice?" I ask, finding it hard to recognize the keen-witted woman I knew in their descriptions.

Sonia shrugs. "Who knows? They all look alike under their habits, don't they?"

"And most of the nuns in the order had died by the time the

Church closed the monastery," Greg adds. "When we took over, the rest were moved to a more modern facility in Florence, where I am sure they are more comfortable than they were here. I'm sure you, too, will find it more comfortable. In your book you describe the . . . um, rather primitive accommodations. I hope that if you write about Castellarosa again you will let your readers know that they can expect a truly luxurious experience here. In fact," he leans in a little closer and I smell his lemony aftershave and a hint of cigar smoke clinging to his tux, "I'm sure we can come to an arrangement . . . perhaps free accommodations for you and your husband whenever you are in Italy . . ."

His voice trails off as he tilts his head and smiles. Has he just offered us a bribe for an endorsement of the hotel? It wouldn't be the first time we've been offered an exchange for product placement. Fred had always been all for accepting them—*as long as we're writing commercial fiction we might as well go full hog*—but I have always been queasy about the arrangement. On the other hand, when I looked up the hotel website, I noticed that the nightly market rate for the suite we're staying in gratis was over a thousand euros.

"I love this place," I tell him honestly. "The best moments of my life happened here. I'm sure whatever Fred and I write about it will be appealing to future guests . . . as long as they don't mind staying where there have been a few murders."

He looks alarmed for a moment—I forget that ordinary citizens don't joke about murder the way those of us in the mystery community do—but then he smiles and laughs, rather too loudly, as if anxious to show he's in on the joke. "You're talking about the pretend murders in your book. Of course, there have been real murders here as well. The history of Castellarosa is quite bloody—"

"You mean Bianca Rosa and the curse," I say. "Yes, I suppose if your guests don't mind sleeping over the bones of two star-crossed lovers buried alive in the crypt, then what's a few fictional homicides?"

He turns white as those bones I just referenced. *Crap*, I have gone and offended him now. So much for our free fancy suite. We'll probably be downgraded to one of the old nuns' cells. Before I can think of a way to smooth things over, I feel someone clutch my arm and find myself being crushed against the plastic name tag of a woman in a bright pink ponte pantsuit and lime-green platform espadrilles. I don't need the name tag to recognize Joan Acosta, bestselling author of a cozy series set in the Texas Hill Country (and several other series under assorted pseudonyms) and practically my best friend in the business.

"Thank Gawd you're here," she drawls, as if I'm the fabled knight come to rescue the castle's damsel in distress. "We have a lot to catch up on." Then, turning to Greg Wilson, she addresses him as if he were the headwaiter instead of the co-owner of the hotel. "The bartender just told me that you're out of ice—*again*—and that the prosecco for the toast is getting warm. And speaking of the toast, we need to agree on a signal for when the waiters should serve the prosecco . . . What's the magic word, hon?" she asks turning to me.

"Um . . ." I dither. "I guess when I give my speech . . . I'll say *full circle*."

"Full circle," Joan repeats. "Got that, Greg?"

Greg Wilson pastes on another smile but with considerably less wattage, as if he's been switched to energy-saving mode. Joan arrived early to help the conference committee set up and I can well imagine that with her exacting standards and demanding perfectionism she has run the staff ragged.

"Of course—" Greg begins, but Joan cuts in. "And would you please tell the catering staff to bring out more of those cute little fried fishes and those stuffed mozzarella things? If you don't keep these mystery writers fed, they'll eat each other."

Joan steers me away before I can see the urbane Greg Wilson react to the news that he's hosting a bunch of cannibals. "If they want a good Yelp review they'd better stay on their toes. All their folderol about being inspired by true love won't keep the lights on and the prosecco chilled," Joan mutters as she flags down a waiter and replaces my empty glass (*when did that happen?*) with a fresh Pomegranate Spritz. "If you ask me, they've overextended themselves and rushed their opening. I told Deb it's always risky staying at a hotel that's only just opened."

She suddenly switches her gaze onto me and I feel the force of her laser-sharp attention like a tractor beam aimed on an unsuspecting alien subject. Under Joan's regard, I feel every one of my forty-eight years, no doubt accentuated by jet lag. Joan herself, a decade my senior, looks like she spent her day at the spa getting Botox and a seaweed facial. Catching a glimpse of myself in one of the splotchy antique mirrors is like seeing the ghost of the girl who was here twenty years ago, my blond hair (*Botticelli blond,* Fred had called it back then) beginning to tarnish silver, my complexion, which had turned gold in the Tuscan sun that summer, now a shade of paper white from months spent in my study doing revisions.

"You look a little peaked, darlin'," Joan says softly. "Is everything okay?"

"I've just been working hard on the book," I tell her. "You know how that is."

She regards me another moment and then mercifully switches her focus away from me and onto the crowd. "Oh, look, there's that handsome husband of yours with Nadine St. George—can you believe she's nominated for a Poirot after only three books to her series?" I follow her gaze to see Nadine in an elegant bone-white sheath—*when did she get a chance to change?*—standing next to Fred. "But then, she seems to get everything she wants. I hear she got that Oxford gig of hers by sleeping with a don—or maybe it was someone named Don?"

I choke on my drink and slap Joan's arm. "Joan, that's terrible," I say, secretly delighted; I can always count on Joan to spill the tea. "That's what they always say about successful women."

"No one ever says that about me," Joan deadpans.

"Because we all know how hard you work." It's true. Joan is one of the hardest-working writers in the industry, producing two to three books a year while still having time to organize conferences, judge contests, and promote other authors in her newsletter and blog. She took me under her wing at my first Bouchercon (while Fred was getting drunk at Noir at the Bar) and has been guiding me through the industry ever since.

Right now, she guides me over to a buffet table laden with

trays of mozzarella, tomato slices drizzled with olive oil and studded with basil, a rainbow of olives, crusty bread, assorted charcuterie, and tiny fried fish. Joan plucks up a fish and devours it headfirst. "And yet," she says, daintily extracting a tiny fried tail, "I'm not the one nominated for a Poirot."

"You should be. Hill Country Homicides is a great series."

"Cozies never win these things," she says. "And according to Buck Orson they shouldn't even be in the same category." She tilts her chin toward a large, loud man in a Hawaiian shirt who's waving a beer bottle at a shorter, thin man who flinches at each wave. Buck Orson writes an international espionage series with a hunky former-CIA protagonist. The man he's threatening is Pete Tyler, a mild-mannered, retired high school history teacher who writes a historical World War II series. They're both nominated for the Poirot and Buck is this year's toastmaster.

"Talk about qualifying," I say. "How is he toastmaster *and* nominee this year?"

"Talk to Deb Andersen. She headed the committee and tried to get him disqualified but she was overruled. As if he shouldn't be disqualified for what he said about Shay last year."

"Wait, what? What did he say about Shay?" I glance around the room and find Shay Armstrong, a tall Black woman in a stunning floor-length orange dress who's been cornered by a an older-looking man in red suspenders festooned with badges from a dozen mystery conferences. I recognize the man as a habitual conference-goer who loves to tell authors that he guessed whodunit in the first chapter and what facts they got wrong in their books. The Gotchas, Fred calls readers like him. Shay, with medical degrees from Harvard and Johns Hopkins, who writes an incisive and meticulously researched series starring a forensic pathologist, is looking at him as if considering where to insert her scalpel first. Shay's also nominated for the Poirot and, for my money, the one who should win it.

"He said—" Joan moves in closer and lowers her voice. "That she won the Anthony because she's a woman of color—although that's not exactly how he phrased it."

I gape at Joan. "And that didn't disqualify him?"

"Nope, Deb wanted to—wait, there's Deb now—" Joan starts pulling me over to where Deb Andersen is waiting on a drinks line. A retired librarian from Minnesota, Deb writes a mystery blog called *Miss Marple's Handbag* as well as basically running International Murder Writers. She's one of my favorite people in the industry—smart, generous, and funny—an oasis of kindness in a sea of sharks.

As Joan steers us in Deb's direction I steal a look around for Fred and see he's still deep in conversation with Nadine St. George, and now Aleister and Penelope have joined them. When Fred catches my eye, he holds up his glass and taps his finger on the base. Oh, right, we were supposed to play Drinks Roulette. I grab a fresh Pomegranate Spritz from a tray, reach into my bag for my lipstick, deftly mark the bottom of the stemmed glass, and then place it on the next drinks tray that goes by. I look over to Fred to confirm he saw me marking the glass but he's too busy laughing at something Nadine is saying. Probably some witty anecdote about life at Oxford. Penelope catches my eye instead, raises one finger for me to wait, and starts walking toward me, but she's waylaid by an attendee who's no doubt pitching a novel to her. Poor Penelope, she hates these conferences for this very reason, but she came to support us. The least I can do is go rescue her, but I, in turn, am waylaid by a vaguely familiar looking woman in a dress patterned in tiny skulls and crossbones and a red cardigan adorned with a pin shaped like a silver scythe, just like the one the Grim Reaper carries on the spines of all the Death Takes a Holiday books. She's a fan. "I bet you don't remember me," she says, as if daring me to admit I don't.

This is my least favorite conversation opener. The *polite* thing to do, I think, studying her round face dominated by black-dyed bangs above heavy horn-rimmed glasses, is to introduce herself and tell me her name and how we know each other, but I gamely dive in. "We met at a conference, didn't we?" I say, angling for a view of the name tag dangling from a lanyard around her neck, which gives me her name and informs me that she's from Portland, Oregon, and is part of a group called the Goth Librarians. "Lindsay, isn't it? Or did we meet at a reading at Powell's?" I venture.

She waits a beat as if I'm going to say which conference and recall every little thing we said to each other, but then she smiles. "That's right. I told you how much I loved *Death Takes the Castle*. It's my favorite book. It's the book that made me want to become a writer."

Uh-oh. She probably gave me a manuscript and expects me to tell her how much I loved it. "Thank you so much, that means a lot to me," I say, truthfully. I *am* grateful, even though there is something a little disheartening about the exuberant praise of one's first book, written twenty years ago. Perhaps it's the suggestion that nothing you have written since has quite measured up, a suspicion I sometimes share. It's doubly hard, standing here in the place where Fred and I wrote that first book and remembering how exciting and magical it had been to write it, the way the ideas and words had flowed along with the wine, as if we had been possessed. I have sometimes wondered if Fred and I mistook falling in love with writing for falling in love with each other.

I sign a copy of *Death Takes the Castle* for Lindsay and point her in Fred's direction to get his signature, watching with malicious pleasure as she interrupts his confab with Nadine. She's replaced by a retired English teacher from Indiana named Barb who tells me that her book club, the Midwest Mavens, has read every book we've ever written and that she personally preorders each book and enters every presale giveaway on Goodreads. "I don't know what I'd do without the next Rick and Dora book to look forward to," she says, placing a hand over her bosom, on which is pinned an anatomically correct bloody heart pierced with a dagger. I take her info to pass on to Ava to make sure she gets an advanced reader's copy of the next book and try not to feel bad that she's going to have to find something else to look forward to after this last Rick and Dora.

I look around for Penelope but can't find her, so I head over to Deb and Joan who have been joined by the man in red suspenders—Robert "Bob" Robertson, according to his name badge—who's moved on from Shay and is now accosting Deb about some imagined error she's made in the treasure hunt, the instructions for which have been handed out in the conference tote bags. Deb's narrow shoulders are taut beneath the slightly pilled weave of her rose-patterned cardigan. I can see two little dimples on the back of her sweater where the hanger has made dents, like the buds of angel wings, and feel a sudden swelling of love for Deb and all the librarians and schoolteachers and book clubbers, who are really the ones who keep books alive.

"I'm sure Deb wouldn't have made any mistakes in the treasure hunt," I say, glaring at Robert "Bob" Robertson.

"She would have if she wanted to win it herself," Bob replies.

I splutter at him but Deb calmly replies, "I'm not even allowed to participate in it—and besides, I double-checked the map with Fred Morgan-Lane, who coauthored the book about finding the treasure. So, if you have any beef, go take it up with Fred."

Bob storms off, and Joan and Deb burst into squeals of laughter, which I join. When I catch my breath I say, "Fred told me he helped with the treasure hunt. You know," I lean in confidentially, "we didn't *really* find the treasure. I hope Fred hasn't been misleading you."

"But Rick and Dora find it in the book," Deb says.

I laugh. "We made that up. I don't even believe the treasure really exists."

"Oh, I do," Deb says, squaring her narrow shoulders so that the dimples on the back of her sweater flex like wings, and then winks at me. "And I think I know where it's hidden, only . . ."

Deb's brow furrows and she leans toward me so close I smell the rosewater she always wears and whispers in my ear. "There's something that's been bothering me that I wanted to talk to you about—"

Before she can tell me what it is, Greg Wilson glides soundlessly up behind Deb in his soft, expensive Italian shoes. Deb looks up at him, visibly awed by the tall, handsome hotelier. "I have been sent to escort you, Ms. Andersen, to the dais, where you will receive your lemon prize."

Deb blushes and beams at Greg and explains that it's the *Miss* Lemon Prize for Outstanding Service in the Mystery Community, named for Hercule Poirot's loyal and efficient secretary. She straightens her cardigan and I realize that it's modeled on the rose-jacquard cardigan Miss Lemon wears in the Poirot television series. I bet Deb knitted it for the occasion.

"And well deserved," I say.

"Absolutely," Joan seconds. "No one does more for the mystery community than Deb. Wait till you see the treasure hunt she's devised."

"Ah, the treasure hunt," Greg Wilson purrs, suavely tucking Deb's hand through his crooked elbow and smiling down at her. "You will have to tell me more, signora. Perhaps I can provide some clues, although I have to warn you that I believe the treasure is a myth." Then he deftly steers Deb toward the dais. She glances back over her shoulder and mouths, *I feel like I'm at the* Oscars!

"I think it's time for you to get up there, too," Joan says.

"Sorry you don't have a tuxedoed escort—Oh, but look, your husband is coming to get you. Good luck, sweetie, my money's on you and Fred."

I squeeze Joan's hand and turn to Fred, whose face, I notice, is oddly flushed. *What has he been talking to Nadine St. George about?*

"Hey," he says, grabbing my arm with none of the elegance of Greg Wilson. "There's something I want to tell you before we get up there."

"Then you shouldn't have spent the whole reception chit-chatting with Nadine," I say, immediately hating how I sound. Joan's influence, I realize. I love Joan, I really do, but sometimes after I've spent too much time with her, I feel like I've absorbed her cynical worldview. "What were you talking about anyway?"

"That's what I wanted to tell you—" Before he can continue, a booming voice comes from the dais.

"Come on, Fred," Buck Orson announces through the microphone, "quit hogging that beautiful wife of yours and get on up here. Last one on the dais buys drinks at the bar, and we know you hate to be the one to pony up."

"*Asshole,*" Fred mutters under his breath, nevertheless hurrying us up onto the dais. There are five chairs set up in a row for the Poirot nominees. There should be six, I think, but then realize that Buck, who's pacing the dais, mic in hand, has no intention of sitting. Nadine St. George is sitting smack in the middle, with Pete Tyler to one side and Shay to the other, which means that Fred and I won't be able to sit together. Shay, seeing the situation, gets up to move over, motioning for Nadine and Pete to move over as well, which they do, but while Shay is still standing, Nadine motions for Fred to sit next to her, forcing Shay to move to the end so I can sit between her and Fred. As I sit down, I hear Shay whistle under her breath. *"Some people!"*

I squeeze her hand and tell her I think her series should win.

"Ditto, hon. Hey, look where they've got Deb seated. What's up with that?"

I turn my head and see that Deb is sitting *behind us* next to Sonia Wilson. What's Sonia even doing on the podium? "Well, that's not right," I say. "Should we get them to rearrange the chairs?"

"I think that would just embarrass Deb," Shay says. "And at least she's out of Buck's line of fire."

I see what she means. Buck Orson has interpreted his role of toastmaster as roast-master. As he introduces each of us nominees—starting with himself—he makes bad jokes about each of us: Nadine gets her sociopath research from her own high school journals, Pete's series has lasted longer than the war that inspired it, and there are more dead bodies in Shay's than on the beach at Normandy. I feel Shay stiffen next to me and I get ready to be the brunt of his next joke but he moves on to Fred. "Do you ever notice that it's always Rick who gets them into trouble but it's always Dora who gets them out?"

The crowd laughs and I feel Fred tense beside me. Deb leans forward in her seat and whispers something in Fred's ear, and I thank God for her gentle influence. If anyone can keep him calm, it's Deb. Instead of moving on, Buck gives illustrative examples from each of the Death Takes a Holiday books. "Remember the time Rick took control of a Cessna but then realized he didn't know how to fly a plane and Dora had to google it and play a YouTube video?"

"That's not the way that scene goes," Fred mutters beside me under cover of the crowd's laughter.

"And what about the time Rick steers a cruise ship into an iceberg? I mean, had the man not watched *Titanic*?"

"You wrote that scene to punish me," Fred says. "For San Miguel."

He's not wrong. If truth be told I've gotten my revenge over the last six years by writing Rick into some pretty compromising situations. Mea culpa. "And yet it only made your fans love you more," I point out, which is also true.

"What I'm saying," Buck tells the crowd, "is if you're feeling at all in danger during this weekend—and let's face it, you're in a room filled with people who dream up murders for a living—the one to go to"—he points at me—"is the brains of the operation, Dor—I mean Thea."

I grimace. That is going a little too far. And Buck isn't done yet.

"Honestly," Buck says, turning to look at me and Fred, "I'm surprised Dora didn't kill off Rick ten books ago. I know I would have. But I hear that Thea has an announcement. Is it that Dora finally kills Rick in the next book?"

I can feel heat rising off Fred beside me as Buck hands me the microphone. This is *not* the way this was supposed to go. Did someone tell Buck we were planning on ending the series? The mic feels slippery in my hand and I have to force myself not to wipe it off.

"Wow," I say, "even on Goodreads reviews there's a warning for spoilers."

There are a few nervous titters around the room—writers love to slam Goodreads—but it's subdued because I've just given away that there's some truth to what Buck said.

"I am going to begin by thanking International Murder Writers for this nomination. It's especially a thrill and honor to be here at Castellarosa, where Fred and I met twenty years ago and began our series—" I look toward Fred, expecting at least a performative husbandly concurrence, but he's too busy listening to something Nadine is whispering in his ear, so I go on gamely.

"I also want to thank Greg and Sonia Wilson for making their beautiful hotel available for us—trust me, it's a lot cushier than the monastery I stayed at twenty years ago."

There are a few more polite laughs but I can sense the crowd's impatience. Damn Buck Orson for spoiling our moment.

"And I want to thank all of you, the writers, readers, and fans, for coming all the way to Italy to share this moment."

There was a contest for free travel to the conference, but it's true that most of the attendees have shelled out airfare, conference fees, and lodging costs to be here.

"This felt like the perfect place to announce that our next book in the series will take place here at Castellarosa, where we began, bringing the series full circle."

I pause. *Full circle* was the cue I'd given Greg Wilson to distribute drinks for the toast. At least that is going according to plan. I can see the waiters making extra loops with their trays to make sure everyone has a glass and I notice Joan whispering to a waiter and signaling him to bring a tray up onto the dais. I reach for a glass and notice that it has a lipstick mark on the bottom of its base. I almost laugh out loud. How perfect that the marked drink—*our poisoned chalice*—has made it all the way around the room and back to me. It's a sign, I think as I take the marked glass, that things have indeed come full circle. We have come back to Castellarosa to finish what we began here.

I turn to Fred, holding the glass up to show him, hoping this sign will soften the blow. But he isn't looking at me. He's still whispering with Nadine, who, thinking that I'm offering *her* the drink, waves it away with the mic in her hand. *Wherever did she get another mic? Does she travel with one in her purse?*

She stands up and smooths her elegant white sheath. "I'd like us all to raise a glass to Fred and Thea for bringing us so much reading pleasure over the years. I know that *Death Takes the Castle* was the book that made my teenage self want to write a mystery."

My teenage self? Oh, come on! I'm not that much older than she is!

"So it is with the greatest humility and honor . . ." Her voice thickens and she pauses to swipe at her eyes and emit a shaky laugh. "That I announce that while Thea is stepping down, I am so honored that Frederick has asked me to step into the breach to continue the series with him."

It must be the jet lag, I think, that makes me feel as if I have left my body and floated up to the heavy oak rafters above us, where I am looking down on the gathering. For a moment I picture the room as it must have looked for centuries when it was the great hall of the castle and the knights gathered here for their meals. *Get up,* I want to yell, *there's an invader at the castle walls. The barbarians are at the gate—*

What I see, instead, is a jumble of bodies on the dais—Nadine leaning in to whisper something to Fred, Fred bending back to hear something Deb is saying, Sonia Wilson handing Deb a handkerchief, Shay leaning over to pat my hand (which I can't feel), Pete not looking at anyone, Buck standing to the side, smirking and whispering something to Greg. It looks, from this impossible angle, like a Celtic knot in a medieval manuscript.

Then I am back in my body and Fred, looking sheepish, is holding up his glass to clink with mine. *Like hell am I going to toast to Nadine St. George stealing our series!* I notice Deb doesn't have a drink in her hand, so I give her mine. Then I turn around to look for a waiter to get another one for myself but the waiter has vanished. When I look back at Deb, I see that her pale blue eyes are confused and I realize that she's hurt I hadn't told her that I was leaving the series. I take a step back to explain but she lifts the glass to her lips, her light pink lipstick clashing with the lurid red spritz, and takes a surprisingly long gulp. I can't blame her. I'm wishing I hadn't given away my drink and I glance around again for a waiter. Behind me Deb clears her throat and tugs on my sleeve. She is going to ask me, I guess, why I didn't tell her I was leaving the series. Maybe I can pretend not to have heard her—

She coughs and tugs harder. "I'm sorry, Deb," I say, turning around.

Deb is staring at me with wide, horrified eyes. She lifts her handkerchief to her mouth again and coughs—

A stream of red spews out of her mouth, soaking her handkerchief and the front of her rose-patterned cardigan. *Has the drink made her sick? Maybe she's allergic to something in it!* I grab her arm but she is already slipping to the floor, her thin frail hands scrabbling at her throat. Carmine-colored froth bubbles on her lips. She goes down hard, face-planting on the dais floor, her neck bent at an unnatural angle, light blue eyes glazing over. The little hanger dimples on her cardigan flutter once and then subside. She's dead before I touch my fingers to her neck, poisoned by the drink meant for me.

CHAPTER FOUR

Is she—?"

I look up into Nadine St. George's wide green eyes and notice meanly that her white sheath is splattered with red gore.

Shay answers for me. "She has no pulse and she's not breathing. I'm going to administer CPR."

"But if she's been poisoned—" I begin, but Shay has already extracted a small red kit from her purse, taken out a clear plastic guard, and strapped it over Deb's mouth. As she lowers her face to Deb's, I hear Joan shouting at Sonia Wilson to call an ambulance.

Thank God for Joan, I think, grateful she's on the scene. And for Shay, who apparently keeps a first aid kit in her purse where most of us just carry lipstick and breath mints. I scoot back from where I'm kneeling to give her room—and something sharp stabs painfully into my right knee.

"Be careful, Thea!" Fred is suddenly by my side, extracting a shard of glass from my knee. He holds it up and I see a smear of blood on its sharp, jagged point that instantly makes me woozy.

Some mystery writer you are, Fred said to me when we were blocking out a katana duel in *Death Takes a Bullet Train* and I passed out after cutting myself, *fainting at the first sight of blood!*

He must be remembering the moment, too, because he's there to catch me as I slump sideways. When I come to, I'm lying against his chest, staring blurry-eyed at a scattering of broken glass and purple berries, my ears ringing.

"She's gone," Shay says, sitting back on her heels.

"What was it?" Nadine asks. "An allergic reaction?"

"I read over the forms each of you submitted detailing your many allergies and food preferences, and no one mentioned being allergic to any of the ingredients in our signature Castellarosa Pomegranate Spritz," Sonia, who's come back from calling the ambulance, says with an affronted sniff.

"I don't remember Deb ever mentioning any allergies," Pete Tyler says, also sniffing. His sniff, I suspect, is because he's on the verge of tears. Pete and Deb were so close that at times I wondered if they were romantically involved.

"We ought to save the broken glass so the police can check for poison," Joan says, reaching for the broken stem.

"Don't touch that!" Buck Orson barks. "That's evidence. We have to preserve the crime scene."

The absurdity of all of us mystery writers playing at detective produces a fit of highly inappropriate nervous giggles from me, which turn almost instantly into choking sobs. *Deb is dead. How is that even possible?*

"Is Thea okay?" Joan asks. "Did she drink from Deb's glass?"

"I saw her give her glass to Deb," Nadine says, a note of suspicion in her voice. *Is she suggesting that I am responsible for Deb's death?*

I clear my throat and sit up. "I'm fine," I say, pushing myself away from Fred. "I gave Deb my glass because she didn't have one for the toast." I stare at the shards of broken glass, searching for the lipstick mark I'd noticed, but there's so much red spilled over it between the drink and the smashed pomegranate seeds that I can't make it out. Had I imagined it? Did it matter? It was only a game, after all. Surreptitiously, I nudge the broken glass stem with my knee as I push myself up. A fat, purplish-black berry rolls out of the mess toward me and stops next to my hand. Something about the berry bothers me, and before I can stop myself, I pick it up and close my hand around it.

I look around quickly to see if anyone noticed, but they're all too busy arguing over which steps we should take next to "secure the crime scene" to have noticed. I look past our little circle at Deb's prone body, the pupils of her wide staring eyes as fat and black as the berry I plucked from the ground, her head haloed by the scattering of broken glass smeared in blood. It could be the cover of one of the cozy mysteries Deb loved—*Death at MurderCon*. But it's not a book cover or a conference poster or a game. Deb is dead. Tears sting my eyes and I have to look away or I'll dissolve into hysterics again. Which is when I notice that the room has become strangely empty, devoid of fans and writers.

"Where'd everybody go?" I ask.

"Greg suggested that the guests go into the dining room until the ambulance comes," Sonia tells me. "If you would like to join them—"

"You mean they're eating lunch?" I ask incredulously.

Sonia looks both apologetic and affronted. "Where else are they to go? The food is prepared."

"She's right," Joan says, patting my hand. "We needed this room cleared. We can't move Deb until the ambulance comes—"

"And the police," Buck adds, glaring at Sonia. "You have called the police, too, haven't you?"

Sonia looks at Buck as if he's an idiot. "Of course we've notified the *polizia*. They are sending someone from Florence so it may take some time to get here. I will have a member of my staff stay to make sure that nothing is moved and that your friend—"

"Deb," I say. "Deb Andersen."

"That Deb is not disturbed."

She has made it sound as if Deb is having a private spa treatment rather than lying dead in a pool of her own vomit. I suddenly remember that in one of our email exchanges, Deb had cut and pasted an offering from the spa menu: *Medieval herbal facial and hand treatment featuring beauty secrets of Catherine de' Medici.* Below it, Deb had written: *Didn't Catherine de' Medici kill someone with poisoned gloves?* Which makes me think of something.

I sway slightly as if I'm going to pass out again and Fred comes to my rescue. "Thanks, sweetheart," I say. "I think I just need some air. Can we go out into the garden for a few minutes—" I gesture feebly toward the open French doors, and Fred grabs my elbow and propels me forward, telling the others that we'll be right back. At least he remembers Rick and Dora's safe word—*sweetheart*—code for *Get me out of here now!*

The need for air was a ruse, but when we step out onto the veranda, I gulp mouthfuls like a drowning person.

"Are you okay?" Fred asks, sounding worried. Does he think I really called him sweetheart? That Deb's death has softened me into a needy pile of mush ready to forgive him for everything? Does he think this reminder of our mortality is going to propel me into his arms? But that's not what he's worried about.

"Is this about Nadine's announcement?" he asks. "I tried to tell you, but you wouldn't listen to me and then you were going to announce that the series was over."

"That's *not* what I need to talk to you about," I say, striding off the terrace and toward a wall of tall yew hedges. "Do you think I'm worried about your dalliance with Nadine St. George with poor Deb lying dead in there?"

"I loved Deb, too!" he cries, as if I had accused him of callous disregard for the Minnesotan librarian. "We all did! That's why I'm sure it must have been some allergic reaction. Who could possibly want to kill Deb?"

"No one," I say, looking for an opening between the overgrown hedges, "but I don't think that glass was meant for Deb."

I find a gap and strike off on a narrow path between the shaggy bushes. The hedge maze is in need of trimming but I hope it's still navigable. We come to a crossing between two paths marked by a statue of a girl holding up her hands as if to say *Don't ask me which way to go!* I glance down both paths to check for eavesdroppers and then turn left, hoping I still remember the way.

"What do you mean?" Fred asks.

"I tried to show you but you were too busy canoodling with Nadine—"

"Thea, it's not like that—"

"I don't care," I say, turning left again at the next crossing and hurrying ahead so he can't study my face for too long. "What I was trying to show you was the lipstick mark on the base of the glass."

"Wait, what? It was the glass you marked?"

"Yes. It made its way around the room and came back to me, which is a little weird, don't you think?"

"It happened once before," he says. "Remember? At Bloody Scotland."

Of course I remember. We'd attended the Scottish mystery festival as the culmination of a two-month research trip to the Scottish Highlands for *Death Takes a Reel*. We were sunburned and toned from long hikes over the moors and mellow from days spent writing and nights spent sipping peaty scotch in a little thatched hut on the banks of the River Tay. The series was doing great, we'd just signed a new contract with our publisher for another five books. Life was good. So good that we'd finally felt secure enough in our future to think about having children. Fred had been the one to put it off at first on the grounds that we should be free to travel, and then I had put it off because I was afraid that I might not be able to keep up the writing schedule with a baby. But that summer in Scotland

I was forty-one and I'd realized that it was probably now or never.

Although I hadn't mentioned it to Fred, I'd missed my period two weeks earlier. And so, before the festival reception, I'd slipped away to take a pregnancy test. I'd come into the reception hall looking for Fred to tell him the results and found him laughing with a young, pretty girl. Someone had handed me a drink and I'd said—my eyes on Fred—*No thank you, I'm not drinking* and put the drink back on the tray after marking it. Fred had hooted and left the pretty dark-haired girl (*Fiona*, I later learned) and spun me around the room in a Scottish reel. And then at the end of the dance, Fiona had dashed her drink in Fred's face and handed me the empty glass, which had turned out to be the "poisoned" one. Apparently, Fred had been flirting with her on his research trips to the National Library in Edinburgh. When I miscarried three weeks later, I couldn't shake the superstitious dread that the "poisoned" drink Fiona had flung in Fred's face and then handed to me had come with a hex.

"I'm not sure that counts," I tell the one-armed statue at the next path intersection. "I always suspected that Fiona picked up the marked glass on purpose or marked it herself. You probably blabbed about our game to her, too." And then, before he can tell me for the hundredth time that nothing had happened between him and Fiona—as if that mattered now—I add, "Just like I suspect that someone arranged for that drink to come back to me tonight. Have you told Nadine about Drinks Roulette?"

"Everyone knows about Drinks Roulette since Joan wrote

about it on her Substack," he says, not quite answering the question.

"As if anyone ever reads those," I say, which isn't totally fair; people do read Joan's because they know she always includes some juicy bits of gossip. "Still, Joan knows, and from Nadine's broad hints about me giving Deb my drink it's clear she does, too. We'll have to mention it to the police."

"Why wouldn't we?" he says. "It's not like you really poisoned the glass when you marked it."

I notice he's said *you* and not *we*, as if the game were something I played alone.

"And we don't even know Deb was poisoned," he adds.

We've made so many turns that I feel dizzy—and lost. Castellarosa's hedge maze is famously difficult; what had made me think I would still be able to find my way in it? I'm just about to admit defeat when we take another turn and come face-to-face with a stone wall. It's made of the same pinkish sandstone as the castle walls and looks as if it might have been part of an earlier castle that fell into ruin. Chunks of stone, some with Latin inscriptions, and fragments of carved statues half sunk into the ground and overgrown with weeds and moss scatter the ground like the detritus of a lost civilization. And there, at the center of the wall, is an ancient oak door. I remember when Fred and I first found it we'd both simultaneously exclaimed: *Just like the Secret Garden!* And it was a secret garden, only not the kind in the children's book. As Fred tries the door, I half hope it's locked—it *should* be locked—but it opens with an ominous creak. That and the weathered sign partially hidden beneath a spill of ivy stating *Periculo! Piante Velenose All'Interno!* are the only warnings about what lies inside. Even the funereal yew trees bordering the walls of the small square and the lugubrious veiled statue at its center fail to adequately advertise the garden's contents.

I remember that when I begged permission of Sister Beatrice to visit the garden, explaining that it was research for a murder mystery that Fred and I were writing, she had lectured me on *playing with death,* as she put it. *If you play with death, death will play you for a fool.*

I can't help wondering if that day has come.

I follow the winding spiral path to the center of the enclosed courtyard. Sister Beatrice had explained to me that it had been laid in stone by the first abbess of the abbey in the twelfth century, much like the labyrinth of the same period in Chartres Cathedral, and that the spiral pattern extended out through Castellarosa to the village walls and beyond. Walking it was meant to provide a meditation on death and everlasting life. *Media vita in morte sumus,* one of the stones underfoot says. "In the midst of life, we are in death." Here it is literally true. The plants on either side of the stone path could send you to that death. There's innocent-looking white hellebore and purple-belled foxglove, pendulous yellow angel's trumpet and spiky Italian arum. Any one of them in the right quantity could sicken or kill. The queen of them all, though, is at the center of the circle, where a marble figure kneels in a bed of purple flowers. She's draped in a veil obscuring her face and holding her hands up as if in prayer. But she's not praying. She's not even a saint, as

I had first assumed. She's much older, Sister Beatrice told me, from the ancient Greeks. *See what she holds in her hands?*

I kneel in front of the statue, the cuts on my knee stinging. When I look down I see that the marble slab is inscribed with the words *Mors semper hic nobiscum*. "Death is always here with us." No kidding, I think, looking closer at the statue's hands. In one there is a ball of yarn, in the other a pair of scissors. She is about to snip the thread. She is Atropos, the third Fate, "she who cannot be avoided," the one who snips the thread of life.

"Don't blame yourself," Fred says, kneeling beside me. *Does he think I've come here to seek forgiveness for Deb's death?* "It's horrible about Deb but she must have been allergic to something in the drink—or she choked on one of those damned pomegranate seeds. There were tons of them in her glass."

"They weren't all pomegranate seeds," I say, opening my hand and holding up the black berry that rolled out of the broken glass—as if I'm offering it to the veiled goddess. Not that she needs another one. The fat black berries grow all around her. "This was in the marked glass," I say. "It's from this plant—Atropa bella-donna—otherwise known as deadly nightshade. Deb was poisoned."

CHAPTER FIVE

"Who would poison Deb?" Fred asks.

"I don't think the drink was meant for Deb."

Fred's eyes open wide. "You think it was meant for *you*?"

"I think it's possible. It was on a tray meant for the people on the stage so it really could have been for any one of us—" Fred blanches as he realizes that he could have been killed. "But it was in the glass I marked so whoever put the berries in the glass might have counted on me reaching for it."

"But they wouldn't know for sure you would," Fred points out.

"No, so it must not have mattered to them if someone else died."

"It's like that Agatha Christie novel, the one where the old priest dies in the beginning—"

"*Three Act Tragedy.*"

"Right. The Reverend Babbington keels over at a cocktail party and it turns out he was just a test run for the poisoner to see if he could pull it off." I shiver, imagining someone cold-blooded enough to have such little regard for human life. From beneath her veil Atropos seems to smile at me. All it takes is a little snip—

Fred settles his jacket over my shoulders.

"I'm glad you decided to tell me first," he says, "but we'll have to warn the others. Any one of the writers on the stage could be a target; it could be a jealous wannabe author or a disgruntled fan."

"Or it could be one of us," I say, turning to Fred. "I noticed that Nadine didn't take a drink."

"She doesn't drink alcohol," Fred says automatically. "She says it's inflammaging."

I glance at him to see if he's kidding. We used to make fun of people who followed fussy health regimes and used trendy wellness terms like that—but he continues with a straight face.

"And besides, what reason would Nadine have to poison any one of us? She had a very successful debut and the next two books in her series are doing well."

"Is that why you want to collaborate with her? You think some of that new author energy will rub off on you?"

"You did say our sales were lagging."

"And you think our readers will accept someone else writing Dora?"

"Well, she wouldn't necessarily be writing Dora. We were thinking maybe a new character—perhaps a younger assistant to appeal to a younger demographic."

"Then who would be writing Dora—" I begin, but then I catch his sheepish expression. "Are you planning to kill off Dora?"

"Hey," he says, holding up both hands, palms out, as if I had just accused him of plotting to murder me and not just my fictional avatar. "You were the one who was planning to kill off Dora *and* Fred."

"In a romantic finale for both of them. You're planning to knock off Dora so Fred can hook up with his hot young assistant!"

"That's not—"

"So why not just knock off Dora's creator at the same time? After all, according to our collaboration agreement I still get fifty percent of the royalties if you go on with the series without me. Did you explain *that* to Nadine? Is she happy to share your fifty percent? Maybe you both thought it would be easier if I wasn't in the picture."

I get to my feet, planning on storming off, but my dramatic exit is ruined by the labyrinth path, which is designed to be walked slowly and contemplatively. All I can contemplate right now is how ridiculous I look treading in a circle like a rat in a maze while my husband plots my demise.

Well, my fictional demise, but still.

Fred doesn't bother following the labyrinth. He leaps over the low hedgerows to catch up with me. Fortunately for me, he trips over a shrub and goes sprawling in a bed of nettles. *Ouch.* I glance back to make sure he's not mortally injured—*I'm not a monster!*—and hurry out the door. Let him pick thorns out of his own damned ass, I think, hurrying down the graveled path, or he can wait for Nadine to help him, if she can even find her way in here. Let's see how good she is at navigating a hedge maze, let alone a mystery plot. The success of her big debut relied on the reveal that her narrator—mirabile dictu!—was a lying sociopath. Like that had never been done before! As her Goodreads reviews have pointed out (okay, yes, I do sometimes read other authors' bad Goodreads reviews), her next two books in the series have rehashed the same material. She really doesn't have the skill set to plot a traditional mystery. Did she plan to have her avatar kill off Dora and then pair up with Rick? Our readers will never stand for it. I won't stand for it! According to our collaboration agreement, I have to agree if Fred wants to go on with the series. The kill clause, Penelope had called it when we drew up the contract, because either one of us can *kill* the series. At least, I think that's what it says. I have to find Penelope and ask her as soon as I get back to the hotel—

Which I should have reached by now.

It only took ten minutes to walk to the poison garden but I've been walking fast for at least twenty and am nowhere near where we started. I've come out of the hedge maze, sweaty and breathless, gulping in sweet, sticky air, but instead of facing the hotel I'm standing in front of a formal sunken garden full of roses, which means I've come out on the south side of the hedge maze. I must have gone the wrong way from the poison garden. I take a few steps forward, following the heady scent of late summer roses, a perfume tinged with leaf mold and decay.

We leave the roses in this garden until they are just past their first bloom, Sister Beatrice had explained to me when she showed me the sunken rose garden, *to add a touch of decay. That is why this garden is called the Memento Mori Garden, as is the perfume that is made from its roses.* Now the scent delivers a pang of guilt that I'm worrying about my own marital and professional problems so soon after Deb's death. As if to censure me for my callous disregard, a voice comes from behind me.

"I don't think we should be doing this so soon after Deb's death."

It's Barb, one of the Midwest Mavens, I realize, turning guiltily to explain to her what I'm doing here. But there's no one behind me. I'm about to conclude that I've manifested my own guilty conscience when I hear what sounds like Bob Robertson's voice coming from behind the hedge maze.

"Deb would want us to follow her treasure hunt to honor her memory." As if Bob, who'd argued with Deb about the treasure hunt minutes before she died, has any desire to honor her! Bob is the last person I want to see at the moment. I can hear their voices getting closer. Just before they exit the hedge maze, I duck through the arch leading into the Memento Mori Garden, into an expanse of white roses, their creamy blooms stirring in the breeze like whitecaps on a restless sea. I remember the first time I came here I was surprised that a convent maintained such an elaborate formal rose garden, but Sister Beatrice had told me the legend that the red-tinged white roses had sprouted from the white and red roses on Bianca Rosa's tomb and had been cultivated by the nuns since the twelfth century. Then she'd added more practically that the revenue from their signature fragrance, Memento Mori, paid for the upkeep of the convent and its charitable works. Back then, the convent's rosewater and scented lotions were sold in a small apothecary in Florence, but since then Memento Mori has gained a cult following among celebrities and trendsetters. I wonder if Sonia and Greg bought the licensing rights to the fragrance along with the convent and whether the profits still go to charitable works.

"Here it is!" Bob's voice intrudes on these speculations, as if to remind me that I am once again thinking about money instead of poor Deb. "I told you this was the way to the rose garden and the first clue points to an 'invisible rose.'"

It occurs to me that not only will Bob and Barb find me if I don't move, but they'll also think I followed Deb's treasure map here. I hurry quickly down a trellised path, hoping that the thick screen of climbing roses will hide me from them as I look for cover. Luckily, I spy a familiar-looking statue at the far end of the garden—a veiled woman half hidden by a cascade of hanging roses—and recall what's behind her. I step past the veiled woman, parting the curtain of thorny roses, into a cool, dark cave. It's the Memento Mori Grotto, a shallow apse carved out of the native tufa rock and meant to provide seclusion for meditation and contemplation.

And a bit of shade on a hot day of weeding, Sister Beatrice had confided when she showed it to me.

When my eyes adjust to the dark, I make out a narrow, curved bench fitted into a shallow niche. I sink onto the worn, cool marble, the cold of the stone traveling up my body like a chill reminder of death. I chafe my bare arms, remembering Sister Beatrice's words—

If you play with death, death will play you for a fool.

Deb died drinking from a glass I marked as "poison" in a

Drinks Roulette game Fred and I played. It's our fault that Deb is dead. I can't hide from that. I have to get back to the hotel and talk to the police. I rub my arms one more time, hoping to stir myself to action. I wipe my face, expecting tears, but my skin is dry. Why aren't I crying for Deb? I start to stand but then I hear footsteps on the gravel outside the grotto and sink back into my hiding place. As the steps approach I make out another familiar voice.

"All I'm saying is that we have to look at this from all angles."

It's Aleister, using the soothing, reasonable voice he employs when explaining why a plot point doesn't work in the latest Death Takes a Holiday draft. *His* hostage negotiator voice, Fred calls it, *as if he's talking someone down from a ledge*. I have always found it comforting.

It doesn't sound comforting now, though. Who is Aleister talking down? What needs looking at from all angles? Deb's death?

"You can't possibly think this is a good idea," says my agent, Penelope.

"It's a surprising one," Aleister concedes, "and I admit I was taken aback when Fred suggested it, but you have to admit it's intriguing—as if Hercule Poirot teamed up with Miss Marple."

"Only if Miss Marple were a sociopath serial killer."

"I think you underestimate Nadine. I'm sure she can write more than sociopaths."

Wait, I want to interrupt. Are my editor and agent seriously discussing Nadine St. George taking my place in the Rick and Dora books? Never mind the fact that they're talking about it right after poor Deb's death, aren't they supposed to have my back?

"Maybe," Penelope grudgingly admits, "but it's an unproven partnership and I don't see the readers accepting a substitute for Dora. Besides, Thea's the real brains behind the operation. She does the lion's share of the work from initial idea to final draft."

Thank you, Penelope!

"Sure," Aleister says, "Thea's the workhorse of the pair—"

Workhorse?!?

"—but I think you underestimate Fred. He's the real stylist of the two. His first drafts are messy but inspired—at least they were until the two of them became estranged. Do you know what happened to them?"

"It was something that went down the winter they spent in San Miguel de Allende. I've always assumed that Fred must have strayed, but Thea's never wanted to talk about it. I thought you might know more?"

Her voice tilts up at the end in an open question and I tense. Does Penelope suspect what happened between me and Aleister? But Aleister, always the gentleman, only says, "No, you know Thea, she's old-school loyal, what my aunt Charlotte would have called a real lady, which is why I think that she might be convinced to go along with Fred and Nadine's proposal if she thought it was the best solution for all involved."

"That a big *if*," Penelope says. "What's the upside for Thea?"

"Think about it—we get to keep the series, which sells the backlist, Fred's happy because he gets to write with a new partner who's not mad at him for something he did years ago, and Thea still gets fifty percent—and you get fifteen percent of that, more if Fred stays with you and Nadine switches over to your agency, which I will suggest."

I expect Penelope, who's never at a loss for words, to immediately object, but instead all I hear for a long minute is the crunch of gravel, during which time I imagine that Penelope is adding up percentages and royalties.

"I don't know," she says at last. "Why should Nadine St. George settle for twenty-five percent when she had such a strong debut?" It's not the stinging rebuke I'd been imagining but it's a good, solid question and one I'm curious about as well.

I lean forward to catch what Aleister says next but he's lowered his voice and all I hear is the crunch of retreating footsteps on the gravel followed by a loud, braying noise.

"It has to be the rose garden; the clue says so."

Bob. Followed by Barb's plaintive voice, "We've looked everywhere."

"Read the clue over again."

"'To see what can't be seen is the aim of our quest, so begin your search with the rose that lies invisible.'"

"See, it has to be in the rose garden."

"There are more rose gardens—the whole place is covered with roses," Barb complains.

"Yes, but according to the map this garden has a Latin name: Memento Mori. Something to do with death."

"'Remember you must die.'" Barb supplies the reference like the good high school English teacher she must have been. "As if we could forget that on a day like today. Poor Deb! One minute she was so alive and so happy to be winning the Miss Lemon Prize and the next she was choking on her cocktail!"

"That is if she's really dead," Bob says. "It could all be part of a ruse to trick us."

"But Shay said she was dead and she's a real doctor."

"Some doctor." Bob scoffs. "She had a slew of medical errors in her last book and when I pointed them out to her, she asked me where I went to medical school. These celebrity authors think they're above us all. I wouldn't put it past them to think they can fool us with a faked death and a rigged treasure hunt."

"Well, there's nothing here but these creepy statues. This one looks like she's lost part of her face."

She must be talking about the veiled statue in front of the grotto, which depicts Bianca Rosa, who, according to the legend, wore a veil in life to ward off potential suitors. She could be the "invisible rose" of the clue. Once Bob and Barb realize that they'll discover the grotto behind her. How will I explain what I'm doing hiding in here? I could claim I'm grieving for Deb but I haven't shed a tear.

"There's a chapel of Santa Bianca Rosa in the monastery," Barb says. "And I think there's a statue of Bianca Rosa in it. Let's go look there."

I could tell Barb that the statue in the chapel doesn't fit the clue because Bianca isn't wearing her veil, but Bob must accept Barb's theory because I hear their footsteps crunch away, leaving me alone. Only, not entirely alone. Standing inside a shallow niche scooped out of the stone is a small statue of the veiled

Bianca Rosa, an unlit votive candle, and a box of matches. I lean forward and light the candle. As the wick catches, the niche fills with a pale creamy glow and the scent of honey and roses. The candle is one made in the monastery's gift shop from white roses and beeswax. I can make out the shape of a small card propped up next to the statue. I pick it up and hold it in the candlelight. It's made of heavy creamy stock and decorated with a border of roses. Handwritten in delicate copperplate calligraphy (which I recognize as the product of a class Deb took at Michael's last year) are a few lines of poetry:

Only when he's drawn away the veil
Does he see that his quest's to no avail;
At last, he knows it is his gloomy fate
To understand his heart an hour too late.
His thirst for wealth and fame has left him dry
Beside a barren well, to weep and sigh.

The lines are from an anonymous twelfth-century poem called "The Quest for the Rose." It's the poem that brought me to Castellarosa in the first place. I had hoped to find evidence that the author was the monastery's patron saint, Bianca Rosa. Instead, I found Fred and together we used the poem as a clue that led Rick and Dora to the treasure in our first book. When I told Deb that story she said, *So you found the treasure after all.*

But we didn't, I tried to tell her, but she had only shaken her head and said, *You found the real treasure—love.*

I had never had the heart to tell her that things hadn't worked out much better for Fred and me than they had for the doomed lovers of the poem.

And now Deb's gone and based her treasure hunt on our book—on our "love story."

I put the card back beside the candle so the other treasure hunters can figure out where the next clue will be (I already have a guess) and blow out the candle. In the sudden dark I imagine all of us following Deb's steps around Castellarosa, like the knight sent out on a quest by his beloved. The smoke from the extinguished candle wafts into my eyes and I wipe my face, which is wet now. The tears have come at last, but whether they're for Deb or myself, I'm not sure.

CHAPTER SIX

Making my way back to the castle I pass other treasure hunters combing the grounds for Deb's clues. It seems dangerous for everybody to be roaming the grounds when there might be a murderer on the loose. I should speak to—

I catch myself thinking I should speak to Deb. She would have had the most sensible solution, but without her, who can I turn to? Joan is president of the International Murder Writers and worked closely with Deb planning and organizing the conference. I'll talk to her and suggest to Sonia and Greg Wilson that they lock the poison garden so no one has access to the dangerous plants in there. Surely, they will agree that the treasure hunt be called off. Bob might think it's a tribute to Deb but I can't help feeling that her death is being reduced to a game. But then, that's how this all began. A game that Fred and I invented so we could ditch everything—my dissertation, his unfinished novel—to spend all our time together.

"How can we not?" I'd posed rhetorically that first night in the taverna. "It's the perfect setting for a mystery. A confined space—"

"You should see my room—it's a cell!"

"Bit soon to be inviting me to your room, isn't it?" I'd quipped and then was chastened by the flash of red—like a torch flaring on a watchtower—in his cheeks. I quickly added, "It was probably one of the nuns' cells."

"The nuns must have spent half their lives wandering the halls looking for their rooms," he said, recovering his equilibrium quickly. "I've gotten lost so many times I had to draw a map."

"Sister Beatrice says the corridors were designed to confuse an invading army."

"*Sister Beatrice*," he repeated teasingly. "You must be on good terms to know her name. I didn't think the nuns even talked. Are you thinking of joining up?"

It was my turn then to blush. "I don't think I've got the knees for it—or the back. The sisters tend all these acres of gardens themselves and harvest the olives and grapes. They make the wine we're drinking"—I held up my glass and then a slice of bruschetta—"and the olive oil we're eating. They're really well educated, too. Sister Beatrice has been telling me the legend of the monastery." I told him the story of Bianca Rosa and her knightly lover.

"He walled himself in with his dead girlfriend and the treasure he brought back from the Crusades? Has anyone found it?"

"No," I told him. "Sister Beatrice believes it's still hidden somewhere in the castle or on the grounds."

"The treasure can be the motive for our murderer—our MacGuffin, like the Maltese Falcon! And our detective will be a world-weary knight in the tradition of Sam Spade and Philip Marlowe—you know Chandler named him Philip Malory at first—"

"After the author of *Le Morte d'Arthur,*" I chimed in, charmed that he knew his King Arthur *and* his Chandler. "What makes you think our detective is a man?"

"Don't we need one of each?" he'd asked, as if that were obvious. "A crime-fighting duo like Nick and Nora Charles—"

"You can be Rick," I said, "short for Frederick."

"And you can be Dora, short for Dorothea."

"Great, you sound like Humphrey Bogart in *Casablanca* and I sound like the ditzy blonde."

"Which will catch everyone by surprise when Dora turns out to be a total badass and the real brains of the operation."

And then he gave me that smile that would win my heart and excuse every trespass—until the last one. But I didn't know that then; all I knew was that instead of spending my days slaving away at medieval Latin in my tiny cell like a Benedictine nun, I was exploring the castle with charming and boyish Fred Morgan, who made me feel like the badass brains of the operation. In addition to the ruins of the old castle and monastery, we explored the cloisters and gardens and surrounding woods. We made up stories about the statues in the garden and pored over maps and floor plans in the library, inventing clues from the cryptic medieval carvings of mythical beasts and flowers and herbs and skulls and skeletons. We even went down into the crypt below the chapel, searching for Bianca Rosa's grave, but it was disappointingly small and severe, as befitted the burial site of monks and nuns, and none of the gravestones or sarcophagi bore the name of Bianca Rosa. There was, however, one truly frightening statue of what at first appeared to be a beautiful woman but when you followed the curve of her cheek, you caught a glimpse of bare skull beneath the veil.

"Creepy," Fred remarked when we came across it. "Do you get the idea that these nuns were obsessed with death?"

"I guess they were supposed to be focused on the next life," I said, trying to sound scholarly while the truth was that I was unnerved by the statue, by the coy turn of the woman's head, concealing bones beneath her veil, as if death were a game of hide-and-seek. A flirtation. "Which makes this the perfect setting for a murder mystery. Shall we call it *Death Takes the Castle*?"

"You really are a badass," he'd said, leaning toward me to brush a cobweb from my face. And then he kissed me, there among the crumbled sarcophagi and moldering bones. I should have known that a romance begun among the detritus of death was doomed from the start.

WHEN I REACH the hotel, I find that the conference attendees have spilled out onto the veranda and into the gardens. They're drinking prosecco and murmuring in hushed voices, subdued by the events of the day, but there's still a party-like atmosphere that sets my teeth on edge. All of this was orchestrated by Deb! From the paper lanterns to the red and black bunting and the skull-shaped candles on the tables—all the macabre touches that the mystery community delights in seem in poor taste now while Deb's body lies in the reception hall.

Is she still there? Have the police come? I'm torn between wanting to know more—and telling the police about the belladonna berry—and fleeing the scene like a criminal. Thank God Joan spots me and comes to my rescue.

"There you are!" she says, grabbing my arm and pulling me toward the chapel and cloisters on the north side of the building. "I've been looking all over for you. The police have come and they want to speak to all the people who were on the stage. Buck's in with them now so you can bet they'll be stuck listening to him spouting theories on whodunit for a while, which gives you a chance to go up to your room and"—she eyes my bedraggled state with pity—"freshen up."

"I haven't even checked in yet," I point out, "or gotten my room key."

Joan gives me her most winning smile, the one she uses for publicity photos, draws a key out of her pocket, and dangles it in front of my eyes. "I got Sonia Wilson to give it to me so you wouldn't have to deal with anybody before you're ready."

"You're a lifesaver, Joan," I say, taking the heavy metal key from her. It looks just like the key to my room last time. "I'd have thought Sonia and Greg would have updated to electronic key cards."

"It's certainly a choice," Joan says in exactly the same tone I've heard her use to dismiss a book she doesn't think much of. "Sonia says she thinks it's more atmospheric, but *I* think it's a cost-cutting measure, like skimping on fresh towels because it's more environmentally conscious and charging an arm and a leg for the spa treatments and bottled water. Come on. I've also discovered the back way up so you don't have to go through the lobby. This place is laid out like a cornfield maze."

She takes me through an arched doorway into a narrow stone corridor that runs between the wall of the chapel and the colonnaded arcade of the cloister. The only sound besides our footsteps—Joan's loud on the marble flagstones—is the drip of water in an old fountain and the hum of bees among the herbs and flowers. The sight of all those medicinal herbs reminds me of what I found in Deb's glass.

"You said Buck would be giving the police his theory of what happened to Deb—what are people saying?"

"The general consensus is that she had an allergic reaction to something in her drink—at least that's what Sonia is spreading about."

"But she said that she personally checked all the forms we turned in for allergies."

"And Deb didn't list any, but someone told her that Deb was allergic to pepper and apparently there's a dash of cayenne in those drinks, which if you ask me is just showing off. Give me a good old-fashioned Old-Fashioned any day. All these drinks with parsley, sage, rosemary, and thyme sound more like hippie folk songs than cocktails to me."

She looks askance at the herbs growing in the cloister as if they're personally responsible for the modern-day corruption of mixology. I could tell her that the Benedictine nuns brewed an herbal liqueur that was the toast of crowned princes throughout Europe (and rumored to have aphrodisiac properties) but instead I dig in my pocket and take out the belladonna berry.

"Deb didn't die from pepper," I say, "she was poisoned with belladonna. I doubt that was one of the approved ingredients in Sonia's signature cocktail."

"Oh my!" Joan gasps, splaying her fingers over her bosom. "You're right! I killed off a character with one of those in *Biscuits and Graves*. And you found it in Deb's drink?"

"In the wreckage thereof," I reply.

"You have to tell the police right away." We've reached a stairway at the end of the cloister. "Do you still want to go up to your room first?" She looks doubtfully at my rumpled clothing.

"Yes," I say, "I need time to think."

"That's probably smart—besides, you want to look your best in front of the carabinieri," Joan says, heading up the stairs. It's a narrow back stairwell that the abbess used to reach her private quarters. It took me a whole summer of exploring the monastery to discover it but Joan has found it after a week and is racing up the steep stone steps as if they're her own personal StairMaster.

"If Deb really was poisoned, that changes everything. The police will be looking for a murderer. Anyone who had access to Deb's glass—"

"I handed it to her!" I wail.

"That's right," Joan concedes, as if just remembering that little detail, "but I sent the waiter up to the stage, remember? Anyone could have taken that glass."

"It was marked," I say, pausing for breath on the landing

beneath a faded fresco of some saint who's been stretched out on a rack and is being visited by a winged angel who doesn't seem to be offering much help. "I had marked the bottom with my lipstick earlier. Fred and I were playing Drinks Roulette."

Joan widens her eyes, looking as surprised as the saint on the wall. "Oh my gosh! And the glass came back to you? How strange!"

"That's what I thought," I say. "But what if someone marked it so I would pick it up?"

"You mean—" Joan lays her hand on my arm. "You think the glass was meant for you?"

"Maybe. It doesn't make sense that Deb was the target since it was just by chance that I gave the drink to her. Besides, who would want to kill Deb?"

"No one," Joan agrees, eyeing the long-suffering saint on the wall. "The woman was a saint. You on the other hand . . ."

"Thanks a lot. But you're right. I can think of a couple people who might want me dead. Nadine St. George is top on my list. You heard her announcement."

"I *was* surprised. I knew you were thinking of ending the series but I couldn't imagine you'd sign off on someone else taking your place, especially not Nadine St. George. I can't see that ice queen writing Dora."

"She wouldn't be," I say. "Fred just told me that the plan is to kill off Dora and give Rick a new, younger assistant."

Joan gasps, seemingly more upset over the threat to my fictional alter ego than to myself. "The nerve of that bitch! After all the work you've put into that series! And believe me, everyone knows it's your work and brains that make it as good as it is. How could Fred—"

"To be fair," I say, "I was planning to end the series, as you know. I told Fred on the plane coming over."

"How'd he take it?"

"Not well. I knew he'd be upset but I hoped he'd see it as a chance to return to the literary fiction he always wanted to write."

Joan rolls her eyes. "*Men*. They all think they've got the Great American Novel stashed in their briefs. As if the Rick and Dora books weren't twice as good as what gets passed off by some uptight editors at *The New York Times* as *lit-ter-a-chure*." She pronounces it like the name of a rare disease. "Fred was probably terrified that you'd call his bluff and he'd actually have to sit down and write some obtuse five-hundred-page monstrosity. But to plot Dora's demise with another woman!" She shakes her head sadly but then brightens. "Wait, don't you have a kill clause in your collab agreement? I certainly did when I wrote those books with Pete."

I'd forgotten that Joan and Pete had collaborated on a couple of romances set in World War II Paris. Joan had seen it as a way of breaking into the more lucrative world of suspense but the books had died on the vine and she'd confided that collaborating with Pete had felt like studying for finals with the nerdiest boy in high school. "Of course. They can't go ahead without my approval and I'd still get fifty percent of the royalties, which means—"

"Nadine and Fred would have to split the remaining fifty

percent. I can't imagine either of them would be happy with that. Oh, honey—" She gives me a look so full of pity I feel like I might be that saint stretched out on the rack. I expect her next words will be to warn me that my own husband is trying to kill me, but instead she says, "You'd better make sure you have a good lawyer."

JOAN LEAVES ME at the door to my suite, cautioning me to be careful. "If you need me just text and I'll be there. I'm right below you. And if you want to stay in my room, there's always Deb's bed . . ."

I'd forgotten that Joan and Deb had been sharing a room, which must feel weird for Joan now. I turn to Joan after I've opened the door to ask if she'd feel better staying in our suite, but she's already shaking her head. "Never mind, my room looks like a nun's cell in comparison to this. Let me know if you want to switch. I'd risk a murder attempt for that view." She wiggles her fingers at me and continues on in the opposite direction from where we came, toward the main staircase.

When I turn back to the suite, I see that it is indeed impressive. Taking up the whole floor of the tower, this had been the abbess's quarters when I was here, and before then it had been the duke's private quarters. A marble mosaic floor, its design so faded it's hard to make out, stretches to the floor-to-ceiling French doors framing a view of the Tuscan hills to the east. Burgundy damask couches and chairs float above the marble design like ships sailing off to sea. A whiff of jasmine and rose wafts in from the French doors—the *open* French doors. I freeze. *The staff wouldn't leave the doors open, would they? Has someone been here? Is anyone here now?* "Hello?" I call. "Fred?"

I open the door to one of the bedrooms. It looks like a cyclone has swept through it. Fred's suitcase is splayed on the bed spilling out clothes, books, and toiletries like a gutted corpse. There's a hint of musk in the air and the mirror above the bureau is steamed over. The bathroom door is open, the floor strewn with damp towels. Fred must have gotten back from the garden before me and taken a quick shower before going down to talk to the police. I should do the same.

I look for my luggage but realize that of course he's moved it to the other bedroom. Since San Miguel, we've used the excuse that he snores as a reason to always book a suite with two bedrooms. He'll have given me the bigger room. He might be planning to murder me but he'd never act like anything less than a gentleman.

I pick up the towels from the floor and hang them over the rack before I leave Fred's room—to spare the maid extra work, I tell myself, which is the same reason that I pick up a discarded shirt from the floor and place it on top of the bed, where I can't help but brush against the piles of paper spilling out of his briefcase, dislodging one that flutters to the floor like a dying swan. I stoop to pick it up. It's a page from our original collaboration agreement. *Why does he have it with him?* He didn't know I was ending the series until we talked on the plane.

One paragraph has been circled in red.

I take it over to the window because it's too dark in the room to read and I suddenly feel a need for some air. I lean against the window frame and in the fading light I see that it's a subsection of the kill clause. The sickly sweet smell of roses past their prime fills the air—*memento mori,* indeed—and a pair of mourning doves coo a soulful refrain like the final aria of a tragic opera. *Shall one of the partners predecease the other,* the clause reads, *the full rights to the series shall revert to the surviving partner.*

CHAPTER SEVEN

I take a quick shower, as much to cool myself down as to freshen up. Standing in front of the steamy mirror I catch my own reflection. I've been so immersed in memories of my time here twenty years ago that I'm half expecting to see my twenty-something self in the mirror. And for a moment I think I do see her, like a ghost hovering behind the veil of steam, a cloud of gold hair hovering above a pale face. But when I wipe the condensation from the glass, I spot the glint of silver in the blond and deeper lines around the eyes.

Memento mori, I say silently to my reflection. But then I hear Joan's voice reply with the only bit of Latin I've ever heard from her: *Nolite te bastardes carborundorum. Which is Latin,* she would add, *for you just need a little concealer and foundation.*

I comply, then quickly dress in black capris, a silk tunic, and a cashmere pashmina—elegant but casual and warm enough to ward off the chill of the old stone building. It's something I recall from my time here twenty years ago; even in summer these old stones hold the cold of centuries.

I walk down the corridor toward the main stairs, past a row of closely spaced doors. These were the nuns' cells when the building was a convent, but now each one has a number on it, and when one of the doors opens, I peek inside and see two double beds with puffy duvets and brocade drapes at the window. They must have knocked down some walls and combined the cells to make normal-size rooms. And gotten rid of the bars on the windows.

I start down the main stairs quickly and nearly go flying on the slippery marble. The helical staircase demands attention. The marble steps have been worn smooth by centuries of castle servants, heavy-footed knights, and the weary tread of nuns. The staircase, Sister Beatrice told me, had once been inside the original tower of the castello and remained when the building was later renovated. The tightly coiled steps can make you dizzy. In the first draft of *Death Takes the Castle* we killed off the officious academic Hal Grazer (a bald-faced stand-in for my adviser, Fraser Halliday) by pushing him down the stairs (we later gave him a more gruesome end).

I stop, gripping the banister, and look up to where the stairs coil above me. A shadow falls across the gray marble. Is someone on the floor above? I listen for footsteps but all I hear is the beating of my own heart amplified in the stairwell as if I'm trapped inside a marble tomb.

Like Bianca buried alive in the crypt below the castle.

I shake off the notion—we never did find her tomb; it was just a story—and continue walking down, gripping the banister and stepping slowly like the careful old woman I will someday (Deo volente, I hear Sister Beatrice say, *God willing*) become.

The helical stairs empty out into the lobby, which is still decorated with the macabre red and black bunting and grinning skulls. Someone should have had the good sense to clear away all the trappings of death in the wake of a real death . . . but then I realize that the *someone* who would have had that good sense is dead.

Oh, Deb, what will we do without you?

I approach the desk, thinking to ask the clerk about having the decorations removed, but I'm intercepted by Sonia Wilson midway across the lobby.

"Ah, there you are, dear Thea!" She grasps my arm and pulls me into an alcove. "How are you holding up? All of this is so shocking! I am beside myself!"

I notice that rather than looking "beside herself," she has changed into a somber dove-gray suit (Prada, I suspect) and swept her dark hair into a modest and elegant chignon that shows off a pair of demure pearl studs. Apparently, she has also been inspecting my wardrobe change.

"So smart of you to dress warmly and comfortably," she says. "These hallways are so drafty. You would not believe what we spent on updating the heating system this year and yet still the place is cold as a tomb—Oh!" She splays her fingers over her mouth. "I did not mean . . . At any rate, I was just coming upstairs to find you. The detective is waiting for you in our office. He has asked to see each of the guests who were on the stage and you are the last remaining."

She's somehow made it sound as if I'm the "final girl" of the Poirot nominees.

"You and Greg were on the stage, as well," I point out. "Have you both had your interviews with the police?"

"Of course! Greg and I have put ourselves and the entire staff of Castellarosa at the service of the Florentine police. Thank God for Greg! He is so good with the locals. You know, the Italians really respect a strong man in these situations. You must have found your husband such a help over the years with all the travel that you do. Don't you find that it's easier to manage all of life's bumps with a strong partnership? Greg always says that I am the velvet glove and he is the iron fist. Take your friend, Deb, for instance. You know she was here all week setting up for the conference, and while she seemed a very independent and capable woman, I thought at times that the strain of doing it all on her own was a bit much for her."

"Joan was here helping her," I point out, unsure of where Sonia is going with this character dissection of Deb. Is she suggesting that a woman needs a male partner?

"Oh yes, Ms. Acosta is such a capable woman, only a little . . . demanding, no? I'm afraid she was a bit brusque with some of the staff, who are all so lovely but don't always understand American English, especially Texan-American English. I was a tad worried, too, that she was running your friend Deb a bit ragged."

"Running her ragged?"

"Yes, Deb seemed quite overwhelmed—almost obsessed with this treasure hunt of hers and so secretive about it—but then you probably know all about that. Did she talk to you about the treasure hunt?"

"Not really," I say. "Fred was more her point person on that—"

"But surely he must have discussed it with you as well? After all, you are partners."

I find myself suddenly embarrassed to admit that Fred and I had barely seen each other all summer, let alone that he hadn't even told me he was working on the treasure hunt with Deb. "He knew I was working on the revision of our next book and so spared me all that," I say instead.

"Ah, so thoughtful. You see what I mean, then. If Deb had had a partner who'd made sure she told me that she was allergic to pepper . . . well . . ." She spreads her hands as if to indicate the future that Deb could have had.

"Oh," I say, "I don't think it was pepper that killed poor Deb."

She raises both eyebrows and regards me expectantly, but instead of explaining my theory of belladonna poisoning, I tell her that I'm ready to see the Florentine detective, which I think, as she shows me the way to her office, could have been the title of a book Deb would have loved.

SONIA WILSON ESCORTS me down a long narrow hallway adorned on both sides by a fresco mural depicting the life of Santa Bianca Rosa. Here she is as a medieval princess wearing a pointy hat at her father's banquet table, entertaining a horde of knights preparing to embark on their crusade to the Holy Land. While the knights drink and cavort, she keeps her eyes demurely lowered. In the next scene, though, her attention is caught by a humble squire, cowering from the blow of a blustering knight. In the next she stands above the knight, one hand raised to stay his blow. A ray of light streams through an arched window above her and illuminates her hand and the face of the cowering squire as if a heavenly force were uniting them. *Shipping them,* as they say in fan fiction. In the next picture, the princess and the squire sit in a secluded garden full of lush red roses. Peering through the rosebushes is the face of the bellicose knight. The next pictures take us through the squire's proposal, the king's refusal, and the squire's promise to his beloved to return as a wealthy knight worthy of her hand in marriage.

The rest of the story is told on the other side of the corridor, but we have reached the manager's office, which had been Sister Beatrice's when I was here twenty years ago. I know that she is long gone, but still, it's startling when Sonia opens the door to reveal a man sitting behind her desk. A big man, too, I see, when he rises and extends a long arm toward the straight-backed chair in front of the desk. He must be well over six feet tall, with wide shoulders that strain his rumpled suit jacket and a broad craggy face that could have been stamped on a Roman coin. I sink down into my chair feeling a bit like that squire cowering beneath the brawny knight.

Sonia Wilson is still hovering at the doorway. "Do you need anything else, Detective?" she asks. "*Un espresso? Acqua minerale*? I can have the kitchen make up a tray for you—"

"Non, grazie," he says, waving a heavy hand in dismissal.

I sneak a look back to catch Sonia's miffed expression—not so fun to be on the receiving end of a *strong man's* dismissal—before she bows herself out and shuts the door behind her. Then I turn to the detective.

"*Buona sera, signora.* Thank you for taking time out of your busy schedule to meet with me." His English is stiff but flawless and laced with a hint of mocking condescension.

"Of course. I want to do everything in my power to apprehend Deb's killer, Detective . . ."

"Bardi," he barks. "Detective Bardi. And why do all you mystery writers assume she was murdered? Is it because every death in your books is a murder? Already today I have listened to the most preposterous theories involving lost treasure, spiteful vendettas, and something called"—he looks down to consult his notebook—"*fridging*, even though Signora Andersen's death occurred nowhere near a refrigerator."

"It's a mystery trope," I say, wondering who had brought it up. Nadine, maybe? She actually did kill a victim by locking her in a walk-in freezer. "It's when a beautiful woman is summarily dispatched for the sole purpose of providing the male narrator with a tragic backstory. I don't see how that would apply to Deb, though—not that she wasn't a beautiful person—but who's supposed to be the tortured man? Pete Tyler was sweet on her . . ." I let my voice trail off and wait for a reaction. I'm rewarded with a twitch of the eyebrow that tells me it was Pete who offered up the fridging theory. "Oh, poor Pete," I say. "But I don't think that's why Deb was killed—"

"We will not know for certain whether Signora Andersen's death will be ruled a homicide until we receive the medical examiner's report."

"Well," I say, digging into my purse and extracting the wrapped belladonna berry. "Spoiler alert. I found this in the glass Deb drank from." I unwrap the berry and hold it out for

Detective Bardi to see. He looks down at it as if I have shoved something foul under his nose. Which I suppose I have.

"You are showing me something spoiled? Something rotten?"

"It's belladonna," I say. "I went to the poison garden to check—"

"The poison garden?"

"Some of the nuns called it the medicinal garden as the plants have useful properties in small doses. But enough Atropa belladonna could definitely kill you."

"And you removed this from Signora Andersen's glass?" he growls, leaning toward me. "You tampered with evidence on my crime scene?"

"It rolled out of the glass straight at me," I say. "It would have gotten trampled if I hadn't picked it up."

"And I'm supposed to take your word for that?"

I shrug, trying to look offhand, but I suspect the effect is more of a cringe. "I'm sure you'll find more when you examine the remains of the glass. Um . . . you'll also find my fingerprints. I handed the glass to Deb."

"Yes, I have already been informed of that. And now you tell me you are familiar with the poisonous plant that you believe killed Signora Andersen. I suppose I will find your fingerprints on the handle of the door to this poison garden. You do realize that you are making quite a convincing case for your own guilt."

I sigh. "Yes, of course I realize that, but what choice do I have? I loved Deb. Whoever murdered her has to pay so I have to tell you everything or—"

"Or you would look more guilty when I found out these things without your help. Or did you not think I was capable of discovering 'the clues' myself? Perhaps you fancy yourself like the English Miss Marple, who must help out the bumbling detective."

I'm too startled by being compared to Miss Marple—I'm hardly old enough to be the elderly spinster!—to respond right away. But then I see from the smile creeping over his face that that was the hoped-for response. He wanted to put me on the defensive.

"I don't think there's anything bumbling about you, Detective Bardi," I say. "I suppose you also noticed the lipstick mark on the base of Deb's glass."

The smile spreads wider. "*Ma certo, signora,* and your husband has already told me about the little game you two like to play."

Of course he has.

"So, you see," I say, trying not to show my annoyance that Fred has stolen my thunder, "the poisoner's intended target must have been me."

The smile vanishes from the detective's face so quickly I find myself doubting it had ever been there. "Or you wanted me to think that you were the target. The marked glass could be what we call *una falsa pista.*"

"*Pista?*" I repeat, searching my mind for the English translation. I vaguely recall the word has something to do with bowling alleys.

"A false lead," he translates helpfully. "Or what I believe you mystery writers call a red herring."

I LEAVE FEELING as if the detective has gotten more out of me than I have gotten out of him. Some Miss Marple I am! He already knew about Drinks Roulette (*damn Fred!*) and was waiting to see if I would bring it up. I come out of the office as backfooted as when Sister Beatrice called me in to talk about my *love affair,* as she called it. I had thought she was going to lecture me on sneaking a man into my room, but instead she'd wanted to warn me against treating what Fred and I had too lightly.

I don't even know what it is we have yet, Sister, I'd told her.

She'd held my gaze before telling me what it was. *It's love,* cara, *a blind man could see that. It is a rare and precious commodity; be careful not to waste it.*

Good thing Sister Beatrice isn't here to see what's become of me and Fred. Speaking of the devil, I wonder where he's gotten to.

I follow the sound of voices down the hall and into the lobby, where the conference attendees have clumped into small groups in the seating areas. I spot Lindsay in her skull dress laughing with two other women in bookish cardigans and overstuffed canvas book bags sporting the MurderCon logo of skull and quill pen. They also all wear the same silver scythe pin Lindsay wears, designating them as the Goth Librarians. One spots me and waves a copy of *Death Takes the Castle,* miming a request for an autograph. Does she want me to sign it *So nice meeting you at MurderCon on the occasion of Deb Andersen's murder?*

Although librarians are pretty much my favorite people in the world, I can't face making small talk right now. Instead,

I pretend not to see her and duck down another hallway toward the library. It had been my refuge twenty years ago, the reason I'd come to Castellarosa. I'd spent days poring over the old manuscripts—hymn books and devotionals, translations of classical works, bestiaries and herbariums, account books from the monastery going back to the twelfth century—hoping to find a scrap written in the same handwriting as the fragment of what I hoped was Bianca Rosa's poem, which had been discovered in Florence during the great flood of 1966.

The fragment had been bound into a fourteenth-century handbook on raising bees, one of the books damaged when the Arno flooded in 1966, swamping libraries and museums, damaging priceless art and rare books. Youthful volunteers from America and around the continent—the so-called mud angels—had rescued many of the damaged books from the Biblioteca Nazionale. A young nun working on restoring the damaged books had found the poem fragment beneath the marbled endpaper and, recognizing its similarity to the legend of Castellarosa, had written a monograph on it.

That nun was Sister Beatrice.

The light vanishes as I step into the library. I remember that there were clouds and cherubs painted on the coffered ceiling but they're invisible in the gloom. Standing in the dark, I fear that the library has fallen victim to the Wilsons' renovations. Perhaps the old books have been packed up and shipped, like the nuns, to Florence. They probably should be in climate-controlled archives accessible to scholars in the Biblioteca Nazionale anyway.

Wouldn't these books be better off in Florence? I'd asked Sister Beatrice when I first arrived at Castellarosa, a little put out that I'd had to take three buses to such an out-of-the-way place to do my research.

So they can be swept away in the next flood? she'd replied, blinking through Coke-bottle-thick lenses. *And besides, how would you find the treasure of Castellarosa sitting in a library in Florence?*

But, of course, there was no treasure.

As my eyes adjust to the dark, I make out a thread of light on the far side of the room—the seam between heavy drapes. I strike out for it across the cold stone floor, my footsteps echoing hollowly in the high-ceilinged room.

This floor was part of the Roman villa that was here before the medieval castle, before the monastery, built with pipes beneath it to heat the room. You can still see the Latin inscriptions in the stones that they used, she had said, pointing to the worn, honey-colored slabs that made up the floor. *That is why it is so dry. It's the perfect place to store books and paper. This was the scriptorium where the nuns transcribed the great books of antiquity—*

I pause with my hand on the heavy drapes, smiling at Sister Beatrice's history of the convent. I was familiar with the theory that the convent of Castellarosa was one of the few places where nuns worked in the scriptorium, but I also knew there was no evidence supporting the idea. Looking back, I can see how the story fit into the old nun's romantic notions—just as she thought I had found some special bond with Fred that I must be careful not to waste. Oh, Sister Beatrice, I think, it hasn't worked out and now I'm afraid that he might be trying to kill me—or at least his girlfriend is—and that policeman thinks I killed Deb. What should I do now?

Instead of the nun's raspy old voice I hear a young, strident one. "No, it hasn't gone exactly according to plan but we can still fix it—"

A slim figure, silhouetted against the light, appears in the doorway, one hand to her ear and the other splayed open as if imploring the painted cherubs above her. A modern Botticelli might paint her as *Venus on Her Cell Phone*. In fact, I notice now, with her long blond hair hanging loose to her waist, she could be me twenty years ago. I wonder if that's what drew Fred to her.

"I don't think Thea will give us any trouble—" She halts mid-sentence when she sees that the object of her conversation is lurking in the shadows. Instead of looking embarrassed, she looks annoyed, as if I've interrupted her private conversation. "Speak of the devil," she says into her phone. "I'll have to get back to you, Jade. I think Thea and I are going to have a little chat."

She pockets her phone and steps into the library, arms folded over her chest. "Were you waiting for me here?"

"What?" I snap, backfooted by her taking the offensive. "How would I know you were headed for the library, Nadine?"

She shrugs. "I thought Fred might have told you. We were talking about using it as a backdrop for a promotional Insta reel. But I see the books are all gone. It's pretty dreary, really."

"I'm sure you can find a more dramatic backdrop. Did you get any footage of Deb's death? Isn't that more your brand?"

She takes a sip of air as if practicing a Zen meditation technique and folds her palms into a namaste salutation. "I can understand how upset you must be, Thea. First, learning about my collaboration with Fred and then seeing your friend die—"

"They're hardly comparable," I snap. "Although I can't help wondering if they're connected."

"Connected?" She looks genuinely surprised and I'm glad that she's the one backfooted now. "How?"

"You must have known that I'll still get fifty percent of the royalties for all the Death Takes a Holiday books going forward, and I can't imagine you'd want to share the royalties—or share Fred, for that matter."

She laughs, but the sound, echoing in the lofty room, sounds forced. "Share Fred? You don't own him, Thea, as much as you've acted like you do all these years."

"Is that what Fred told you?" I demand, bristling.

"He didn't have to," she replies. "Once I got to know him it was clear how much you've been calling the shots since day one, dictating what he should write—"

"It's called an outline, Nadine, but wait, you don't do them. Good luck collaborating with another pantser."

"I'm not talking about the Death Takes a Holiday books," she says. "I'm talking about Fred's freedom to be the writer he was always meant to be—and the *man* he was always meant to be."

"And you think I've been holding him back?" I ask, taking a step forward. She flinches as if she's physically afraid of me, and for a moment I see myself as she must see me: an aging writer and jealous wife.

"I think you've cared more about the series than your marriage," she replies, "or about Fred's welfare."

"Oh my," I tut, "didn't anyone at your fancy MFA program teach you to avoid clichés? You've fallen for the oldest trope in the book—poor, underappreciated husband. Did he tell you *my wife doesn't understand me*? Do you think things will be different with you? That you'll be able to bring out Fred's undiscovered genius?"

"Is that what you're afraid of, Thea?" she asks coolly. "That if you let him have his freedom, he'll outshine you and everyone will know you were never the real brains of the operation after all?"

So that's the role she's cast me in, even worse than the jealous wife: the aging desperate diva clinging to the shreds of her reputation. Bette Davis in *All About Eve*. "Well," I say, "I guess he won't have that problem collaborating with you."

She colors as my remark sinks in and for a moment I regret my words, but then she rallies. "So you won't stand in the way of our working together?"

I laugh. "Not on your life! I've got a kill clause and I plan to use it."

She nods. "If that's how you want to play it," she says. "But you may want to remember that you're not the only one here who's plotted a few murders."

And with that, she turns and leaves.

CHAPTER EIGHT

I stand in the library listening to Nadine's retreating footsteps on the stone floor fade, her last words echoing in my head.

You're not the only one who's plotted a few murders.

Was that a threat? What kind of murders was she talking about? The fictional kind? We were all used to talking blithely about murders. Surely that's all she meant, and yet . . . Someone killed Deb with a drink meant for me. Could it have been Nadine? But would she really try to kill me so she could take over my place in the Death Takes a Holiday series?

Unless it wasn't just about the series. Unless it was about Fred. Just how well did she and Fred know each other?

Yes, he'd greeted her with a hug at the airport, but that could have been because they bonded at ThrillerFest earlier this spring. Now that I think of it, I do remember seeing them together at the bar at ThrillerFest but that was back in May. Had they been spending time together since then? But wasn't Nadine in England at her Very Important Oxford Gig? I remember seeing her posting pictures of herself hiking on the moors (of course I follow her on Insta; she'd followed me and it would have been rude not to follow her back!) and then at some posh writing residency in Scotland and taking tea with some minor royal in London. She'd clearly been in the UK the last few months while Fred had been in New York City—

Or had he?

I stand in the library, searching my memory of the last three months. Fred had been hard to get in touch with but we had emailed and texted . . . but had I seen him since ThrillerFest? I'd had a busy summer getting ready for this trip, correcting the copyedit and galleys of our nineteenth book, and writing the outline for the twentieth. Our cat Tuppence had been in and out of the vet all summer with kidney problems. Fred had sent a lot of concerned texts about her, but now that I think of it, it was a little funny that he'd never suggested coming up from the city to Rhinebeck to visit or help out. Was that because he wasn't in the city?

Had he gone to the UK without telling me?

Not that he was obligated to tell me if he left the country. There was nothing in our distribution-of-assets agreement that stipulated informing the other party when crossing international borders. Over the last six years, though, we have done each other the courtesy of sharing our plans. After all, as far as the world is concerned, we're still married. And not *just* married; we're famous as a married writing couple. It would be embarrassing if some reporter mentioned they'd seen one of us at the Venice Biennale or fly-fishing in Montana and we didn't know about it. Especially if the other one was spotted hanging around with a beautiful younger writer.

Which might be why Fred would keep a trip to the UK a secret from the press—but would he really keep it a secret from me?

Maybe.

If things had gotten serious with Nadine.

I look around the library as if the answers to my questions are here on the shelves, but the shelves are bare. The collection of Castellarosa has been moved. There are no answers here at all. But I have an idea where I might find at least one.

THE SHELVES MIGHT be bare but not all the library's secrets are gone. Pressing a carved gargoyle on the third shelf from the top releases a false bookshelf that swings open to reveal a secret passage. When I showed it to Fred, he had all sorts of ideas for how we could use it in *Death Takes the Castle*. It would be how the real murderer got to the library to commit the crime even though they were supposedly locked in the tower room. It would be how the returning knight discovered his beloved Bianca Rosa. It would be how Rick and Dora escaped the villain in the final scene. Little had Fred known it would be how his suspicious wife would avoid the crowds to find out if her husband was cheating.

Not that it would be cheating, exactly, I remind myself as I go up the steep, narrow stone steps. Although we hadn't discussed it in the lawyer's office, Fred and I had a good long, mature talk afterward in the Royalton bar near Grand Central before my train back to the Hudson Valley. Over a bottle of Venere Rose, the signature sparkling wine of Castellarosa, which

Fred had touchingly ordered specially for the occasion, he told me that he just wanted me to be happy and I told him that that was all I wanted for him as well—plus an Edgar Award and a Netflix deal, of course.

To which he had laughed and said, *Well, obviously.*

And then I told him I understood that of course there'd be other women and he feigned disinterest and remarked that the men would be lining up for me, starting with the lawyer who handled our agreement, and I scoffed at the idea (he was right; the lawyer asked me out a circumspect three weeks later). After we had both assured each other that we had no interest in dating other people, we agreed that if we *did* meet someone, we would be discreet, and that if it got serious, we would tell each other.

Then, over the last glasses of wine, he told me that he'd never feel the same about anyone else, that what we had together at Castellarosa was unlike anything he had felt about anyone else, and that there was still time to change our minds. *Isn't that what the ending of* Death Takes the Castle *is all about? That there's always time for a second chance?* Then he told me that he had booked the penthouse suite.

I blame the Venere Rose. Sister Beatrice confided to me that the grapes were watered by a spring once sacred to Venus and that it was renowned for its aphrodisiac properties. I'd been shocked to hear a nun talking about such things and even more shocked to find myself following Fred up to the penthouse suite, where another bottle of Venere Rose was chilling in an ice bucket along with a plate of Tuscan figs and cheeses. We didn't get to the second bottle or the figs or the cheese. We barely made it to the bed. When he kissed me, his lips tasted of grapes and the Tuscan sun as they had the first time we kissed. It was as if we had gone back to my tiny cell in Castellarosa, where we had to still each other's cries lest we be heard. We didn't have to in the penthouse suite of the Royalton.

In the morning, though, I awoke to stripes of light slashed across the bed, as if a jealous lover had taken a knife to them, and I remembered another room, in San Miguel. When Fred woke up, I told him I was glad we had had one last time together. If he was disappointed he didn't say, he only promised again that he would let me know if there was ever anyone important and asked me to return the favor.

So why hasn't he told me about Nadine? Did that mean she wasn't important? Or that he thought I'd be upset he was seeing a younger and more glamorous writer? I pause at the first landing, winded by the climb, my heart pounding in my chest, my face damp—

I wipe my face and find it's wet with tears once again.

Stupid, I tell myself, sprinting up the rest of the way. It's not like I haven't had lovers. There was the lawyer, who was very sweet but ultimately a bit boring (he only read nonfiction!), a painter up in Rhinebeck who didn't read at all and asked me to loan him money, and Aleister for a hot minute during the Frankfurt Book Fair last year, until we had decided it wasn't professional. Which had pissed Fred off when he found out about it. In fact, now that I think about it, I never did discover how Fred found out about Aleister. I thought we'd been so discreet.

Our rooms were on the same floor but we never spent the whole night together; we'd traveled separately after the fair to a sleepy little village in the Austrian Alps, and I'd been careful not to post anything from there. But when I got back to New York, Fred had been waiting in Rhinebeck for me, where he'd been watching our elderly cats, Tommy and Tuppence, and he'd been *furious*.

You've crossed a line, he'd fumed. I'd mixed the personal with the professional (as if our entire lives weren't a fatal mix of the two) and I'd betrayed our agreement.

But he's not important, I'd wailed, even though I'd told Aleister differently on our last day in the Alps, and I'd been planning on telling Fred about what had happened when I got home. As soon as I said the words, though, I realized they were true. The whole time we were in the Alps I'd tried to convince myself it was as romantic as those first days with Fred in Castellarosa. But it wasn't.

It's over anyway, I told Fred, meaning it.

But Fred had been angry ever since. So angry that he'd decided to get his revenge by sleeping with someone he knew I was jealous of already? (*Oxford!*) So angry that he'd plotted with her to take over the series from me? So angry that he'd plotted with her to *poison* me?

No.

I was letting my imagination run away with me. *You have a really dark imagination,* Fred had said appreciatively when I outlined how we could murder our next victim by strangling them with the pull ropes in the bell tower. *I'd hate to be on your bad side.*

Over the years, though, he'd come up with some pretty grisly scenarios himself. *I've learned from the master,* he'd quipped on a panel once. *Don't ever cross Thea; she knows a hundred ways to commit murder without leaving a trace.*

The secret passage takes me straight to the fourth floor next to the door to my suite. *The abbess used it to go down to the scriptorium at night to check on the work of her novices,* Sister Beatrice told me, *and to read the books they were working on.*

I open the door to the suite gingerly and listen for any sound. All I hear are church bells tolling from the village far below us in the valley. I pad softly to Fred's room and tap on the door. A chime from my phone nearly makes me leap out of my skin. So much for skulking around. When I look down, though, I see it's a photograph of Fred at the bar with Pete and Buck, waving beer bottles at each other. *FYI,* Joan has texted me, *your hubby is trying to convince Buck it's not appropriate to hold a wake for Deb at Noir at the Bar.* I reply with an eye roll emoji and namaste hands. At least I know where Fred is, and if experience is any guide, once Fred and Buck get into it they'll be at it for a while.

I open the door to Fred's room with impunity and walk in. I see immediately that he has been back up and straightened the mess he'd left before. I'm glad I left the collaboration contract where I found it. He may suspect I saw it but he won't know for sure. He's put it away somewhere. I open up his wardrobe and look for his laptop case. There's always a chance he's got it with him—or, I realize as I spot the room safe, that he's locked it away. In which case I'm out of luck . . . unless, he still uses the same combination we always used when we'd shared a room safe. Unlikely, but . . .

I key in the numbers 071705 and the safe springs open.

He's a creature of habit, I tell myself, refusing to be touched by the fact he still uses our anniversary, but does he still keep his passport with his laptop? I reach in and close my hand around the slim booklet and experience a frisson of self-doubt. Have I really become this kind of wife—*this kind of person*—who rifles through her husband's private papers?

A passport is hardly a private document, though. Anonymous immigration officers paw through it, looking back and forth skeptically between you and your picture, trying to match up your past and present selves with a gimlet eye. When I open to Fred's picture I feel a sharp pang. His passport is in its last year—I should remind him to renew it, I think before remembering that it's no longer my job—so the picture is nine years old. I remember that punk haircut from our trip to Iceland when we wrote *Death Takes the Plunge.* That had been a good trip. We'd soaked in hot springs and ridden Icelandic horses and stayed in an ice hotel, where we huddled under the eiderdowns for three days.

Can Death go someplace warm next year? Fred had implored.

Hm, I'd said, pretending I needed convincing, *I hear there are a lot of ways to die in the Azores.*

I thumb past Fred's photo to the first pages of stamps. There's Reykjavik and then Lisbon. That trip had started well, but had become tiring as we moved from city to city. I had sensed a restlessness in Fred. He decided we should set the book in Spain instead of the Azores (I thumb past the stamp for Madrid) and that it should be an homage to Ernest Hemingway's *Death in the Afternoon*. He immersed himself in the master's books (master to Fred, that is; I had mixed feelings about Hemingway). *If we're going to riff on Hemingway, we'd better know our stuff.* I think it reminded him of his college days and the literary ambitions born there. He began to drink more and write in an affected Hemingwayesque style. One afternoon at a train station between Madrid and Barcelona, after I'd been reading over his edits of my section, I complained that he'd slashed my draft to bits.

You have to kill your darlings, he replied.

You know that's Faulkner, not Hemingway, I pointed out.

Do you think our readers know the difference?

If you feel that way maybe we should call it quits after the next one.

We had one more book on our contract. Fred had taken a slow sip of his beer and replied:

Why not call it quits now.

Because we have a contract for one more book.

Lots of writers pull out of their contracts.

Do you want to give back our advance?

That had given him pause. In the last two years we'd bought the house in Rhinebeck and a co-op in Washington Heights. The books had been selling well, we had a film option that looked promising, but still we'd managed to overextend ourselves financially.

Let's finish out the contract, then, he said, *but we'll talk again before signing the next one.*

That's fine, I said.

We finished *Death Takes the Bull by the Horns* and I have to admit, it's one of our best books. Fred stopped drinking so much and started reading Val McDermid and Iain Banks in preparation for our trip to Scotland. I thought we'd weathered a rough patch—all marriages have them—and were stronger for it. We even started talking about having children.

I turn the page and find the stamp for Glasgow. I can almost smell the heather, remembering our summer in the Highlands writing *Death Takes a Reel*. Everything was perfect until bloody Bloody Scotland and Fiona's curse.

I flip the page and see an entry stamp for Mexico marking our winter in San Miguel. The next stamps are dated two years later, after the pandemic, then there's a slew of them—Brazil, Tibet, Japan, Nigeria, Hong Kong, Thailand—our travels becoming more exotic as we searched for new angles for the books. I find I can barely remember these places or the books that came out of them. All the hotel rooms and airports and murders and suspects and plot twists blur together. Then I turn the last page—Fred really does need a new passport—and there it is. Heathrow Airport, this June, and an exit stamp from Glasgow in late August. Fred spent the entire summer in the United Kingdom without telling me.

CHAPTER NINE

My phone pings again as I stand there gobsmacked. *You're never going to believe this,* Joan has texted.

Oh, Joan, I think, there's nothing that would surprise me right now.

Try me, I text back.

Nadine wants to go ahead with tonight's panel. She says it's to "honor Deb."

Joan adds an eye roll emoji and continues.

She's got Buck and Fred on her side but Pete and Shay are against it and want you to weigh in. Buck's arguing that you and Fred only have one vote between you.

The nerve of that bitch, I think. As if she had any interest in honoring Deb.

I'll be right down, I text.

I hurry out of our suite but pause at the head of the stairs to send Joan another text. *Remind me what the panel's called?*

That's the tackiest part of it, she writes back. *It's called "Kill All Your Darlings."*

I WALK QUICKLY down the curving stairs, my footsteps echoing with Nadine's words.

You're not the only one who's plotted a few murders.

Images of Nadine and Fred together—hiking the moors (Fred knows how much I love *Wuthering Heights*! How dare he go to Brontë country without me!), drinking pints in cozy pubs in front of peat fires, snuggling together in some thatched cottage on the Isle of Skye—fill the stairwell like a miasma rising from the crypts below. By the time I reach the bottom I am as tightly wound as a child's top, primed to spin out of control.

I walk down the corridor that runs along the cloister to the old chapel, where the panel is being held. I pause for a moment on the arched threshold of the chapel, recalling the peace and quiet that used to reign here, the voices of the nuns at evening vespers as soft and ancient as the ground fog that crept up the hills from the valley, like a moat cutting Castellarosa off from the world and turning the castle into an island floating in a vaporous sea. I remember one of the nuns saying that the neighboring mountain, Monte Cetona, had magnetic properties that drew storms to it. I wonder if a storm is percolating now. I feel a tingle of electricity in the air that stings my fingers as I pull the iron door handle.

Like everyplace else at Castellarosa, the chapel has been transformed. But here it's not just the arrangement of furniture—rows of chairs where there once were pews, a long table on a raised platform where the altar stood, a heavy velvet curtain behind it where once had hung the fourteenth-century triptych of the Annunciation—that has changed; it's the very essence of the room that has been altered. The chapel would have been deconsecrated when the church let go of the property and the holy relic—a lock of Bianca Rosa's hair—would have been removed. I wouldn't have believed that could make any difference, but standing on the threshold looking toward the figures on the raised platform—Shay and Pete on one side of the long table waving their arms at Buck and Nadine on the other, Fred sitting in the middle like Solomon hearing the testimony of the two mothers—I feel an emptiness in the crowded room that rhymes with the emptiness inside my heart since learning that my husband and his new girlfriend may be plotting to murder me.

"Here's Thea," Joan says, rising from the front row of seats, "let's all see what she has to say."

As I walk forward it occurs to me that I, and not Fred, am being cast in the role of Solomon here. *What a ridiculous story,* I'd told Sister Beatrice, *as if even the false mother would want half a baby?*

She doesn't want the baby at all, she'd replied. *In her grief for her own dead child, she can't bear to see another mother happy.*

I understand that now as I walk toward Nadine. Since I saw her in the library, she's changed into a clingy long red dress that reminds me of the one Kate Bush wore in her *Wuthering Heights* video. As if she's mocking me for her time on the moors with Fred! What gets me more than how gorgeous she looks is the smirk on her face, like she's reveling in the position she's put me in. As I make my way to the stage, I realize we have an audience. The conference attendees have already staked out their seats. Barb is sitting in the front row and Bob is standing in the aisle arguing with Greg Wilson about the arrangement of chairs, I guess, from Bob's pointing at the rows and Greg's thinly disguised impatience.

Lindsay and her coven of Goth Librarians are filling the middle rows. They're all draped in some kind of gauzy gray scarves. Some kind of mourning garment for Deb? I suppose they might mean to honor Deb, but the effect is ghoulish. As I pass by, Lindsay jumps up and rushes to my side. She's holding one of the filmy scarves in her hands and before I know what she's doing, she's tossed it over my head as if I'm a butterfly she's snaring in her net.

"What the—" I splutter.

"Look!" she cries triumphantly, holding up her phone to show our twin faces swathed in diaphanous shrouds. The effect is downright creepy. It's as if we're walking corpses from a Hammer horror film.

"It's just like in *Death Takes the Castle*!" she crows. "We're the ghosts of Bianca Rosa."

Ugh. I claw at the clingy shroud to get it away from my face and make my way up to the dais, where I notice that Nadine is also wearing one of the shrouds. "Isn't it clever?" Nadine says. "What devoted fans you have!"

Great. Now I'll look ungrateful if I take the damned thing off. Just as I'll be the killjoy if I refuse to do the panel. Nadine knows this; I can see it in her self-satisfied smirk.

"What a fabulous idea," I say when I reach the stage, "to honor Deb this way! After all, she was going to be our moderator. But now . . ." My eyes rove over the crowd and land on Joan.

An ally in a sea of enemies. "Didn't she go over her questions with you, Joan?"

"She did," Joan answers, winking at me. Of course, whip-smart Joan gets my idea immediately. "Obviously, no one can take Deb's place, but I'd be honored to step in for her."

WHILE JOAN EFFICIENTLY taps in a message to the conference WhatsApp group announcing that the panel is going forward in honor of Deb Andersen while simultaneously ordering Greg Wilson to set up more chairs, I stop at a side table where Ava is setting up promotional material. I realize I haven't seen much of her since we arrived, and I use the excuse of helping her arrange the postcards and bookmarks promoting our series to talk to her. "I guess this hasn't turned out to be the promotional opportunity we all thought it would be," I remark.

She gives me a sharp look that startles me. "I hope you don't think I'd capitalize on poor Deb's death like that," she says.

"Of course not!" I say, taken aback at her unfriendly tone. Have I done something to offend her? "I only meant that the trip hasn't turned out how any of us expected."

"No, I suppose especially not for you," she says, her hands busily arranging cards in a fan shape.

"What do you mean?" I ask warily.

She regards me for a moment with a look that's almost pitying. "You didn't know about Fred and Nadine, did you?"

I feel the hot sting of blood coursing to my face. She must notice because she nods as if my blush were confirmation. "I didn't think so. You were more worried about me, weren't you?"

"What?" I ask, appalled. "Have I ever given you any reason to think that?"

"No, you've never acted in any way less than professional with me—nor has Fred, for the record—but I saw the way you looked at me sometimes and I guessed that you were jealous. It's okay—at least you never tried to get me fired. Did you know Nadine has already asked that her publicist take over for the series?"

"That's outrageous!"

"I know." Ava tilts her chin toward the stage where Nadine is whispering something to Fred. "I'd watch your back with her."

I turn to ask what she means but she's retreating to where Aleister and Penelope have staked out seats in the back row. I notice that Greg and Sonia are standing at the rear door to the chapel, their heads together, whispering. I feel a stab of envy at their marital concord. Fred and I used to whisper together like that at conferences, sharing gossip and editorial comments about our fellow writers. But now he's up on the stage, whispering in Nadine's ear as if they're plotting something. My murder?

Just then Nadine lifts her head up and calls to me in an artificially sweet voice, "Thea, your seat is over here next to Fred."

"You take it," I tell Nadine. "If you're going to be Fred's new collaborator, you'd better get used to fielding his questions."

My remark is met with a low murmur from the audience and a raised eyebrow from Joan, who is taking the moderator's seat next to me. It's Fred I'm watching, though—he has gotten to his feet and is whispering something in Shay's ear. Shay starts to get up to move so I can sit next to Fred, but I grab her arm and give her a sharp look that she reads quickly, and she sits back down. Fred shakes his head, puzzled, but then takes his seat at the end of the table next to Nadine. I smile back at him and turn to Joan.

"If we're done playing musical chairs, let's get the show on the road, shall we?" Joan says briskly. "I thought we could begin with each of us saying something about Deb. I think I knew Deb longest so I'll start. I met Deb at the very first Malice Domestic I attended. She was head of the debut-author breakfast committee and greeted me like an old friend. She'd read my book and even tried out the recipes in it. She told me that I might not get rich writing cozies but I'd always have a place in her private library of good books—" Joan's voice thickens and for a moment I'm afraid she's going to cry, something I've never seen Joan do. But then she laughs instead. "Then she signed me up to run the debut-author breakfast for the next year and got me to volunteer for her mentorship committee. She had a way of getting you to agree to anything."

A friendly murmur goes around the room as we all remember Deb's persuasive powers. I pat Joan's hand and draw one of the two mics toward me. "She signed me up for her Prison Partners Book Drive within five minutes of meeting me at my first Bouchercon. She told me that publishing could be a tough business so it paid to have good friends in the community, and then she spent the next twenty years being the best friend anyone could ask for."

Shay takes the mic from me, giving my hand a squeeze before I can start to blubber. "She told me that writing could be a lonely business but that I'd always have a friend in her. When I proposed founding a writers of color scholarship, she was the first one to contribute."

The crowd breaks out in applause. When it dies down, Pete whispers into the mic, "She was the best," and passes it on to Buck. I hold my breath, waiting for Buck to make a crude joke and ruin the mood. After all, it had been Deb who had tried to get him removed as toastmaster, but instead he recites in a clear and surprisingly sweet voice "She Dwelt among the Untrodden Ways" by William Wordsworth, substituting Deb's name for the Lucy of the poem. By the time he gets to the last stanza—

She lived unknown, and few could know
When Debra ceased to be,
But she's in her grave, and, oh,
The difference to me!

—there's not a dry eye in the room, and it occurs to me that the chapel has been returned to its original use, our grief for Deb resanctifying it. Then Joan leans over and whispers in my ear, "The difference to Buck is that no one's left to hold him accountable for his actions," and I remember that the person who poisoned the glass Deb drank from may well be in this room. Whether it was meant for her or me, there's a murderer at large in Castellarosa.

As if echoing my thoughts, Fred says, "What always impressed me the most about Deb was her sense of justice and fairness. I asked her once how a nice girl from Duluth got involved with such a ragtag group of murder-plotters and she told me she loved mysteries because they set the world to rights. That's what Deb did—she set the world to rights, and without her I feel that it's tilted askew."

That's exactly right, I think as he passes the mic to Nadine, because we haven't yet gotten to the part when the killer is unmasked and justice is done. We're in the middle part, still reeling, in a world where Deb is dead and Nadine St. George is about to deliver an oratory for a woman she hardly knew.

"I didn't know Deb as well as the rest of you, but in the brief time we knew each other she gave me the best advice anyone's ever given me. She told me that writing an edgy protagonist might make a big splash but if I wanted real staying power, I needed to learn to write from the heart."

She looks straight at Fred when she says *heart* and then, for just an instant, her eyes flick toward me and I detect the hint of a smirk. It's gone so fast I'm not sure if I imagined it; only Joan's low whistle in my ear confirms my suspicion. *That snake!* Is she actually suggesting that it was Deb who steered her toward taking my place with Fred and the series? Before Nadine can continue, Joan pulls out a stack of three-by-five cards from her conference tote bag and raps them smartly on the table.

"Well then," Joan says, "now that we've shared our thoughts and prayers for Deb, *Deb* has some thoughts and questions for y'all."

I look over at the cards in Joan's hands and recognize Deb's neat handwriting. I knew Joan and Deb had talked about questions for the panel but I wonder how Joan has acquired Deb's actual cue cards. Then I remember that they had been sharing a room so she must have known where they were.

"Deb's first question for you is: What was the hardest character you ever had to kill off? Nadine, hon, why don't we start with you."

"Oh!" Nadine says, flinching a little as Joan raps the cards on the table again. Or maybe it's the question that makes her jump. It's a disconcerting one coming from a dead woman—perhaps all the more so if you murdered that dead woman. Did Joan suspect that Nadine poisoned Deb? Is that why she's baiting her? It certainly seems to have worked. Nadine appears tongue-tied. Joan takes advantage of her silence to add, "Or maybe you've never had a qualm about killing any of your characters?"

"Well, they *are* fictional," Nadine says, rather lamely, I think.

"Hm," Joan hums. "Interesting answer. Would you say your narrator treats people as if they weren't real? That might explain why she has no compunction about deceiving and lying to everyone whose path she crosses."

"My narrator lives in a world where nothing is certain," Nadine says, bristling. "And in a world where all certainties are gone, what do we have left but lies and deception?"

"What indeed?" Joan concedes, letting the question hang in the air for a moment before turning to Fred. "What about you, Fred? Hardest character you've ever had to kill off?"

"That's easy," Fred says. "Sister Benedetta in *Death Takes the Castle*."

There's a collective hum in the room as everyone recalls the final scene when the elderly nun sacrifices herself for the lives of the young couple, Rick and Dora.

"That *was* a heartbreaking scene," Joan says, "and I suppose that killing a nun is right up there with killing cats and children."

"Never kill a cat," Buck solemnly intones. "Your fans will never forgive you."

"Is that your answer, Buck? The hardest character you ever killed off was the kitty in *Die, Die Baby, Baby Die, Die*? Not the little girl in that book?"

"Hey," Buck growls, "that kid had it coming."

There's a smattering of amused chuckles punctuated by a little gasp. Buck's tough guy persona is his brand and usually goes over pretty well with the murder crowd, but it reads a little differently in the wake of a real death. I shoot Joan a warning look, hoping to convey my concern that this line of questioning—even if it did originate with Deb—is heading for trouble, but Joan avoids my gaze and continues on to Pete.

"I've got a note here for you, Pete, from Deb, to say that you're exempt from this question because we all know it hurts you to kill each and every one of your characters. Instead, she asks: How'd an old softy like you ever get into the mystery-writing biz?"

The question sounds so much like Deb that for a moment I'm afraid Pete will be too overcome by emotion to answer it, but he surprises me by responding in a steady, calm voice. "Deb and I talked about this a lot," he says. "She told me that she thought I was writing to honor my parents' generation, who put their lives on the line for our freedom. I've always written to honor the dead and now . . ." He pauses, and in the silence that fills the room I can hear him swallow and I'm afraid he won't be able to go on, but he does. "Now I'll write to honor Deb."

There's a heavy silence in the room, interrupted at last by Shay dryly remarking, "Oh heck, I only kill the bastards who've got it coming in my books so I don't have any qualms at all."

Relieved laughter greets her remark and I breathe easier, sure Joan will move on now. After all, Fred's given an answer for both of us—

"Thea?"

"I'll go with Fred's answer," I say. "Sister Benedetta." What I don't say is that when we killed off the sweet old nun, I felt as if I'd betrayed the trust of Sister Beatrice, whom she was based on.

"Not so fast, hon. Deb's got a specific question for you, too." She peers down at the card in her hand as if she can't quite make out the writing even though Deb's handwriting is immaculate. "Uh, Deb wanted to know if you'd ever kill off Fred or Dora in your books."

"Oh!" I say, surprised. Had Deb suspected that I was thinking of ending the series? I remember now that when Deb was telling me about working on the treasure hunt that there was something bothering her she wanted to talk to me about. She was poisoned before she ever got a chance to. What if—

My mind spins.

What if Deb suspected that Fred and Nadine were plotting to kill me and they killed her first?

"Thea?" Joan's voice breaks through the swirling fog of speculation I've gotten lost in. "I didn't realize it was such a hard question."

"It's the wrong question," I say abruptly, emerging so suddenly from the fog that I'm nearly blinded by the light. "The real question is who would prevail if Rick and Dora tried to kill each other."

Buck guffaws. "Dora, obviously."

"Exactly," I say, rewarding Buck with a smile that leaves him blinking in surprise. I lean forward and peer down the long table toward Fred, who's staring at me as if I've lost my mind. Maybe I have, and yet as Polonius says in *Hamlet, Though this be madness, yet there is method in't.* I'm beginning to glimpse the method. Fred leans forward toward the mic but Nadine gets to it first.

"I think it depends on who Rick has on his side," she purrs.

A low murmur goes through the crowd and I sense a percolating electricity in the room. I almost expect someone to hiss and shout *Catfight!*

"Well then," Joan says, "this has taken an interesting turn, perhaps we should see what the audience thinks—"

Before she's finished, Bob is on his feet with his hand up. He doesn't wait for Joan to call on him before shouting out, "Was Deb killed because she knew where the treasure is buried?"

I see Joan close her eyes briefly as if she's praying for patience. "None of us know what happened to Deb, Bob, and it's not helpful for the *polizia* or any of us to speculate or spread rumors—"

"Is Deb even really dead?" The question comes from one of the Goth Librarians. In her shroud she looks like an emissary from the underworld risen to challenge Deb's inclusion in her tribe.

"Wh-what?" Even Joan is thrown by this. Pete grabs the mic and demands to know what she's talking about.

Lindsay gets up and puts her arm around her friend as if she needs to be protected from Pete. "It's just we couldn't help noticing that Deb died just like the first victim in *Death Takes the Castle* so we wondered if this might be a publicity stunt."

I take the mic from Pete to answer. "Absolutely not. We would never exploit anyone's death—especially not the death of a dear friend like Deb—for publicity."

"But isn't that what you do all the time?"

The question comes from someone standing in the very back of the room. I try to see who's talking—the gravelly female voice is vaguely familiar—but she's standing in the shadow of one of the side chapels, half blocked by a poster advertising tomorrow's "Killer Speed Dating Contest" and wearing one of Lindsay's shrouds.

"I'm sorry," I say, half standing to make out the interlocutor, "I don't understand—"

"Haven't you exploited death for your own profit?"

A chill goes through me as I catch a glimpse of a veiled face that for all the world looks like the ghost of Bianca Rosa.

CHAPTER TEN

The room erupts into a loud commotion that even Joan is unable to quell. Everyone in the audience has turned to look at the veiled figure who has asked such an incendiary question, but before anyone can ask what she meant by it, the figure vanishes through the side door into the cloisters. A few people rise to go after her but Greg stops them at the door and says that the cloisters are off-limits because of construction. While they argue with Greg, I get up, whispering to Joan that I'll be right back, and slip unobserved behind the curtain and out a back entrance into the cloisters.

It takes a moment for my eyes to adjust to the dark after the bright lights of the chapel, but when they do, I'm confronted by a row of tall white-robed figures, as if the veiled figure had multiplied. I blink away the illusion and see that it's only a row of marble columns glowing white in the moonlight, bordering a long narrow arcade, each column topped by a capital carved with fantastical creatures—griffons, dragons, basilisks—an entire bestiary of medieval monsters.

The arcade is purple and fragrant with lavender. The veiled figure must have escaped through the arch at the end. I head toward it, the moonlight drawing a clear path on the uneven marble paving stones, many of which were salvaged from the old Roman villa and have archaic Latin words carved into them. I remember that Fred and I spent a whole day crawling around and making rubbings of Latin inscriptions that we would later use as clues in *Death Takes the Castle*.

The cloisters at Castellarosa are unique. A convent will usually have one or two cloisters to provide a private sheltered place for exercise and contemplation. They're often planted with herbs and flowers with a fountain or a well in the center to provide the convent with fresh water. At Castellarosa, though, the central cloister is shaped like a labyrinth, like the one in the poison garden, only here instead of being marked by low hedges, the labyrinth is formed of high stone walls.

"I told you it wasn't a good idea." Not Sister Beatrice's voice, but Fred's, entering the cloister from the chapel, where Greg Wilson has apparently lost the battle to keep the guests out.

"Don't worry," Nadine tells him, "it will all work out. She must have gone through this arch, let's catch up—"

What will all work out? I wonder, stepping into a shadowed apse. I'm afraid they'll see me but they walk right by me and through the arch, Nadine's filmy gray shawl, which she's draped dramatically over her head as if now she's the *ghost* of Cathy in *Wuthering Heights*, nearly brushing me as she sweeps by. The moonlight is so bright in this arcade that everything in the shadows is nearly invisible. Before I can step out, I hear another pair of voices.

"Do you think that girl might be right and Deb's alive?" I recognize Barb's plaintive voice and then Bob's as he answers her.

"I wouldn't put it past them. I knew something was wrong the minute I saw the treasure hunt. I bet that veiled figure is someone dressed up like a ghost to scare us and this is all part of the treasure hunt. The last clue said something about a well and I think there's one in here."

They pass right by me and disappear through the arch as if through a stage door. As soon as Bob and Barb have exited stage left, Lindsay and her coven enter stage right.

"Oooh," one of the Goth girls, wrapped head to toe in her winding sheet, coos, "look at all the cool gargoyles."

"They're not gargoyles," Lindsay corrects her acolyte, pointing up at a carved capital. "That one's a basilisk—a mythical beast that's a cross between a cock and a scorpion."

The other girl giggles at that but Lindsay ignores her and goes on to point out other mythical beasts—a manticore, griffin, unicorn, and then an amphisbaena. "That's a dragon that eats its own tail. I think that's a clue that these cloisters form a circle. If we follow them, we'll find the next clue at the center."

Lindsay strikes off through the moonlit arch and her friends follow, one hanging back to make an off-color joke about cocks and tail-eating that I can't even follow but which seems to entertain the rest of the coven as they pass by me. The lavender arcade is quiet after they go but the peace is ruined by the thought of running into the crowd if I follow them. Besides, there's no telling if my veiled figure even went that way. In my shadowed apse, I've remembered something. Everyone has gone through the arch at the end of this arcade because it's lit up by the moonlight, but there's another path to take to the center.

There are always two ways to walk the labyrinth, Sister Beatrice had told me enigmatically.

I wait a moment to see if there are any more intruders to the cloisters and then I leave my hiding place and cross quickly to the shadowed arcade leading to an arch in the wall. I can barely make out the carved creatures above it but I know they're pelicans, plucking at their breasts to feed their young with their own blood.

Every true quest begins with a sacrifice, Sister Beatrice had told me.

I hadn't been sure I agreed with her then, but as I pass under the arch now, I think of all the hard work and sacrifices I've made along the way and I have to admit that the old nun might have been onto something. The next arcade is pungent with the smell of thyme, which, according to medieval herbalists, stood for strength and courage for the journey ahead. And there, standing across the beds of thyme from me, is the veiled figure, as if she has been waiting for me. As soon as she sees me, though, she passes through the next arch and I wonder if I have imagined her. I hurry along the colonnaded path and follow her into the next leg of the labyrinth. The beds here bristle with thorns and purple spikes. Thistle for bravery because every journey has its rough patches. The capitals in this cloister are carved with lions, for loyalty, because the only way to get through the thicket is to stay loyal to one's companions on the journey.

So much for that, I think, following the elusive figure through another arch. What if you're loyal and your lover is not? I'd like to ask Sister Beatrice . . . Could the veiled figure be Sister Beatrice? I wonder. The old nun could still be alive and the voice had sounded familiar. She might have come back to warn me—or to upbraid me.

Haven't you exploited death for your own profit?

Yes, I think, passing through the next arch, where I find another figure standing in the moonlight. Only it's not Sister Beatrice—it's Fred, looking up at the face of the statue in the central fountain. It's a marble girl, holding a sprig in her hand, the same herb that grows here. Rosemary, for remembrance.

What do you think she's remembering? Fred had asked me when we came here twenty years ago to block out the scene for the second murder in *Death Takes the Castle*.

Her lover, I said, *her knight errant.*

She doesn't look very happy about it, Fred said.

I guess because she misses him.

Yeah, but shouldn't she at least look happy when she's thinking about him? Or else what's the point of all this—he'd waved his arms at the fragrant herbs—*remembrance? I hope that when you look back on these times—us being together, running around the castle, plotting murders—it makes you happy.*

It had sounded as if I'd be looking back alone. I had suddenly realized that although we'd been spending all our time together *plotting murders,* we had never talked about the future. We'd never plotted out *our* story. I was supposed to go back to New York in the fall to turn in my dissertation, which I hadn't done a lick of work on since I'd met Fred, and start looking for academic jobs. As far as I could tell, Fred had no place he had to be. He'd spent the last few years drifting from place to place, wherever the muse took him, looking for the next inspiration for his novel. He supported himself writing travel articles and blogging. Maybe I was just another adventure along the way—a chapter in his picaresque novel.

Are you planning on heading off for the Crusades*?* I'd asked, trying for a joking tone when what I really wanted to ask was *Am I part of your plans? Do I have a place in your future?*

Aren't we already on a crusade? He'd replied in a similarly light tone. Only I thought I detected a note of bitterness.

I guess you'll be wanting to get back to your novel, I said. *This must all seem silly, like a game of* Clue*.*

He shrugged, looking uncomfortable and distinctly miserable. How could I have been so stupid? I wondered. I'd been ignoring my dissertation to play detective with this cute boy—because even if he was a year older than me he was, essentially, still a boy—thinking . . . what? That I meant something to him?

I like Clue, he said. *This has been fun—*

Yeah, fun, I said, turning to walk away. *I'm sure you'll look back on it fondly when you move on to your next adventure.*

I'd gotten three steps away when I felt his hand on my arm. I stopped but didn't turn around because I didn't want him to see that I was crying. *Stupid,* I berated myself. *How could I have been so stupid?*

The thing is, he said, *I was hoping . . . I mean . . . I know you have more serious things to do . . . like your dissertation. But I thought maybe we could . . . I don't know . . . keep doing this, too? I mean, you're really good at this mystery thing. We could finish this book at least and then when you finish your dissertation—*

If I don't go back in the fall I'll lose my funding, I said.

Oh, he said, the word like a stone dropped in a well, *I didn't realize. I guess I can see why that's more important. It was silly to think you'd want to keep doing this.*

Keep doing this? I'd turned then and found that Fred's eyes were sparkling in the moonlight. Were those tears? Was he just as frightened of losing me as I was of losing him? Because that's what I'd realized, here amid the rosemary, which symbolized love as well as remembrance—I was frightened of losing Fred because I was in love with him. *You mean, like keep writing the book?* I asked.

Was there, for a moment, a dimming in his eyes? Or had it just been a cloud passing across the moon?

Well, he said, *Rick and Dora haven't even found the treasure yet. We can't stop now.*

And we hadn't. We'd finished the book and on the day we typed *The End* (I typed *the* and he typed *end*) Fred had taken me back here and asked me to marry him. At our wedding, I carried rosemary in my bouquet and pinned a sprig of rosemary to Fred's lapel. This was where we'd pledged ourselves to each other. Is that why Fred has stopped here? Is that what he's remembering?

I take a step closer to see if he's remembering with sadness or joy—and my foot grates against the gravel path. He spins around and I see a look of fear on his face—

Of me?

What does he have to be afraid of, I wonder, even as I feel an answering spike of fear that sparks another memory—the fear I'd felt of losing Fred when I knew I loved him.

Or had I been afraid *because* I loved him and I knew that loving someone as handsome and charming and mercurial as Fred was bound to end in disaster?

"Thea?" he says, stepping toward me, his voice so low I can feel its vibration percolating up through my body like a spring bubbling up through the ground and bursting into the air.

A scream rends the air as suddenly as that imagined spring. For a moment I think it has come from me. Fred is staring at me as if it has, but when it comes again, he whips his head around toward the arched doorway.

"Stay here," he says, running toward the sound.

I'm damned if I'm going to let him tell me what to do. I follow him into the next arcade, which is full of bitter-smelling yellow flowers. Rue, for regret, of course; what else would follow remembrance? I get it, I think, passing through the next arch and into the central cloister, which is full of flowers that glow bloodred in the moonlight. Poppies, symbols of sleep—and death. A figure bends over a large round well at the center like a marble personification of mourning. For a moment I think it's the veiled figure I followed in here but then I realize it's only Nadine with her shroud thrown over her head. Her red dress, I notice, matches the poppies so well I can't help wondering if she staged the whole scene.

Fred goes to her and puts his arm around her. She sags against him as he looks over her shoulder into the well. His face, in the moonlight, looks completely drained, as if all the red around him was his own life's blood ebbing away into the earth. I walk to the opposite side of the well and look down.

"What is it?" someone behind me is asking. The words echo hollowly in my head as if I am the one down in the well, legs skewed sideways, neck broken, mouth bloodied, already wrapped in her own funeral shroud. Lindsay was right that Deb died just like the first victim in *Death Takes the Castle,* and she has proven her point by dying just like our second victim.

CHAPTER ELEVEN

"Oh my God! I was right, it's just like the second murder in *Death Takes the Castle!*"

The words echo my own thoughts so precisely I wonder if they're in my own head. Then I turn around and fear I've gone *out* of my head. Lindsay is standing in front of me, her face as gray as the shroud wrapped around her head and shoulders. I look back down into the well. The moon now shines full on the face of the dead girl and I realize my mistake. It's one of the other Goth Librarians; not Lindsay, just someone dressed like her.

"Poor Kailee!" Lindsay wails. "She was so determined to find the next clue that she rushed ahead of us!" I notice that the two remaining Goth Librarians are standing a few feet away clutching each other.

"Is that what you were doing in the cloisters?" I ask, remembering now that Kailee had been the one to make the off-color joke about cocks and tails. "Playing a game of treasure hunt?"

"Well," Lindsay huffs, looking more affronted than grief-stricken at her friend's death, "you were the one who came up with the game in the first place. The first clue came right out of *Death Takes the Castle* and led straight to the well." She points to the cast-iron frame above the well. Hanging from the pulley is a clear plastic sleeve. An empty plastic sleeve. "That must have had the clue in it and Kailee fell taking it out. So you see—" She sniffs. "It was really all your fault."

"My fault?" I snap, rounding on her. "You and your friend are the ones who dressed up as corpses and chose to go treasure hunting when there's already been one murder." My voice, steadily rising, cracks on the word *murder*. Fred, who has deposited Nadine on a nearby bench, moves next to me and puts his hand on my arm. I shake it off and round on him. "And what was your girlfriend doing hanging over the well?" I demand.

"Nadine heard a scream and came to see what had happened," Fred says.

"I thought it might be you," Nadine says, lifting her head. "Because of the shroud."

"I bet you were thrilled," I snark. "You wouldn't have to share your royalties with me."

Nadine stands up, no longer prostrate with shock, and turns to Fred with icy dignity. "I'll go alert the authorities that there's been another death. You might want to calm her down before they get here." As she turns to leave, tossing her shroud over her shoulder with the insouciance of a runway model, she's met by Pete and Joan.

"What's all the hubbub?" Joan demands.

"A young woman has fallen in the well," Nadine informs her.

"I'm going to go tell the Wilsons to call Detective Bardi. You should probably talk to Thea before the police arrive." She casts a pitying look over her shoulder toward me. "And explain to her that it's always the one slinging baseless accusations around who turns out to be the guilty party."

Joan's carefully penciled eyebrows shoot up and she looks toward me as Nadine sashays out of the cloister, followed by the Goth Librarians. I take a step forward, intent on following her—*how dare she spout Mystery 101 theory to me!*—but Fred lays a restraining hand on my arm.

"Thea," he says, "you don't actually think that Nadine had anything to do with this?"

"Don't you dare defend her," I spit out. "I know you've been going over our contract. I saw it on the bed with the kill clause circled in red."

I hear Joan gasp and watch all the blood drain from Fred's face. "You're the one who demanded that clause in the first place. It always hurt that you thought so badly of my character that you couldn't trust me. I'd hoped that after twenty years you'd have gained a better opinion of me."

"Ha! As if cheating on me in San Miguel was a testament to your character!"

"I didn't—"

Before he can repeat his excuse that it wasn't really cheating because I caught them before they had sex, I cut him off. "And what do you mean, I demanded that clause? Penelope suggested it."

"Because you asked her to."

"I didn't, but I'm certainly glad she thought of it, even if it has given you and Nadine a motive to kill me."

His face, so pale a moment ago, flames red as if I had slapped him. "Do you really think that I'm capable of that?" he whispers in a low, husky voice.

He sounds so wounded that I feel a moment of doubt. Do I really think my husband of twenty years is capable of plotting to murder me? It doesn't matter if I do or not. The moment of hesitation is as good as a yes. Fred gives me one reproachful look and turns on his heel to leave.

As soon as he's gone, Joan comes over and puts her arm around me. "Why, you're shaking like a leaf, hon. Come over here and sit down."

She leads me to the bench recently vacated by Nadine. Pete looks uncomfortably between us and the well and then points toward the plastic sleeve hanging from the pulley. "I was with Deb when she put this clue here. The well was covered then. She'd never have put it there if it hadn't been. She'd never have done anything that would put anyone in danger."

"Of course she wouldn't, Pete," Joan says soothingly. "Why don't you go see if you can find that nice Italian detective. Thea and I will wait here for the police and make sure no one goes near the well. We wouldn't want anyone else getting hurt."

For a moment Pete doesn't look as if he's heard her. He's staring at the empty plastic sleeve suspended above the well. Maybe he's remembering being here with Deb. Maybe he, too, has some fond romantic memory of these cloisters like the one I had with Fred—

At the thought of Fred, I start to sob. Joan tightens her grip on me, and Pete, stricken by the sight of a weeping woman, mutters something about "getting help" and flees.

"Men," Joan tsks. I'm not sure if she's talking about Pete or Fred or the gender in general. She lets me cry it out, rocking me slightly in her tight grip and murmuring a soothing *there, there.* When my sobs abate, she digs a tissue out of her pocket and hands it to me. "All done?" she asks.

I'm not sure I'll ever be done but I can tell by the brisk tone in her voice that she's suggesting I'd better be. The police are on the way and while a few dainty tears might serve me, I'd better have my wits about me. I nod.

"Good," she says, nodding back. "Now, tell me what the heck happened in San Miguel."

I GIVE HER the short version. Even if we had time for the whole San Miguel story, I don't think I could go through it all here. I tell her enough so that she knows I caught Fred in a compromising position with the assistant of a prominent writer and that the marriage effectively ended back then.

"You mean you've been shamming your marriage vows since then?" she asks. I'm a bit startled by the way she puts it. I forget sometimes that just beneath her modern progressive surface lies the girl who was brought up a Southern Baptist. Some of that fundamentalist sense of justice and values poke out in unexpected ways.

"I'm sorry I never told you," I say. "Part of our agreement was not to tell anyone. If it got out—"

"It would hurt the brand," she finishes for me, the practical business side of her firmly in place again. "I get it. I sometimes think the biggest fiction we writers spin is our own authorial persona. I'll let you in on a little secret—" She looks around to make sure we're alone and then mock-whispers. "I hate grits."

I snort a surprised laugh. "Half your books include a grits recipe!"

"Hate 'em. Can't stand Southern cooking in general—fried okra, chicken-fried steak, Jell-O mold—blech!" She grimaces. "But don't you ever let my readers hear that. You know what else? I hate cats."

"Don't you have three?" I ask, recalling Joan's Insta feed. "Oolong, Earl Grey, and Lapsang?"

"They belong to my housekeeper. She lets me photograph them. I'm allergic."

I gape at her and then shake my head. "That's not as big a secret as pretending to be happily married."

"Nor do I think those cats are out to kill me, although I wouldn't put it past 'em if they were just a little bigger. Why do you think Fred is?"

"I found the contract," I remind her, "with the kill clause circled in red."

"Oooh, well, he might have just been thinking of consulting a lawyer."

"And then someone dressed in the same shroud as me gets pushed in a well? And remember, Deb was poisoned by my drink."

I'm hoping that level-headed, practical Joan will refute me—

she could at least point out that several people were dressed in shrouds—but instead she shakes her head and, giving me a pitying looks, says, "Oh, hon, it looks like Fred and that hussy are trying to get rid of you."

SONIA WILSON IS the first back to the cloister. She runs to the well, gasps, and covers her mouth. But not, as it turns out, because of the body at the bottom. "What is this doing open?" she demands, whirling on me and Joan as if we have personally sabotaged her hotel. "We made sure to cover it." She casts her gaze around the moonlit cloister until her eye alights on a circular piece of plywood leaning against a wall. "There! This is the lid. Someone very strong must have moved it." She looks at me and Joan as if about to accuse us but before she can, Detective Bardi enters the cloister barking out an order to another officer to carry a large battery-operated lamp to the mouth of the well. The light leaches his face of color and carves deep, shadowed grooves beneath his eyes and mouth, making him look as if he's wearing a tragedian's mask. When he turns that face on me, I shudder as if Death itself has come for me—which I suppose, in a way, it has.

"Another body, Signora Morgan-Lane. You seem to attract them."

"I didn't find her," I object. "Nadine St. George did."

"I've spoken with Signorina St. George and she told me you preceded her into the cloisters tonight. What were you doing in here?"

"I was following someone," I say. "I thought it was Sister Beatrice."

"Who?"

"I . . . I don't know. I thought . . ." What had I thought? "They were wearing a shroud."

"Like the one you're wearing?" he says, pointing to my shroud.

"No—I mean—maybe?" I claw the shroud off my head and shoulders. I'd forgotten I was still wearing it. "One of the fans put this on me. It's supposed to be like the one the ghost of Bianca Rosa wears in *Death Takes the Castle,* only she turns out not to be a ghost—" I stop myself before rehashing the entire plot of the book, which it turns out is unnecessary anyway. Detective Bardi retrieves a cheap mass-market Italian edition from his pocket. "Yes, I've been reading your little book."

"Kailee was wearing one just like it," I say, pointing to the well. "Her murderer must have thought she was me. I think someone is trying to kill me." I look at Joan for courage. Am I really going to accuse Fred to this policeman's face? She squeezes my hand and does it for me.

"Have you ever heard of a kill clause, Detective Bardi?" Joan goes on to explain Fred and Nadine's motive to kill me. Detective Bardi listens with growing disgust and skepticism on his face.

"And you say you found this contract in your hotel room?"

"In my *husband's* room," I clarify. "We don't share a room anymore."

"Very well," he says. "Can you show me this contract with its incriminating red circle?"

"It was gone when I went back," I say. "But you can ask Fred to show it to you."

"You must be angry that your husband will be writing your books with another woman, especially one as beautiful as Signorina St. George—"

I flush at the implication that I'm just a jealous wife.

"It's not like that," I say. "My husband is free to do what he likes—" He raises an eyebrow. "I mean, we're not really together anymore. We're getting a divorce."

"Ah! The divorce can cause much . . . bad feeling. The drink that Signora Andersen drank, did you not offer it to Signorina St. George first?"

"What?" I say, thrown off by his sudden pivot. I think back to the moment on the stage and remember that I had held the marked glass out to Fred but Nadine had waved it away as if I were offering it to her. "I wasn't offering it to her; I was showing it to my husband—" I see immediately by the narrowing of the detective's eyes that that doesn't sound much better.

"And then you gave the poisoned drink to Signora Andersen. And then tonight—" He looks sorrowfully toward the well. "This young woman who was wearing the gray shroud was killed."

"That's right, she's dressed just as I am. Don't you see? Nadine St. George pushed her into the well because she thought it was me!"

"Or," Detective Bardi suggests mildly, "you pushed her into the well because you thought she was Nadine St. George."

CHAPTER TWELVE

"Honey." I look down and see, although I can't feel it, that Joan has her hand on my arm. "I think maybe that you shouldn't say anything more without a lawyer present," she whispers. Only, Joan's whisper carries.

"*Certo*, that is of course your choice, signora. I would just ask that you not leave Castellarosa until our investigation is complete."

"We're here for the rest of the weekend," Joan answers for me. "Hopefully you'll have this sorted by then and have the actual culprit behind bars. In the meantime, my friend has had a long day and is still recovering from jet lag and shock. I'm going to take her up to her room."

Joan steers me out of the cloister, her hand clamped hard on my elbow, and propels me to the same back staircase we took earlier today. She seems to have committed the floor plan to memory, which doesn't surprise me. Joan's books often come with maps and puzzles, which she designs and draws herself, that turn out to have clues to the mystery. I've watched her do

The New York Times Saturday crossword puzzle in minutes *in ink*. The woman has a mind like a steel trap. I'm relieved to be in her hands.

"You have to watch yourself here, Thea," she tells me as we climb the stairs. "That detective has his eyes on you and I don't mean that in a cutesy romantic way. I did a little looking into him and he's good. He put away a serial killer in Florence ten years ago and a Mob boss last year. He's not going to like a bunch of American amateur sleuths messing up his record. He'll want to close this quickly and right now you're looking like his prime suspect."

"But that's ridiculous. Nadine has a much bigger motive to kill me than I do to kill her."

"Only if you think money is a bigger motive for murder than jealousy, which I do, for the record. But Detective Bardi clearly favors the jealous wife story."

"Misogynist," I mutter, meeting the eye of the saint stretched out on her rack. She gives me a commiserating look right back. Joan's right, though. I can see the appeal of the jealous wife theory for the detective. After all, Nadine is younger and stunning. And, truth be told, I *am* jealous of her, but not for the reasons Detective Bardi thinks. It's not even the Oxford gig that has my blood boiling, it's that she's just starting out her career and can do anything she wants with it. It's her freedom I'd kill for.

We've reached the door to my suite. I take the key out but I'm suddenly afraid to open the door lest Fred is there. I turn to Joan. "What should I do?" I ask. "How can I prove my innocence?"

"Innocence is a hard line to sell, hon," she says, taking the key from my shaking hand. "Better to prove someone else guilty. Let's see what your husband has hidden in his drawers, no pun intended."

"Please," I say, following her into the suite. "You're a cozy writer; every pun is intended."

UNFORTUNATELY, WE FIND Fred's drawers empty. His whole room, in fact, has been vacated of clothes, toiletries, papers; the safe yawns open and even the scent of him is gone. All he has left is a note written on a sheet of hotel stationery and weighed down by the heavy room key. *I wouldn't want you to feel unsafe in my presence,* it reads in red ink, *so I've taken my presence elsewhere.*

"*Unsafe,*" Joan scoffs. "He sounds like a human resources officer." Then, seeing the stricken look on my face, she asks, "Do you want me to stay here, hon? So you don't feel . . . *unsafe?*"

It's tempting. We could order room service—*when did I eat last?*—and a bottle of wine. Joan's good company. She's a wicked mimic and can always make me laugh. She'll spin the tattered threads of my life into an embroidered shawl shot through with gold and glitter. But I know from experience that once a story is woven, it's hard to pick apart the threads, and right now I think I've got to follow those threads myself.

"Thanks, Joan, but I think I just need to sleep. I should be safe with the doors locked."

For a moment I catch a flicker of disappointment in Joan's eyes and I realize with a pang that I've been selfish. Maybe Joan wants the company. Maybe she feels unsafe. Not that she would ever admit it. The flare of displeasure is so quickly quenched, though, I'm not sure if I imagined it.

"You're right; sleep's the best thing," she says, hurrying out of the bedroom and checking the locks on the French doors. "Shoot that bolt after me," she orders briskly at the door, "and whatever you do, don't open it for anyone, even if that handsome husband of yours comes begging for makeup sex."

"That's unlikely," I tell her, holding the door open for her. "I think we both know we're a long way past that stage."

AFTER JOAN LEAVES, I double-lock the suite door and check the French doors in the living room. There's another door to the balcony in the bedroom, this one slatted wood, that I lock, as well as the adjoining door to the living room. A maid has been in to turn down the bed and left something on the pillow. I'm hoping for a mint but instead I find a little hat-shaped sachet that smells like jasmine and incense. I toss it on my night table, change into a nightgown, and crawl under the clean white sheets and fluffy duvet. My eyes are so heavy I expect to fall asleep the minute my head hits the pillow, but instead when I close my eyes, I see a white bed slashed with spears of light and hear myself recounting the story of San Miguel to Joan, who has a look of pity in her eyes. I toss and turn, trying to banish the memories, but when I finally do drift off to sleep the scent of jasmine and incense clinging to my pillow carries me straight back there.

It had seemed like the perfect place to heal from the miscarriage and the Fiona incident. Fred swore that nothing had happened between them and that she had misunderstood his friendliness for flirtation. He was so eager for me to forgive him that he offered to keep going with the series instead of taking a break. He even signed the contract for five books that Penelope had sent over to us.

"Why don't we wait," I offered, feeling magnanimous in light of his penance. "I'll tell Penelope we want a break, that we're taking a vacation—a real one, this time, not a research trip."

"I'm not even sure what that looks like anymore," he said. "What do people do on these so-called vacations? Sit around a pool and sip drinks with little umbrellas in them?"

I shrugged. "Why not?" Then I'd taken a step closer to him and in a lower voice added, "I've heard that sometimes couples just stay in their room and have a lot of sex."

"What?" He'd feigned surprise. "They don't just use their rooms for writing? What are the desks for, then?"

I'd led him to the big oak Stickley desk I'd given him for our fifth anniversary, sweeping off the page proofs for *Death Takes a Reel,* and demonstrated its other uses.

That heat lasted through the first weeks in San Miguel. Later I wondered if it wasn't a heat fueled by grief over the miscarriage as much as lust, as if I was trying to prove we were alive when I felt as if Death had reached out his hand and squeezed the new life out of me. As if by writing about death we had invited it into our lives.

If you play with death, death will play you for a fool.

Still, there had been something heady in the mountain air, a combination of woodsmoke and incense. The narrow cobblestoned streets and baroque architecture recalled our first days in Castellarosa, but with a sultrier, sexier air (and with a bigger bed and no nuns lurking in the halls). We spent the mornings exploring the city and hiking in the mountains and took long siestas in the afternoon, the vast four-poster mahogany bed a ship in the sea of slanted light that filtered in through the closed shutters. I can still remember the feel of the polished wood posts I gripped, the spicy scent of geraniums from the flower boxes on the terrace, the chorus of mourning doves, and the bells of San Miguel Arcángel tolling the long, lazy hours. I felt as if we had reclaimed something we had lost. When dusk fell, I would light a candle rather than ruin the mood with electric light and say a prayer of thanks for this second chance and a promise that I would not waste it.

And then the San Miguel Writers' Conference and Literary Festival came to town. Of course, we knew it would. It was one of San Miguel's attractions that the city had a thriving artistic community. I had thought it might be refreshing to attend a writers' event that wasn't a mystery conference, one where we weren't hawking our own books or up for a prize. Maybe, I thought, Fred would be inspired to go back to the novel he'd been working on when we met—or, at least, something more literary. Maybe *Death Takes a Siesta* should be our last Death Takes a Holiday book. It was time to choose life over death.

What I hadn't counted on was that one of the headliners was Jonathan Rooney, a classmate of Fred's from the Iowa MFA program. I thought Fred would be excited. I'd watched him read every one of Rooney's books as they came out. I'd read them, too, although frankly I wasn't sure what the big fuss was. Jonathan Rooney was talented enough, but to my mind his books were baggy and overwritten, each longer than five hundred pages. I could tell Fred was pleased that I was unimpressed by Rooney's oeuvre, but when I told him that Aleister would have whittled them down to a crisp hundred thousand words, he curtly replied: *Writers like Jon don't have to kowtow to their editors.*

Maybe they should, I'd replied.

I should have known Jonathan Rooney's arrival would spell trouble. I should have gotten us out of there, especially when I learned that he would be staying at our hotel. His "team" had commandeered the whole top floor, and the lobby and poolside were suddenly abuzz with reporters and bloggers and fans, all clutching Rooney's most recent book—a pretentiously understated black-and-white-covered eight-hundred-page door stopper titled *Apathy.*

"If the hotel runs out of firewood, we're covered," I joked.

Fred didn't laugh. Instead, he got his own copy and disappeared into its pages, becoming grimmer and thinner as he read, as if the book were sucking out his essential life source. I could see why. I read my own copy at the local café, kept awake only by endless demitasses of espresso. It was a grim tale in which the big reveal was—*Quel surprise!*—that all the characters were dead. I envied them their state by the time I got to the end. When I told Fred what I thought about it—plotless, too long, mean to its characters—he told me that I hadn't understood it. It was an homage to the great founding work of magic realism, Juan Rulfo's *Pedro Paramo.*

"I read *Pedro Paramo* in world lit," I told Fred frostily. "It's brilliant *and* it's a hundred twenty pages. I don't see the point of going on for eight hundred."

"If we rolled all our books together," Fred told me bitterly, "we'd have twice that. So what's the point of *us* going on?"

"Good question," I replied, slamming my copy of *Apathy* down on the table. "When you've got an answer, I'll be down the hall in my new room."

My dramatic exit was ruined by the hotel being sold out for the festival. So I spent the night on the couch in our suite's living room. He apologized the next morning and told me by *us* he meant the series, not the marriage. "Rooney always brings out the worst in me," he confided. "We were always in competition in workshop and now . . . well, he's a National Book Award winner and I write genre. I don't even really write it. You're the one who comes up with the ideas and make the books work."

"I bet our books sell more copies than his," I countered, "and make people happier."

"Maybe," he conceded, "but do they make us happy?"

I had thought so, but clearly, they didn't anymore. Maybe our chance at happiness had vanished along with our unborn child in Scotland.

"You could write something ten times as good as this," I said, peeling the book out of Fred's hands and climbing into his lap. "For one thing, the man doesn't know how to write a sex scene."

So we made up, as we always did, with great sex and drinks afterward, but I could feel Fred's attention drifting even before the night was over. In the morning, he got an email from

Jonathan Rooney's assistant inviting us to dinner that night at the hotel's rooftop restaurant. *An intimate welcome for Jon before the festivities,* she wrote.

"We don't have to go," I said, dreading the encounter, but Fred said it would be rude not to.

I dressed, as if girding myself for battle, in a low-cut black lace dress and a red embroidered shawl that I wore draped over one shoulder like a toreador's cape. I think I wanted to flaunt what Fred had and Rooney didn't, but maybe I was also feeling a little defensive as a "genre writer." What I wasn't prepared for was for us both to be greeted with so much enthusiasm. As soon as we stepped foot on the roof, Rooney broke away from his entourage and came straight for Fred, folding him into a bear hug.

"My man!" he crowed, pounding Fred on the back. Then, stepping back and seeing me, he grinned, his eyes traveling from my neckline to my toes and back again. "You old bastard! I wondered what you were doing writing potboilers, but this solves it; I'd write Harlequin Romances for a woman like this."

I froze, my skin simultaneously hot and cold, an ice statue set on fire. I don't think I'd ever felt so objectified in my entire life. And I'd fallen right into it, dressing up like a damned femme fatale. I looked to Fred for—*something.* A correction, at least. An acknowledgment that *we* wrote the books and that they weren't potboilers. But instead, he laughed and said, "Actually, I'm working on something of my own right now."

He was? That was news to me. I shot Fred an inquiring look but he only had eyes for his bro-pal Jon. A perky young blond woman in a tight black dress sidled up next to me and introduced herself as Jon's PA, Siena. "He's been so looking forward to seeing Fred and meeting you," she told me. "I downloaded all your books for him and read them all myself. I love Rick and Dora! They remind me of the old detective movies I used to watch with my grandmother."

As she gushed over the books—and her grandmother, who had inspired her to want to be a writer, too, and all the wonderful things Jon had said about Fred, and did I think I might consider having a look at something she was writing?—she was gently herding me to a couch-and-chair grouping arranged around a fire pit, as if I were her elderly gran who needed to be tucked safely away. She introduced me to Gunnar, partner of a famous Icelandic poet; Nori, a lifestyle blogger; and Delphine, the mistress of a famous French playwright. I looked over to see Fred and Jon joining the Icelandic poet and the French playwright in a halo of cigar smoke and peaty scotch. I'd been sent to the *wives'* corner, the lit-con equivalent of the kids' table.

"I mean, I know you're awfully busy, and I wouldn't ask except Fred has a reputation for his generosity and I don't want to bother him while he's talking to Jon."

I blinked at Siena, completely at a loss for what she was talking about, until I looked down and saw she was holding a sheaf of typescript in her hands. *Her* manuscript—printed out, for heaven's sake!—which she was asking me to read. No, not me, *Fred,* whose reputation for generosity in blurbing and reading the work of unpublished authors was entirely of *my* making. Not only was I being consigned to the *wives'* table, I had been demoted to Fred's secretary.

"Sure," I said, noticing as she handed it to me that there was a tattoo of a scorpion on the underside of her wrist. She noticed me shudder. "The scorpion represents strength, protection, and transformation," she said rather reprovingly, as if I didn't *get it*, "that's why I've named my book for it."

I glanced down and saw that the title of the manuscript was indeed *The Scorpion's Sting.* I placed it down on the chair next to me and prepared to make the best of the evening. After all, my aim had been to cheer Fred up, and from the raucous laughter emanating from the cigar and scotch cloud, that was succeeding. I attempted to engage my fellow B-listers in conversation but Gunnar spoke almost no English, Delphine was nearly deaf, and Nori was more interested in looking at her phone than me. What galled me even more was that Siena drifted back into the A-lister orbit, positioning herself by Jon's side but with her eyes on Fred. Who was *glowing*, plumped up on scotch and attention, both from Jonathan Rooney and Siena, who seemed to be hanging on his every word. Left with no distractions, I pulled a pen out of my bag and leafed through Siena's manuscript, correcting grammar and striking out unnecessary words, as Aleister always called them.

By the time we sat down to dinner, Fred was on a roll, regaling his audience with tales from slumming with the hoi polloi at mystery conferences. "If some little old lady from Topeka asks me one more time where I get my ideas, I might explode," he complained. "Thank God, Thea fields those questions."

At that, Jonathan Rooney turned toward me, as if remembering for the first time that I was there, and asked, "And what do you say, Thea? How do you explain the creative genius to the masses? Where *do* you get your ideas for your crime stories?"

"From the bad behavior of my fellow human beings," I said, "of which there is never a shortage."

Later, Fred would say that I'd looked right at him when I said this, as if I were accusing him of bad behavior. Maybe I did. He *had* been behaving badly, leaving me at the wives' table while he chummed with his new misogynist friends and ogled Siena. But if I looked at him it wasn't for long. My quip was met with a murmur of approbation around the table and a shifting of Jon's attention. As if he realized there was a head attached to my body.

"Does that include your own bad behavior?" he asked, lazily running a finger along the rim of his wineglass.

"Of course," I replied, feeling the hum of flesh on crystal vibrate through my body. "Write what you know."

Jonathan Rooney grinned at me and I bared my teeth in response. He was mine for the rest of the evening, asking me questions about my medieval studies and writing process. "So, really, you're the idea man of the team," he said at some point, sparing a look toward Fred. "No wonder you hate that question, Freddie."

I should have stopped right then, but I was angry. Fred had abandoned me without a second thought; why shouldn't I feed him to the wolves—or at least to one particular wolf—in turn? My anger sharpened by tequila and spite, I traded barbs with Jonathan Rooney. Later I would realize that it was what he wanted. He was as deeply jealous of Fred as Fred was of him. There'd been a girl back in Iowa that Fred had taken from him and he saw his way to revenge through me. And

Fred, once Jon's attention had shifted from him, turned his attention to Siena.

Which only redoubled my attentions to Jon.

I lost track after that of how many shots of tequila I drank and eventually I lost track of Fred, Siena, and of the night. The sun was coming up over the mountains when I lurched downstairs to our room and discovered Fred and Siena.

In our room!

In our four-poster bed!

The newly risen sun streaming through the slatted blinds, slashing across the white sheets—no, not sheets. Paper. Pages strewn across the bed. Siena in her skimpy dress lying amid the pages like some kind of beached mermaid washed up on a papery shoal.

Dimly I registered that she *was* dressed and that Fred was asleep on the couch. They were reading Siena's manuscript and fell asleep, I reasoned. Then, meanly: *It must not have been that riveting*. But then I picked up a page and read the header. *Frederick Morgan*. And a title: *Death Takes His Due*. Only that wasn't the name of the book we were working on, and why was there only his name on it? And without our hyphenated surname?

I started reading the page.

After she lost the baby, he wondered if it had been because of what they did for a living, if in return for making their living off Death, Death hadn't exacted His share of the royalties.

The scorpion on Siena's arm might have come to life and stung me. Fred was writing a thinly disguised autofiction about our marriage and he had shared his darkest thought about our darkest moment with a stranger.

I lay down the sheet of paper and left the room without waking them. I went downstairs to check into my own room—an adjoining room to Jon Rooney's suite, as it turned out, which he offered to me when I met him at the front desk that morning—and made plane reservations for the next available flight back to New York. Unfortunately, that wasn't for another week since the conference had packed all the departing planes. Massively hungover, I slept for most of the next week, shutters closed, burrowed under the duvet in a chilly room (it had a fireplace to heat it but I couldn't be bothered to make a fire), my only sense of time marked by the ringing church bells that seemed to be tolling the death of my marriage.

At the end of the week, I heard the door to the suite open and then close. Housekeeping, I assumed, checking for signs of life. At least they'd lit a fire in the fireplace to warm the frigid room. When I roused myself, I found a tray with a thermos of coffee and a bag of cinnamon rolls from my favorite bakery and realized it had been Fred, not a maid, who'd come in and stoked the fire. It was a peace offering, as if I would forgive him for some caffeine and pastries. But then I saw the manuscript. A slim typescript—less than 250 pages—tied with a piece of twine as if it were a handpicked bouquet of wildflowers. Fred's new literary masterpiece, *Death Takes His Due,* I assumed. Did he think I'd forgive him for sharing it with Siena first when I saw what literary gold he'd spun out of the wreckage of our lives? But when I flipped through the pages, I saw it wasn't *Death Takes His Due*; it was a Rick and Dora book. *Death Takes a Siesta*. The plot was as skeletal as one of the sugar *calaveras* sold for Día de los Muertos. He'd written it in a week, after all, and it needed a lot of work. My fingers itched to start marking it up. When I turned to the last page, I found the contract Fred had signed in New York. All I had to do was add my signature and send it back to Penelope. We'd go back to the way we were . . . until the next Fiona or Siena showed up.

Or I could toss both manuscript and contract on the fire.

I sat in front of that fire, drinking the coffee and then a glass of brandy, weighing my choices. At some point I picked up the manuscript and started editing. Maybe I could let the book decide what I would do next.

And in a way, it did.

At the end of *Death Takes a Siesta* Rick narrowly avoids dying at the hands of the murderer after taking a foolish—albeit gallant—risk.

There's only so many times you can cheat death, Dora tells him.

Death and I are on good terms by now, he replies. *We have an understanding.*

Which gave me an idea.

I signed and returned the contract. Then I called my lawyer to start drawing up our division-of-assets agreement.

"That wasn't what I bargained for when I sent you the manuscript," Fred had complained. Instead of answering, I referred him to the end of the manuscript. I'd added one more line to the concluding dialogue: *When you make a deal with Death,* Dora warns Fred, *you'd better make sure you've read the fine print.*

CHAPTER THIRTEEN

In my dream I am back in our room in San Miguel de Allende. I can smell the smoke of wood-burning fires on the air. The big four-poster bed is striped in slanted rays of light from the louvered shutters, dissecting the body tangled in the sheets into disjointed parts—an arm here, a leg there—that make no sense. The figure on the bed turns toward me, making a crackling sound. It's not tangled in the sheets, I realize; it's lying on a bed of loose typescript. I try to parse the meaning of the words on the pages as if translating a difficult Latin sentence, but the words swim together like spilled ink. I move closer and a bony hand snatches my arm, a face rising out of the dark, like a rotten apple bobbing to the top of a barrel, and I realize it's Death itself sleeping in my bed.

I startle awake out of the deep coma of jet lag with no idea of where—or when—I am. Sharp white blades of moonlight slice the darkness, laying a path on the marble floor. *Just like in my dream*. Even the smell of smoke is in the air. I have traveled back in time to our room in San Miguel. All I have to do is follow that path of moonlight. I could tear up the contract and end things there and then. Fred and I could have a chance to start over and go our separate ways. At least he wouldn't hate me so much that he's trying to kill me. As if urging me on, the scent of night-blooming jasmine wafts in through the open balcony door—

Open?

Hadn't I closed the door before going to bed and made sure it was locked? As I puzzle through this question, the slatted wooden door creaks open and a shadow falls across the moonlight, stretching toward me like a long bony finger. I freeze, pinned beneath the fluffy white duvet as if sealed in ice, as the dark shadowy figure glides weightless across the marble floor toward me. *It's Death,* I think, picturing the shrouded Grim Reaper that graces every cover of the Death Takes a Holiday series. Death has come to collect on the deal we made all those years ago—

But that was only in the book, I think, struggling out of dream logic. It wasn't real. And besides, hadn't Death already taken its due?

A spark of anger thaws through the ice and releases me from my paralysis. I fling back the duvet and launch myself straight into Death's cavernous embrace, half expecting to be swallowed into a yawning pit of the damned. Instead, I hit flesh and muscle. Something heavy and metal clatters loudly to the floor and I fall hard on my ass beside it on the marble floor. Death utters a deep guttural *oof!* and lands on top of me. I claw at the layers of cloth and peel away its cloak—

Uncovering a grinning skull.

I startle back and Death takes the opportunity to shove me away. I crack my head against the bedpost and the room shivers, the figure rippling in sickening waves as it gathers itself and reaches for the thing that had clattered to the floor. It looks like a shard of moonlight, sharp and silver—

A scythe. Just like the one Death holds on the cover of all our books and that our fans wear to show their loyalty. I am about to be sliced open by my own media brand.

I lurch forward and grab the hem of Death's cloak and yank. The cloth peels away like rotting flesh and glides over me, tangling me in its folds, making me an easily dispatched package. But instead of feeling the sharp blade of the scythe, I hear a crash and shouting and then hands are grabbing me. I struggle, punching through the cloth until it falls away from my face, and I find myself looking up at the face of Detective Bardi.

"*Basta, signora!* That's enough. Your attacker is gone. You are safe."

I stare up at the detective, clutching the remains of the tattered cloak around me, trying to absorb what he's saying. My attacker is gone, fled into the night; that much I get. But safe? When Death itself has come for me? I don't think so.

DETECTIVE BARDI SENDS in a female police officer to wait for me while I dress. He warns me to disturb the scene as little as possible and make note of anything that is missing. "You think this was a robbery?" I ask incredulously. "My assailant was too busy trying to mow me down with a scythe to take anything."

"You say you awoke from a deep sleep to find the cloaked figure at the door to your balcony. How do you know they were just coming in? They might have been here for some time and were just leaving."

The thought that Death had been in my room, pawing through my stuff while I slept, is sufficiently horrifying to silence me. I dress in slacks, a long-sleeved white button-down, and a black cardigan—what Fred calls my dour-librarian outfit—trying to touch as little as possible. Nothing appears to have been disturbed, but then I'd barely unpacked or spent any time in my room before going to sleep. When I come out, I find Detective Bardi talking to one of his officers.

"Shouldn't you be searching for my attacker?" I demand. "And checking alibis to see who is in their rooms? Nadine, for instance, and my husband."

"My officers are doing just that. Your husband is being interviewed right now."

"And Nadine?" I ask. "Was she—?"

The detective's mouth twitches as if he guesses what I'm afraid to ask. "Signorina St. George was *not* with your husband," he says, watching for my reaction.

"Then where was she?" I demand, refusing to look relieved.

"She was not in her room," he admits.

"Aha! You see, it *was* her. She's the right height . . ." I pause, recalling the feel of the body I barreled into and the strength of the arms that pushed me away. "And she does Pilates. Are you looking for her?"

"*Certo,* we are looking for her. Your husband said she mentioned her intention of taking an early morning hike." Again he watches for my reaction to Fred's familiarity with Nadine's routine. I greet it with a dismissive laugh. "Ha! In the dark—" But when I turn to the windows, I see that the sky is lightening. With a pang, I remember that when Fred and I were here twenty years ago we had often gone out before light to hike up into the mountains to see the sun rise. Had he been planning on doing that with Nadine?

"It's the perfect alibi," I say. "She could have gone straight from my room up into the hills and hid the rest of her costume on her way. You have to search the woods!"

"We are searching the hotel and the grounds, signora. Leave the investigation for us. Now, if you please—" He gestures to a chair. "I have some questions for you."

"I have some for you, too," I say, reluctantly sitting down on the edge of the chair he's indicated. "How did you happen to be in my room when I was attacked?"

"I had one of my officers watching your room and they alerted me to the appearance of an intruder on your balcony."

"Why did you have them watching my room?" I ask.

"For your protection," he says and then smiles at my incredulity. "And just in case you decided to slip out and murder one of your colleagues."

I start to express my outrage at his suspicions but I'm interrupted by a knock on the door. A maid comes in with a tray of coffee and pastries. He directs her to put the tray down on a table near me and begins happily chatting with her in Italian as if he were at his favorite café instead of in the middle of a murder investigation. It's a control tactic, I think, to make me wait. I open my mouth to demand that he talk to me right now—

But then I smell coffee, butter, and cinnamon, and my stomach growls. *When did I last eat?* I pour a cup of coffee, add hot steamed milk and sugar, which I don't usually take, but someone is always recommending sugar for shock in British mysteries and I'm definitely in shock. I pluck a warm cornetto from the breadbasket and the flaky hot pastry dissolves in my mouth, practically making me swoon. The first mouthful of coffee sharpens my synapses. I drink two cups and eat three cornetti while watching the sky lighten over the monastery walls, turning the old stone to a rosy gold, barely paying attention to the fast Italian speech passing between the detective and the maid—

Until I hear the words for *door* and *open*. He's asking her if she had left the balcony dooropen. She shakes her head and says she was not in my bedroom tonight.

"But my bed was turned down," I say, "and she left that weird little sachet."

The detective turns back to the maid and asks her another question while miming the turning down of bedclothes. She looks confused and they go back and forth in escalating volume and contention. Finally, he turns to me and says, "She says there was no turning down of the sheets and no sachet."

"It was on my pillow," I say, getting to my feet and heading into the bedroom. There's nothing on my pillow now. The pillow and sheets and duvet lie in a heap on the floor where they fell when I leaped to my feet to attack my assailant. The memory of that moment, of diving into the abyss of black robes and hitting flesh, makes me dizzy. I drop to my knees and run my hands along the floor.

"I know it was here," I mutter. "It reminded me of something—"

The scent of incense and jasmine had taken me back to San Miguel de Allende. That's why I'd been dreaming of finding Siena in our bed. Only in my dream it had been Death in that big four-poster bed. That's what I'd been dreaming of when I awoke to find Death in my room. My subconscious had been telling me that Death was coming for me.

But had I imagined the sachet?

I can smell it now, wafting up from beneath the bed. I lay my cheek down on the cold marble floor and peer into the dark space, braced to find Death's hollow eyes looking back at me. Instead, I spot the sachet. I drag it out and hold it up triumphantly to Detective Bardi and the maid. "This was lying on my pillowcase," I say, brandishing the lumpy hat-shaped thing.

The effect on the maid is instantaneous. She crosses herself and touches the little horn-shaped amulet she wears around her neck. *"Che sfortuna!"* she utters and then lets out a stream of outraged Italian.

How unlucky!

"She says she would never put such a thing on your bed, signora," Detective Bardi says. "It is bad luck to put a hat on a bed, a superstition that comes from the days when the priest was called to the deathbed and would place his hat at the foot while delivering the last rights. Leaving such a thing—" He shrugs and holds up his hands. "It is the same as wishing a person dead."

After Detective Bardi leaves, taking the ill-omened sachet with him, I head down to the lobby, intending to ask for a new room, preferably one without cursed amulets and faulty window locks. I find, however, that the registration desk is swamped by an angry mob. Joan is standing a little to the side, looking on as if she's planning to use the scene in her next novel, but when she sees me, she hurries over to meet me at the bottom of the stairs.

"What's going on?" I ask.

"Rats fleeing a sinking ship," she tells me. "You'd think a bunch of people who read and write mysteries wouldn't take fright at a couple of real-life murders, but half the convention woke up this morning and decided to check out."

"Are the police letting them?" I ask.

"Detective Bardi has given the Wilsons a list of people of interest who are not allowed to leave, but everyone else is free to go. The hubbub is that the Wilsons are refusing to give refunds just because their hotel has been the scene of two murders, and the mystery community is vowing revenge by Yelp. Now, you tell me what happened up in your suite this morning. There's a rumor that there was a break-in and all bets are on it being your suite because it's where all the carabinieri headed this morning."

"It was at the crack of dawn," I say. "Who was up then to see?"

"There was 'Sunrise Yoga and Silent Meditation in the Olive Grove,' which gave everyone a front row seat to the arrival of the carabinieri swarming over your balcony. Here, I'll show you—" She leads me out through a doorway on the east side of the hotel. Instead of formal gardens, this side of the hotel is bordered by an ancient olive grove. Joan takes me to a round clearing and points back toward the hotel, where I can see straight to the balcony of my suite. I make a mental note not to indulge in any nude sunbathing, not that this trip has been conducive so far to any such leisure activities. I'm surprised Joan found the time to take a yoga class, speaking of which . . .

"Since when do you do yoga?" I demand. Joan is fit but more in a kickboxing kind of way.

"Since there were two murders in my hotel. I needed to bring down my blood pressure and I wanted to hear the scuttlebutt."

"In a *silent* meditation class?"

"Please." Joan scoffs. "We're mystery fans. Murder *is* our meditation—ooh, dibs on that as a title. Now, tell me what happened?"

I fill her in on my visit from Death, ending with a description of the ill-omened sachet.

"The attacker must have been in your room before you went to bed," Joan concludes decisively. "I know I checked that the balcony doors were locked. They must have been in the suite hiding."

It's an awful thought but I have an even worse one. "Or they had a key."

"But how—?" Joan, sharp as ever, figures it out before finishing the question. "You mean Fred might have had another key. Oh, hon." She puts a hand on my shoulder. "Wouldn't you have known it was Fred when you tussled?"

Would I? I recall the feel of flesh and muscle under the cloak but there's nothing familiar about it. "I can't be sure. I don't think it was Fred. The police went to his room right after and he appeared to have been sleeping—*alone*. But it could have been Nadine. Was she at Sunrise Yoga?"

Joan shakes her head. "No, but I heard her say something last night about planning to take a morning hike."

"It sounds like she broadcast that around to everyone," I remark. "That could have been her plan, to head into the woods after she had attacked me and ditch the evidence somewhere." I look up the wooded slope that rises above the walls of the monastery. The sun has cleared the peaks in the east and lights up the old bell tower on the nearest hilltop. I remember that Fred and I had explored those woods for hours. There were dozens of paths where deer and wild boar roamed, deep gullies, and thick woods. "She could be anywhere hiding in the woods," I say. "Detective Bardi said he would send policemen to look for her."

"I wouldn't bet on him making that a priority," Joan says. "But there's nothing to stop us from taking a little hike. I need to get my steps in."

"Thanks, Joan, but it's too dangerous. If Nadine is the murderer she could be waiting for me in the woods. We can't just take off by ourselves."

She gives me a puzzled look. "Don't you remember, hon?

There's a nine a.m. hike up to the bell tower, and you and Fred are scheduled to lead it and give a talk."

Of course. Aleister had reminded me of it on the limousine ride just before I drifted off to sleep. "Oh no," I groan, "isn't our talk called—"

"'Finding the Perfect Murder Spot,'" Joan says with a grimace. "You and Fred are supposed to explain how you planned the third murder in *Death Takes the Castle*—aka the famous bell tower strangling."

CHAPTER FOURTEEN

Given how many people have checked out I'm not expecting a big turnout for the hike, especially since there are ominous-looking clouds amassing in the east, so I'm surprised to see a dozen people gathered by the east gate at nine o'clock. I'm less surprised to find Bob and Barb and the rest of the Midwest Mavens. Lindsay is there, too, with two of her Goth Librarian pals. I'm a little surprised to see her after our exchange at the well, but I suppose it was probably just the shock of her friend's death that made her lash out at me. Four retired teachers from Pittsburgh who have been in the same book club for twenty years round out the numbers.

"*Death Takes the Castle* was one of the first books we ever did," a woman named Sue tells me. "We've done every one of your books since then. Being here is a dream come true."

I nod politely, afraid their dream has turned into a nightmare. If I were writing this scene, I'd peg one of them for the next murder victim. I'm tempted to send her away but then I remember that there's at least safety in numbers.

"Won't Fred be here?" Pittsburgh Sue asks. "I have some questions about some of his narrative choices."

You and me both, honey, I think. "He had a busy night," I say instead, the excuse springing easily to my lips. How many times over the years have I explained away Fred's lateness or absence? I'm suddenly tempted to tell her the truth, that's he's too busy plotting my demise with his new girlfriend, but before I can, the man himself comes striding through the olive grove.

"There he is now!" Sue cries, beaming at Fred's arrival. "I knew he wouldn't disappoint us!"

I bite back a retort and turn to my husband, a smile pasted on my face. "Hello, darling," I purr. If *sweetheart* is our "get me out of here" code word, *darling* is code for "you're in big trouble." "Glad you could make it. Everyone would have been so disappointed if you hadn't."

He stares at me as if I've lost my mind. "You mean the hike is still on? Do we really think that's a good idea, *darling*, given what's happened over the last twenty-four hours?"

"Why not? The place is crawling with police so it's perfectly safe. Besides"—I look pointedly down at his hiking boots—"you look like you're ready for a hike. Were you planning on going alone? Or were you meeting up with someone in the woods?"

"Nadine hasn't come back from her morning hike yet," he replies tersely. "I was going to look for her."

"Well, then, we can help you." I turn to the group, who have been tracking our strained back-and-forth volley as if they were at Wimbledon. "The first trick to plotting a murder in a dangerous location is to give your characters a plausible motivation for going there in the first place. So, let's go find Fred's new writing partner. Maybe she's fallen off a cliff!" I say too brightly. Joan gives me a warning look as we head out the east gate and up the steep path, which is lined with tall cypress trees. I cheerily point out their funereal aspect to the group as *good for establishing atmosphere and portending doom*.

"Did the nuns have to make this walk every day to ring the bells?" Sue asks, huffing after only ten minutes. The rest of the Pittsburgh group is lagging behind with Joan, who is selling them on adopting her new series for their book club.

"Three times a day," Fred says at the same time I say, "Seven."

"Sunrise, noon, and sunset," he counters definitively.

"Yes," I concede in my most accommodating voice, "*plus* when the convent was under the Benedectine order they followed the canonical hours: Matins and Lauds at midnight, Prime at sunrise, Terce at the third hour, Sext at noon, None at the ninth hour, Vespers at sunset, and Compline at the end of the day."

"That's a lot of hill climbing," Sue says. "Those nuns must have had strong legs. This is steeper than the highest setting on my elliptical."

"Those nuns had buns of steel," Fred says, a line that's always good for a laugh. He's deflected to humor because he's annoyed I corrected him. Usually I let him have the laughs, playing straight man to his affable trickster, but I'm not in the mood this morning.

"That's nothing compared to the upper body strength needed to pull the ropes. Remember, Fred, you couldn't keep up with Sister Beatrice when you took a turn bell ringing with her."

"I'd pulled a muscle in my shoulder the day before," he says, sounding so wounded that I almost feel bad for goading him until I remember that he's scheming with Nadine to kill me. I'm about to shoot back another embarrassing anecdote when Lindsay, who's weaved her way through the Pittsburgh group and inserted herself between me and Fred, interrupts with a question.

"Why did they build the bell tower so far away from the convent?"

"To torture young novices," Fred quips

"Actually," I correct, "it was originally the castle's watchtower, built during a time of political strife and feudal bickering. It commanded a view over the valley to the east and the Via Francigena, the main road between Florence and Rome, and would have been manned by a watchman twenty-four hours a day to watch for invading armies. If any were spotted, the watchman would ring the bells to warn the castle to close the gates and prepare for battle."

"What happened to the watchman?" Lindsay asks. "Did they at least wait for him to get back to the castle before closing up the gates?"

"Nope," I say, "it was the watchman's job to stay in the tower and keep ringing the bells to call for reinforcements from neighboring allies. This was also, according to legend, where Bianca Rosa came to watch for the return of her crusading knight, who would have been traveling on the Via Francigena on his way back from the Crusades. Before she was walled up alive in the crypt, she begged the watchman to ring the bells in a special pattern if he saw her beloved returning. They say she heard the bells ringing his return as she lay drawing her last breaths—"

I pause to catch my own breath, feeling suddenly as if I am the one trapped beneath the castle's foundation, and see that we've reached the last turning in the path. The cypress trees stop here, yielding to shorter, scrubbier holm oaks and myrtle, allowing for a better view of the valley. Spread out below us is a patchwork quilt of olive groves, grape vineyards, and sunflower fields, punctuated by hills crowned with villas and monasteries, farmhouses and ruins. Once each hilltop would have housed a potential enemy or ally. Now they're home to rival hotels and Michelin-starred restaurants. There's a little shrine here—a brick arch with a white plaster saint against a bright blue ceramic background, below which someone has lain a bouquet of white and red roses. *The local girls leave roses for Santa Bianca Rosa here,* Sister Beatrice had told us, *to pray to be granted a love like hers.*

As the group turns from us to take pictures of the little shrine, murmuring over Bianca Rosa's tragic end, Fred steps closer to me.

"Of course that's all hearsay and legend," he says in a sulky voice, no doubt getting back at me for correcting him earlier. "You were never able to prove any of it."

"No, that's the thing about legends; they're very often unprovable. Maybe that's exactly what gives them their power and makes them so perfect for fiction."

"Perfect for fiction, maybe; not so perfect for a doctoral dissertation."

I squint up at Fred, who's standing above me on the path, his back to the sun so I can't make out his face. His dark silhouette strikes a spark of fear in my heart. He looks, I realize, like the figure of Death I saw in my room last night. *Could it have been him?*

"No," I concede, when what I want to ask is: *Is this our story now, Fred? Is this what our marriage has become?*

"Which is why you abandoned your dissertation, wasn't it?" Fred says.

"I abandoned my dissertation because we started writing *Death Takes the Castle,*" I say.

"Really?" Fred says, tilting his head to one side like an innocent baby deer. "Because as I recall, you were still working on your dissertation until the day we came up here with Sister Beatrice and she told you that she had never been able to find any proof that Bianca Rosa even existed."

"Because," I nearly shout, "the men who took over the abbey after her death wanted to erase her memory!"

"Maybe," Fred says, with an irritating shrug. "But you really didn't have any proof for that either. Don't you remember? You told me that day that without your dissertation you didn't know what you were going to do with yourself. You'd put so much work into it that would just go to waste . . . *unless* you could use it in a novel. That's when you really decided that you wanted to write *Death Takes the Castle.*"

I gape at Fred, completely dumbfounded. "What are you talking about? We were already writing the book when we came up here with Sister Beatrice."

"We weren't, really," he says. "It was just a game to you at that point—a diversion from your dissertation, which wasn't going well. I'm not blaming you; it was a diversion for me, too, from the serious work of my novel and it seemed like the best way to get to spend time with you. But let's face it, neither of us were taking it too seriously until the day we came up here and you finally had to admit that the premise of your dissertation was entirely false. Honestly, I felt bad for you. When all certainties desert us, what are we left with but deceptions and lies."

I'm too shocked by this pompous theory to even respond. I just stand there playing over what he's said in my head as if I'll be able to parse the words into sense . . . and then I realize where I've heard those words before. "Where is this coming from?" I demand.

"What do you mean?" he asks, looking equally dumbfounded. Or maybe a little bit guilty?

"You've never once suggested over the last twenty years that I launched our writing career because I was stuck on my dissertation."

"*Launched our writing career*? You make it sound as if you single-handedly came up with the idea and wrote the books yourself."

"Don't change the subject," I say, recognizing the feint for what it is—a diversion. "We're not talking about who had the original idea—although it *does* sound as if you're suggesting it was me since I was so desperate for a diversion—"

He tries to cut in but I steamroll right over him.

"Because, what? I'd given up finding proof that Bianca Rosa

existed after a few months here? As if that would stop any serious researcher! A researcher who had so little regard for the truth that I . . . How did you put it . . ." I turn to our audience, who has clearly decided our argument is more interesting than the shrine. No, I haven't forgotten that the entire tour group is standing on the path like an invading army listening raptly as we tear apart the edifice that is our marriage and our writing partnership. "Oh yes . . . *When all certainties desert us, what are we left with but deceptions and lies.* Why are those words so familiar? I could swear I heard someone say something just like that here at this conference . . ."

Sue, God bless her, raises her hand. "Yes, Sue?" I prompt.

"I think it's what Nadine St. George said last night," she says, looking torn between being proud that she can identify the source and embarrassed to catch Fred in an act of plagiarism.

"Of course!" I say, wheeling around to face Fred. "And who else would know so much about deceptions and lies? I mean, because of her fellowship at Oxford, of course. She would know all about research dead ends. Did she lend her expertise to this interpretation of my creative process?"

Fred has the decency to blush—or maybe he forgot to wear his sunscreen and he's burning under the bright Tuscan sun. "That's not what this is about—"

"Then what is it about, Fred? Is it not enough that you and Nadine want to write Dora out of the books? Are you going to rewrite *our* history, too?"

"Why not?" he snaps. "You wrote us into existence and that's all we've ever been—a fantasy of a marriage you cooked up to sell books. You're welcome to write the ending you want. I'm done."

"Typical," I say, "to leave the hard writing to me." I turn on my heel and leave before he can. I'm so mad that I practically sprint up the rest of the hill, Fred close behind me. We come around the last turn of the path and reach the bell tower, which Fred storms inside of as if he were taking it by force. Sue and Lindsay follow him more cautiously and then the rest of the group, except for Joan, who lingers behind. "Are you okay, hon?" she asks, patting my arm awkwardly. Joan doesn't do consolation well, but she does do hard truths.

"Do you think he's right?" I ask.

"What? That you cooked up the myth of Rick and Dora's happy marriage just to sell more books?" she recaps with brutal minimalism.

I nod.

"What if you did? More power to you. That's what we writers do—we spin fantasies to make life bearable. Do you think the women who read my books need to be reminded that their husbands don't appreciate them and their kids are ungrateful? Not on your life! They want to believe that if they're clever enough, there's an adventure waiting for them in their Podunk little town at their boring, humdrum jobs. Your readers want to believe that a couple may bicker and get into scraps once in a while but they still love each other. So what if that's a fantasy—it's a fantasy people are willing to pay good money for."

"And when they learn that I made it all up? Not just the books but the happy marriage?"

Joan shrugs. "You'll sell them the next fantasy—plucky woman author survives dissolution of her marriage and her book series to go on to her next adventure—because that's what we do. There's no bad news that can't be grist for the mill and spun into gold—pardon my mixed metaphor. Now, dry your eyes and go show those good women from Pittsburgh who've shelled out their discretionary income to fly all the way here how to ring those damn bells."

Joan hands me a Kleenex from her copious bag and I wipe my face. Then I square my shoulders and follow her into the dim cool interior of the bell tower. The group has formed a circle around the ropes that hang in the center of the space, each one terminating in a loop that looks unnervingly like a hangman's noose. Everyone is looking up at the rickety iron steps that circle upward to the belfry. There's a wooden platform on the top level beneath the bell chamber, but no one looks anxious to risk the ancient stairs to get a closer look. I don't blame them. The stairs appear even flimsier than they did twenty years ago. And besides the work of climbing to the top, the bells are so large that that there's very little room to stand inside the bell chamber. The bells practically touch the floor. Anyone standing too close could be squashed or pushed off the platform.

"Who wants a go at bell ringing?" I say brightly. "We need four people—" I slide one of the loops around my wrist and grasp the rope a few feet higher. Fred and Sue each take a rope. Then Lindsay looks around, puzzled. "Is there supposed to be a fourth rope?"

"Yes," I say, scanning the walls to see if the rope for the

fourth bell has gotten tangled in the staircase. "There are four bells . . . unless one of them has broken." I remember that one of the bells had cracked when I was here twenty years ago and Sister Beatrice was afraid it might have to be replaced eventually. "One of the bells must be out of commission. Still, three bells should sound beautiful. The way Sister Beatrice showed us how to do it was for one ringer to pull down slowly and when the bell rings, the second ringer begins to pull, and so on. Remember that the bells are quite large and very heavy so make sure you take a steady stance before you begin. We wouldn't want anyone getting swept off their feet."

"You begin," Fred says, "then Lindsay, then Sue—" He's gallantly handed his rope to Lindsay.

I grasp the rough hemp rope in my hands, bend my knees slightly, and pull. The weight is heavier than I remember, as if the bell is reluctant to move. I pull harder . . . and something groans overhead. I look up and see flakes of paint and sawdust floating down from the belfry. Something is wrong. But it's too late to stop. The momentum of my pull carries the bell in a wide arc that nudges something off the floor of the bell chamber—a drop cloth or polishing rag, I think, as a bundle of cloth spills over the side of the platform. It looks, I think as I stare up, mesmerized, like an angel in flight fluttering down to earth—

Straight toward me.

Fast.

Too fast for it to be just cloth. It's something heavy, headed straight at me, and it's too late for me to get out of its way.

I barely have time to close my eyes and shield my head with

my arms. But the blow doesn't come from above; it comes from the side and sweeps me off my feet. I land so hard on the stone floor that all the wind is knocked out of me and my head fills with a ringing like a hollow vessel. As if *I* am the bell.

When I open my eyes I'm looking into a pair of slate-blue ones, and what I think is, Oh, the angel of death has Fred's eyes. Then I see it *is* Fred and his mouth is moving but I can't make out what he's saying. I look past him to see a tableau out of a medieval painting. Sue has her hand over her mouth while Lindsay points open-mouthed at a figure suspended in the air—the angel I watched descend from the belfry, only this angel is cloaked in black and wearing the same skull mask as the Grim Reaper that invaded my room last night. It's an effigy, I think, as Fred helps me to my feet. A straw-stuffed dummy rigged up to frighten us. It would have hit me if—

I turn to Fred and realize that the blow I'd felt was him pushing me out of harm's way. If he'd wanted me dead, he could have let that thing hit me. Was I wrong about him? He's not looking at me right now, he's staring at the hanging figure with an expression of horror. *It's just an effigy,* I want to tell him, but the ringing in my ears is so loud I can't hear my own voice, so instead I walk to the hanging figure and peel away the mask—

Revealing the distorted and purplish—and very real—face of Nadine St. George.

CHAPTER FIFTEEN

I can see Fred's mouth moving but I can't hear what he's saying. I can't hear anything but the bells. *Why are the bells still tolling? Are we being invaded? Are the barbarians at the gate?* I look around the tower. Pittsburgh Sue is weeping, Lindsay's mouth is open in a long silent scream, Joan is shouting into her phone.

Oh, good, I think, Joan is on the case. Those barbarians don't stand a chance.

Then I feel something burbling up inside me, vibrating at the frequency of those damn bells. Am I going to be sick? What emerges, though, is laughter. *If only the watchman had had a Galaxy S24 Ultra! They wouldn't have to ring the damn bells in the first place.*

Although I can't hear my own laughter, Fred must because his eyes widen with alarm and he pulls me out of the tower. The crisp hilltop air and sunlight slap me in the face and the laughter dies in my throat. Instead, I feel sick. Knowing that look on my face, Fred steers me around some olive trees to a rocky outcropping perched above the valley and holds my hair while I'm sick over the cliff edge. What a scenic spot to throw up, I think, admiring the view of vineyards and olive groves.

When I'm done, Fred steers me to a comfortable rock beneath an old, gnarled olive tree and hands me his water bottle and a damp bandanna to wipe my mouth. When I've rinsed out the bitter taste, I turn to look at him. His face is stony and gray in the silvery light of the olives, his jaw clenched and his eyes the color of storm clouds. "Oh, Fred," I say, "I'm so sorry about Nadine. I know she was your . . ." The words get swallowed up in the silence; I don't know what Nadine was to him.

"She was a good friend," he says, a tear sliding down his face. "It wasn't what you thought."

"That doesn't matter now," I say quickly, but he shakes his head.

"No, I should have explained everything right away instead of letting you get the wrong idea. Nadine was reading my novel—something new I started this past year—and she told me about a writing residency that she thought would be good for me. That's where I was this summer—at a retreat in Scotland. I wasn't with Nadine. She was reading my book and encouraging me but there was nothing romantic going on."

"It's really none of my business if there was," I say, unable to hide the hurt in my voice. "But why didn't you tell me about the book?"

"I was afraid you'd be angry I was taking time away from Rick and Dora," he says.

I stare out at the valley, trying to digest this. "Let me get this straight," I say. "You were more afraid I'd think you were cheating on Rick and Dora than you were of me thinking you were cheating on me?"

He could easily point out that a romantic affair wouldn't have been cheating since we'd agreed we could see other people, but instead he looks at me sheepishly. "Yeah, well . . . I remember that you were upset I'd shared my book with Siena instead of you."

"That's fair," I say before he feels forced to explain himself. The betrayal I'd felt at the sight of those pages strewn across the bed—*our bed*—sharing *our* pain is still sharp. "I suppose I've prioritized Rick and Dora over you and me. You were right when you said I put the books before the marriage—"

"I didn't mean that," he cuts in. "And I didn't mean that part about you inventing the books because you'd hit a snag in your dissertation either."

"I did!" I cry. "When I realized there was no proof Bianca Rosa even existed I saw my whole academic career going up in smoke! I couldn't make up a love story for my dissertation, but I could make up one for Rick and Dora."

"You didn't make that up," he says, taking my hand. "I was already head over heels in love with you by then. I still . . ." His voice thickens and I see the muscles of his throat working. I lean a little closer to hear what he's going to say, but instead a much harsher voice intrudes into the olive grove.

"Mr. and Mrs. Morgan-Lane," Detective Bardi says, as if pronouncing us husband and wife. "There you are. I've been looking for you. I have some questions for you about the death of Nadine St. George."

"Can't that wait?" Fred says, straightening up and placing himself between me and the detective. "My wife has had a terrible shock. The body nearly fell on top of her—she could have been killed!"

"What a tragedy that would have been for you, Mr. Morgan-Lane, to lose two such beautiful women in one day!"

"I would have been killed if Fred hadn't pushed me out of the way," I say, standing next to Fred.

Detective Bardi looks keenly from me to Fred and back again. "I see the tragic circumstances have at least worked to bring about a reconciliation. If you'll come with me, perhaps together you two can explain how such a monstrous murder could be committed."

"Come with you where?" Fred demands angrily.

"Back to the scene of the crime," Bardi replies, "as you would write in one of your books. To the bell chamber."

DETECTIVE BARDI ESCORTS us back to the bell tower, walking closely behind us as if expecting us to bolt. The thought of going inside nearly does make me bolt. As we approach, a stretcher is carried out by a team of police officers. Nadine's face is, mercifully, covered, but still, as we enter the bell tower I seem to see her bloated face hovering in the shadows.

"Why can't we be questioned back at the hotel?" Fred asks, seeing how green my face is.

"There are some questions I have about the . . . how would you say? . . . the mechanics of how such a grisly crime could be executed, and it appears from your book"—he takes his copy of

Death Takes the Castle out of his pocket—"that you made quite a study of medieval bell ringing."

"Sister Beatrice explained the rudiments to us," I say, looking up to where the bell ropes vanish far above us through holes in the bell chamber floor. An image of that awful angel of death plunging down through the air makes me flinch. "But we're no experts. I'm sure the Wilsons could explain more—"

"I'd like your particular expertise," he says, waving toward the rickety stairs, "as crafters of murder."

"Are those stairs even safe?" I ask.

"Both Nadine St. George and her killer got up them," he replies.

"Couldn't it be possible that she hung herself?" I ask, trying to delay setting foot on those stairs.

Detective Bardi shakes his head. "And bound her own hands behind her back? I think not. Come—unless you have any particular aversion to visiting the scene of the crime?"

"Just a desire not to break our necks on those stairs," Fred says, but then meeting my gaze he adds, "I'll go. Thea can stay down here."

"That's all right," I say, refusing to play the frail female—*Dora would never stay behind!* "Of course we're happy to help in any way to find out who did this to poor Nadine."

Fred gives me a curious look but I only walk past him and to the stairs. The whole structure vibrates as soon as I grasp the rusted iron handrail and start climbing. It shakes even harder as Fred and Detective Bardi follow. It may be true that the staircase supported Nadine and her killer, but we don't know if they climbed up at the same time or whether the staircase can support all three of us. In fact, it occurs to me, the killer could have planned to kill us by loosening a few screws from the struts that hold the iron staircase to the old stone walls. As if to confirm my fears, I spy a spill of sand falling from one of the struts as we make our way up.

If he's worried about falling to his death, Bardi doesn't show it. He launches into an interrogation as we ascend. "When did you see the victim last, Mr. Morgan-Lane?"

I look back and see Fred flinch at the word *victim*, a word we have written a hundred times without it ever conjuring the horror of Nadine's bloated face. I see Bardi, on the step below Fred, register the flinch, and realize that it makes Fred look guiltier.

"As I told you this morning when you woke me, I hadn't seen Nadine since last night after that girl's body was found in the well. She was very upset—"

"Was she?" Detective Bardi remarks dryly. "I spoke with her at some length and she seemed unusually cool and collected."

"She was good at acting calm under duress," Fred says.

"Ah," the detective remarks, as if Fred had said something profound, "I suppose you crime writers are inured to the horrors of death. You sound as if you knew the lady quite well."

"I . . . er . . ." Fred clears his throat nervously and I realize that Detective Bardi's intent in questioning Fred in front of me is to make me jealous. It's also occurred to me that he's fitting Fred up for Nadine's murder, partly because of my accusations against him.

"It's all right, Detective," I say, "Fred has clarified his relationship with Nadine to me. She was helping him with a book."

"Ah," he says, "I see that you two are friends again now that Ms. St. George is no longer in the picture."

"What? No, it's not like that—" I begin.

"Just what are you implying?" Fred demands, the staircase shaking with his anger.

"Only that it seems convenient for you that the woman who caused trouble in your marriage is gone now that you have . . . how do you say it? . . . mended fences?"

"Neither Thea nor I had anything to do with what happened to Nadine. Neither of us have been here to the bell tower before arriving together with the group tour this morning."

"And how do you know your wife had not been here beforehand? Were you with her last night?"

He knows that Fred wasn't in my bedroom when the intruder showed up—or at least, not that I said—but Fred doesn't know that. "No," he says with a tone of regret, "we had had a fight and I was staying in my own room, but I know that Thea would never hurt anyone." His trust in me, after I have suspected him, nearly breaks my heart.

"How inspiring to hear a husband with so much faith in his wife," Bardi says, as if mocking the sentiment. "I'm sorry that your wife has not shown the same faith in you, signore. She told me about the murder clause in your contract."

"Murder clause?" Fred repeats, sounding puzzled.

"I think the detective means the kill clause," I say, glad I can't see Fred's face. I can feel, though, his hurt radiating through the vibrations of the staircase, “which I only mentioned because I found a copy of the contract on your bed. But clearly, I was mistaken. If Nadine and Fred had been plotting to get rid of me so they wouldn’t have to share the royalties, why would Fred kill Nadine?”

“Perhaps since you two had made up, he needed to eliminate her before she accused Fred of murder,” he says.

“That’s preposterous!” I say. “Besides, you know I was in my room last night when the intruder came in, and you checked on Fred right after so you know he was in the hotel when Nadine was still alive—”

“And how do you know what time Nadine St. George was killed?” he asks.

“Didn’t you see what she was dressed like?” I demand. “She was wearing the same black cloak and death mask as my intruder. Clearly it was Nadine who came into my room and attacked me. So she was still alive while Fred and I were in the hotel. Nadine must have fled the hotel and come up to the bell tower. She knew we were coming here this morning—”

“Or maybe Nadine saw your intruder fleeing the hotel and she followed him up here where he turned on her and killed her,” Fred says. “Then he dressed her in the cloak and mask.”

Of course, I realize, Fred still can’t believe that Nadine is guilty of murder.

The final approach to the bell chamber is a steep, nearly vertical flight of rusted steps that disappear through a wooden trapdoor. As I lift the hatch, I’m assaulted by the metallic smell of blood and I feel a rising sense of dread. *It’s a trap,* every nerve in my body screams. Bardi is the murderer and he's led Fred and me up here to dispose of us. Our only chance is to get up here first and bar the door. I climb up into the bell chamber and am immediately enmeshed in a web of light, as if a net has been cast over me. Looking up, I see that the sun coming through the slats in the tower roof is filtered through the great spoked wheels on which the bells are mounted. *The bells*. I had forgotten how massive, how solemn, how . . . *otherworldly* they are, their great mouths gaping open like the slavering jaws of a pack of wolves. Staring up, I feel pulled as if by a magnetic force into their copper-breathed gullets.

Sister Beatrice had told us a story about the bells that day, that when they were cast a man had fallen into the smelting vat and that by the time they fished him out all that was left of him were his bones. Ever since then the bells were hungry for flesh and blood.

"That's how it was done." For a moment I think the bells themselves have spoken, but then a beam falls on the wheel of one of the bells and I see that it's Bardi aiming a flashlight on the mechanism. "Do you see the rope?"

"The ropes are threaded through the wheels to ring the bells," I say, confused.

"Look closer," he says. "There's a second rope on this bell and none"—he swings the flashlight to another bell, where the end of a frayed rope hangs severed a few feet below the wheel—"on this one," he finishes.

"Someone cut off the rope of one of the bells and threaded it on another—but why?" Fred asks.

"It was tied around your friend's neck," Bardi says. "When the bell was tolled the second rope tightened around her neck and dragged her body up onto the wheel, then flung her down through the rope hole." He points his flashlight through the gaping hole beneath the double-roped bell.

"You don't mean . . ." Fred's voice is hollow, as if coming from a great empty space.

"That she was killed when you rang the bells?" Bardi asks, his voice reverberating inside the hollow bells as if they are shivering with pleasure at the horror he's recounting. "Yes, that's exactly what I mean. The autopsy will reveal if she was still alive. If she was, let us pray to God that she was at least drugged or unconscious."

"That's . . . dreadful!" I gasp, shuddering. "Who would even think of such a monstrous thing—"

Fred's hand lands on my arm and squeezes. To comfort me? No, I realize, the full horror dawning on me as if the bells themselves were descending over me; Fred's trying to warn me.

"You did," Bardi says, unable to hide the satisfaction in his voice. "It's exactly how the third murder is committed in your book."

CHAPTER SIXTEEN

Sister Beatrice had given us the idea for this particularly gruesome murder method—one fit for the Spanish Inquisition. There was a legend that an invader to the castle had snuck up into the bell tower and, after subduing the watchman with a blow to his head, had tied him up and fitted a noose around his neck before attaching it to the wheel of one of his own bells. The scheme served two purposes: If anyone from the castle escaped the siege and made it to the bell tower to raise an alarm, they would unwittingly kill the watchman and his body would jam the mechanism and silence the bells.

I had suggested we use the manner of "death by ringing" for a particularly unsavory character. *Really?* Fred had said when I proposed it. *Won't that lose us our PG-13 cozy rating?*

Cozies don't make real money, I'd replied. *We want to go a little darker.*

Afterward, I'd regretted the choice. *A lurid tendency to the macabre,* one reviewer had put it. I suppose that's why I'd forgotten the scene.

"Writing a murder isn't the same as committing one," I tell Detective Bardi now. "And besides, we didn't even come up with the idea. It was part of a legend Sister Beatrice told us."

"The fact remains," Bardi says, "that the three murders so far follow the ones in your book. Am I supposed to believe that is a coincidence?"

"Probably not," Fred admits to my alarm. "I wondered after Kailee died in the well—"

"You did?"

"Yes, that's why I was heading up here this morning—not just to look for Nadine; I wanted to see if the third clue was here. But don't you see, Inspector, it makes Thea and me the least likely suspects," Fred points out. "Why would we incriminate ourselves by imitating the murders in our own book? Isn't it obvious? Someone with a grudge against us is doing this."

"And why would anyone have a grudge against you two?" Bardi asks with feigned innocence.

Fred laughs, the sound unfortunately amplified and distorted by the hollow bells hanging above our heads. "Are you kidding? Writers are notoriously envious and backstabbing. Pick any writer—or better yet, any would-be unpublished writer—here who hasn't had our success and you've got a person with a grudge against us."

"You don't seem to think highly of your peers, Mr. Morgan-Lane. Do you count yourself among the envious and the back-stabbing?"

"All Fred is saying is that we'd hardly incriminate ourselves by imitating the murders in our own book," I say, before we can go farther down the path of besmirching our fellow mystery writers. "And he has a point. The murderer has even imitated the clues in the treasure hunt—" I look around the chamber. "Was a clue left here?"

"You didn't notice it?" Bardi asks with a grin. "It was pinned to the victim's cloak."

"I wasn't really focused on the cloak," I say, shuddering at the memory of Nadine's bloated face.

"Of course," Bardi says, extracting something from his copious pockets. I'm relieved it isn't his copy of *Death Takes the Castle*; I'm sick to death of the sight of our debut work. Instead, it's a clear plastic evidence bag containing one of the now familiar Florentine note cards Deb used for the clues. My vision blurs at the thought of Deb carefully choosing the cards at a Florentine *cartoleria*. Fred reads the clue out loud:

The ominous and weather-beaten gate
Leads to a stony sentinel of fate
Whose fanged mouth spits most terrible red streams
Of victims' blood within that darkly gleams.

The bells above our heads shiver with the echo of the words as if excited at the prospect of blood.

"So, Mr. and Mrs. Morgan-Lane, tell me about the fourth murder in your book."

One of my least favorite parts of author Q and As is when a fan asks a question about a tricky plot point from one of our old novels. After twenty books, many of the details blur together. How can we be expected to remember something we wrote ten or twenty years ago and might have rewritten several times? I'm tempted to plead amnesia here but unfortunately the fourth death in *Death Takes the Castle* rises in all its bloody horror just as Bardi opens his copy of the book to a marked page and begins to read out loud.

"The iron beast was fashioned along the lines of the iron maiden—a six-foot-tall monster with the body of a bear, the snout and tusks of a wild boar, and the claws and wings of a dragon. Hollow as a chocolate Easter bunny, its insides were lined with sharpened iron spikes. When closed on its victim, their agonized shrieks and blood poured through the beast's fanged mouth.

"*Che orrore!*" Bardi exclaims. "Does such an infernal contraption exist in the castle?"

"No," Fred says.

"We made it up," I admit.

The look of horror turns to disdain. "What minds you two have," he says, shaking his head, "to imagine such an abomination. You had best use those minds now to figure out what version of this monster the murderer will use next."

"ARE WE TERRIBLE people?" I ask when we are walking on our own down the hill. Bardi had hurried on ahead after escorting us out of the bell tower as if he didn't want to spend another minute in the company of people who could imagine such horrors.

"You mean because we made up a torture device worthy of the Marquis de Sade?"

"That—and what you said earlier about our fellow writers. Do you really think they're all racked with envy?"

"Most of them, yeah. We might smile and congratulate each other on social media for winning this award or making that top-ten list, but let's face it: Who among us doesn't feel a little stab of envy every time it's not our name on that list or trophy?"

"So you're including us among the envious?"

"Ha!" He laughs, side-eyeing me. "Remember that Bouchercon when we didn't win the Anthony and we plotted how we'd poison each of our competitors?"

"I thought we were joking," I say, although what I remember was the sharp pang of disappointment when Buck's name had been called, relieved only by Fred's snarky whisper, *Do you think he stuffed the ballot boxes?*

"I wouldn't have minded so much if it had been anyone but Buck. His book wasn't half as good as ours. He only won because he schmoozed all the attendees into voting for him—" I stop, embarrassed at the heat in my voice. "Okay, I get your point. None of us is immune from a little envy and these contests that pit us against each other are bound to bring out the worst in everyone. But it's one thing to joke about knocking off the competition, it's another to actually do it."

"Maybe for us," he says. "After all, we've been successful and lucky. But for the writers whose careers are in decline and who may not get their next contract, or who've never had the success we've had, how much would it take for envy to turn to malice? Take your friend Joan, for instance—"

"Joan!" I squawk. "She's very successful! She has three series going."

"I heard her publisher canceled the Hill Country series and that she lost her editor at Windsor Books"

"She told me about that," I concede. "But they assigned her to a new young editor she likes—although she did joke that we have shoes older than her. But Joan's a fighter. She's already got another series planned. She doesn't sit around feeling sorry for herself; she gets down to work."

"She works like a dog," Fred agrees, "because those books don't get the kind of advances ours do. Don't you think that bothers her?"

"Maybe," I concede, recalling Joan's remark that cozies were never nominated for big prizes like the Poirot, "but she's always supportive of other writers."

"She's always networking, you mean. Exchanging favors, courting blurbs, promoting someone else's book to get hers promoted—"

"You make all that sound like a bad thing. She's pragmatic—"

"She's transactional," he counters. "Haven't you noticed that every time she gets in touch with you she has a blurb request or wants an introduction to someone influential or for us to do a giveaway on her newsletter—"

"All of which helps *us*!"

"Sure, and if we didn't cooperate, we'd end up on her infamous naughty list. Pete told me that when he collaborated with her on that series, she refused to put a certain writer in the acknowledgments because she had refused her a blurb once."

"She can be sensitive . . . But speaking of Pete," I add, eager to shift the focus away from Joan, "surely you don't count him in your cast of envious backstabbers."

"Ha! I once spent an evening at Noir at the Bar listening to Pete enumerate how each and every writer there had gotten a historical detail wrong in one of their books—including us."

"He's a perfectionist," I concede.

"He doesn't understand why the most historically accurate book isn't the one that sells the best. But then there's Buck, who thinks that the only reason his books don't win all the prizes is that he's a straight white male who's the victim of the woke mob."

I snort. "I heard what he said about Shay . . . who, by the way, has never displayed a sliver of meanness or envy in the entire time I've known her."

"Shay's a class act," he agrees, "but what do you think it's like having to deal with racist buffoons like Buck and all the inequities of white-dominated publishing?"

"Shitty," I say. "But I don't see her killing anyone over it and if she did, she'd do a better job of it than accidentally killing Deb, whom she loved. In fact, if the killer is motivated by professional jealousy, they're doing a pretty poor job at clearing the field; two of the people killed weren't even writers."

"Kailee was," Fred says.

"Kailee?" I echo before remembering that it's the name of the girl who was killed in the well last night. "I thought she was part of Lindsay's Goth Librarian crew."

"First of all, I don't think all of those women are actual librarians—they just dress like them. They're a writing group, and at least three of them—Lindsay, Kailee, and Zoe—have manuscripts in the Paulson and Pratchett discovery contest. Nadine judged that contest last year and she said she got hate mail afterward from the losers."

"I notice you don't count Nadine among the envious horde," I say, and then immediately regret it. I add, "But then, she didn't seem jealous of anyone."

"You're wrong about that," he says, "she was jealous of you—and not because of me," he hastily adds. "She told me she envied the courage you had to walk away from an academic career and commit yourself to a creative one."

"Ha!" I say. "Or the folly."

We've come to the cypress alley, which stretches down to the east gate of the castle. I stop and am suddenly transported back to the day we were here with Sister Beatrice and I finally realized that the premise of my dissertation was fatally flawed.

Giving up on the Bianca Rosa theory will set me back months and my adviser is already pressuring me to submit, I'd wailed

He sounds like an asshole, Fred, who'd picked up enough of my ambivalence about Halliday to have conceived a jealousy, had remarked.

I didn't think so at first, I confessed, *he was all charm and smiles.* I'd looked down at the east gate and noticed the arch above with its carvings of medieval beasts. *He's like that manticore with his handsome man's face and lovely voice, but a scorpion tail that stings when you're not looking.*

Ooh, Fred had said, *let's use that in our book and kill him like the watchman was killed.*

I'd been about to remind him that we'd already killed Hal Grazer, the stand-in for my adviser, by a fall down the main stairs, but then I registered what Fred had said—*our* book. It was the first time he'd called it that.

I guess in fiction we can do whatever we want, I said.

Exactly, Fred had said, *and we can kill off all the people we don't like.*

It was the moment when I first realized I could walk away from my dissertation and Fraser Halliday—from all of it—and write novels with Fred Morgan instead. It was the moment our collaboration was sealed, born from despair and envy and some pretty gruesome murder methods.

"What did the clue say again?" I ask now.

He has the words memorized, as I knew he would:

The ominous and weather-beaten gate
Leads to a stony sentinel of fate
Whose fanged mouth spits most terrible red streams
Of victims' blood within that darkly gleams.

I look up at the arch above the gates and the fantastical beasts carved there. The manticore bares its three rows of terrible teeth in its human face and flexes its scorpion tail; the winged basilisk stares with its deadly glare; the woman-faced and -breasted harpy beats its bird wings and lures men to their doom with its seductive song; a unicorn pierces an elephant's hide with its pointed horn; a griffin flexes its wings and rends its enemies' flesh with lion claws and eagle's beak; a two-headed dragon-like amphisbaena gnaws its own tail. Each horrible creature of the medieval bestiary teaches a lesson—beware of trickery and seduction; watch out for the sting of the scorpion tail hidden behind the lion's back. Any one of these could be the *sentinel of fate whose fanged mouth spits most terrible red streams*. We had come up with the horrible iron beast right here, but it was made up.

"Did Deb ask you about the iron beast?" I ask.

"She did—and I told her we made it up."

"Did she tell you where she would put the clue?"

"No, she just said the castle was full of monsters."

I shudder at the thought that one of those monsters had killed Deb. "It is," I say, "there are hundreds, remember?"

He nods and I know he's recalling the days we spent scouring every inch of the monastery, discovering every creature carved into the walls of the castle, crowning the capitals of the cloisters, stitched into threadbare tapestries, lurking in the marginalia of the manuscripts, crouching at the feet of prostrate knights on the sarcophagi in the crypts. Weaving the rich medieval world of fantastical creatures into a modern mystery is what had made writing the book so much fun. But now it means that we have no idea where to start.

I look up at the arch that we will have to pass under to enter the castle and feel a sense of dread, as if the fantastical beasts depicted there are really loose inside the castle, prowling the halls, ready to kill with a look, deceive with a song, lash out with a hidden poisonous tail. Just as someone here in the castle is plotting to murder again. Could it really be one of our peers—

someone we've known for years, shared drinks and panels and book parties with, because of some grudge or resentment that they've hidden like a manticore hides its scorpion tail? Could it be Shay, Pete, Buck—Joan even? My mind balks. Joan has been my best friend, always touting our books and making me laugh, and yet . . . I'm recalling now all the snipes and carping she's done over the years. *Cozies never get nominated for these things; her plot was basically the same as a book I did ten years ago; he paid for that* Kirkus *review; none of the recipes in her books actually work; the sales on his last book tanked; she's been recycling the same plot for the last ten years* . . . I always felt a little dirty listening to her gossip but I never told her to stop and, truth be told, I liked it. Liked hearing the dirt and knowing that Joan wasn't including me on her naughty list. But does she include me when I'm not around, with her other friends? Has Joan envied my success—my marriage to handsome Fred, the six-figure advances, the awards—and been harboring a murderous resentment?

I shudder at the thought and Fred puts his hand on my arm. "Are you all right?"

"Just cold," I say. It's true. Since we set out for the hike a bank of clouds has moved in from the east bringing with it cold, damp air, but that's not really the reason I'm shivering. "It's just so awful to think it could be someone we've known for years," I say.

"I'm sorry for suggesting it. I just want you to be safe and it's better if you don't trust anyone. It could be one of these new writers—the debuts—or one of the discovery contestants."

"That's right," I say. "I'll talk to Aleister and get a list of everyone who submitted to the discovery contest."

"That's a good idea," he says. "I'll go look over the emails Deb sent me to see if I can figure out where the next clue should be."

And where the next murder will be, I think.

"Let's meet back at the suite in an hour . . . if that's okay," he adds, looking suddenly sheepish. "Would it be all right if I move back into the second room? I don't like the idea of you staying there alone."

"Sure," I say quickly, reminding myself that it doesn't mean anything. He's asked to stay in the second room, not the primary bedroom where I am sleeping.

We part in the lobby, Fred headed to his room to move his things back into the suite and me to find Aleister to ask if any of the discovery contest entries have raised any red flags—although, considering they're all murder mysteries, I'm not sure what exactly would constitute a red flag.

CHAPTER SEVENTEEN

Checking the schedule, I see that Aleister and Penelope are on a "Business of Publishing" panel in the chapel. On my way there, though, Joan appears as if out of nowhere—*how does she do that*?—and grabs my arm.

"Where are you going? Did you forget you signed up for speed dating?"

"Jesus, Joan, are you serious? Don't you think it's a little disrespectful to do something as frivolous as speed dating after we just found Nadine's body?"

Joan tilts her head and gazes at me in a quizzical birdlike fashion and shakes the conference program at me as if rustling tail feathers. An image of the human-faced, bird-bodied harpy appears in my head. "Frivolous!" she squawks. "It's for charity!"

How many times over the years has Joan roped me into doing something with the same plea? Of course, the charities are all worthy—literacy programs for inner-city children, books for prisoners, scholarships for disadvantaged communities, etc.,

etc.—but did I really agree to *speed dating,* my least favorite conference activity?

"Are people really up for this?" I ask, peering into the dining room. Small, round tables have been arranged with white tablecloths and scattered rose petals—a romantic touch that unfortunately looks like blood splatter—each topped with a charity auction basket artfully crafted from books and artisanal Italian delicacies. I vaguely recall okaying a basket of soaps and essential oils from the monastery's gift shop to go with a signed first edition of *Death Takes the Castle*. Not all the tables are full but there are a scattering of fans at each one, and I see Buck and Pete huddled together at the breakfast buffet and Shay seated at an already full table. At least I'm not the only one who's been roped into this.

"*Our readers,*" Joan intones, as if invoking a higher power, "have paid good money to meet and talk with their favorite authors. And they need a distraction from the unpleasant events of the last two days. Besides, I'm one author down because Nadine's gone."

She makes it sound as if Nadine has skipped out on her duties by being strangled in the bell tower. I shudder at the momentary thought that she's well out of it. I hate author speed dating—a barbaric parody of the singles matchmaking ritual in which authors, instead of potential mates, move from table to table shilling their current book to potential readers in five-minute sound bites. The only thing that ever made it bearable was doing it with Fred—

"Wait," I say, "I was supposed to do this with Fred."

"He texted to say he was otherwise detained and that you'd handle it."

The bastard! All that guff about splitting up so he could reread his emails from Deb! He knew I'd run into Joan and have to do this on my own. I look back into the dining room and am surprised to see Sue and the rest of her book club in attendance. I would have thought they had enough of murder for one morning after what happened in the bell tower, but they're all beaming at Buck as he sits down with them, preening like a strutting rooster. Like the basilisk, I can't help thinking.

"Are we still doing partners?" I ask.

"Yes. I thought you'd pair with Pete—"

I glance toward Pete just as he drops a stack of promotional postcards for his new book. He's drawn a circle of the Midwest Mavens around him to help pick them up. With his fuzzy tweed waistcoat and jacket he looks like a large, awkward bird whose feathers have been ruffled. In the medieval bestiary Pete would be one of the harmless beasts, perhaps the pelican, which selflessly pierces its own breast to feed its young. Not a likely murder suspect.

"I'll take Buck," I tell Joan, who visibly bristles in her surprise. When she turns around to lead me to Buck's table I half expect to spy tail feathers protruding from her St. John knit suit.

ONE ADVANTAGE OF partnering with Buck is that I can sit back and let him do most of the talking. He's a natural at speed dating, so much so I wonder if he's ever tried it to find a romantic partner. As far as I know, he's a confirmed bachelor. As I sit down at the Pittsburgh table, he opens up his book spiel by leaning toward Sue and confiding to her in a deep, husky drawl, "I could tell you about my new book, but then I'd have to kill you."

Sue giggles and then blushes, glancing nervously at me as if she's embarrassed to be laughing so soon after the shock of finding Nadine's body. I smile to reassure her that I'm not judging her. As Joan said, *our readers* have spent good money to be entertained by us. And Buck is certainly doing his best to sing for his supper. He's gone on to spin a tail of jet-setting espionage and daring feats of bravery by his hunky, roguish agent against a backdrop of glamorous international settings, all before the five-minute buzzer rings to signal his time's up.

"Sounds exciting," Sue says, "although frankly, after the events of the past day, I think I've had enough excitement to last a lifetime." The rest of the Pittsburgh ladies chime in their agreement and then they all turn to me as the buzzer rings, signaling it's my turn to start.

"Well," Buck says, overstepping into my time, "I'm sure you'll find *Death Takes the Castle* a much more . . . *sedate* read."

He's practically called my book a sleeping pill. No matter, I'm not trying for sales right now. "I think everyone here has probably read our first book—" All the Pittsburgh ladies nod eagerly. "So I'll dispense with the synopsis and dive right into another mystery. I thought it would be instructive to illustrate how Dora would go about solving a mystery. Alibis first! Let's start with you, Buck. Where were you last night while I was being attacked in my room?"

"What?" The self-confident smile melts from Buck's face like cheap hair dye on a hot day. "What's that got to do with anything."

"I just thought that avid and discerning crime readers like these women would like to see how a real murder investigation is solved. Clearly the first step is providing an alibi."

"I was in bed," Buck says, pasting on a leering smile. "Alone, I'm afraid—"

Before he can bemoan his lack of company and make some wholly inappropriate suggestion for remedying the situation, I cut in. "But didn't you say in a CrimeReads interview last year that you have insomnia and write in 'the wee hours of the night,' as I think you put it?"

"I-I may have been up writing for a while—"

"Uh-huh. And where exactly were you writing?"

"Where?" he echoes, clearly baffled. "My room, of course."

"But didn't you say in that same article that you always smoke a cigar while you write? Cohiba Lanceros, I believe you told the reporter, just like Hemingway." *What a load of crap,* Fred had remarked when he read the article aloud to me, *Hemingway wasn't even a regular cigar smoker.* "Surely you didn't smoke in your room," I say, remembering suddenly the smell of smoke I detected when I awoke in my room last night.

Buck looks like he's going to treat us to a rant on the nonsense of no-smoking rules, but then he glances at the Pittsburgh ladies, who are all regarding him with raised eyebrows and widened eyes. They might be entertained by Buck's bad-boy persona but they will not be amused by his breaking the hotel's no-smoking rule, and Buck knows better than to incur the wrath of the book club women.

"I stepped out onto my balcony for a smoke while I wrote," he says. "No law against that, right?"

"Your balcony is below mine," I say. "I smelled your cigar right around the time someone broke into my room. You must have seen the intruder flee if you were out on the balcony?"

I let the question hang in the air with the insinuation that maybe he had been the intruder, although I don't really think so. Bardi's officer would have seen him climb up to my balcony and I think I would have recognized Buck's beefy frame under that cloak. But I do think he was outside smoking on his balcony and that he may have seen something. Before he can answer, though, the buzzer sounds. "Oops," I say brightly, getting to my feet. "Chapter break! We'll have to wait to find out Buck's answer. Thank you for your time, ladies, and for being such loyal readers. I'll make sure you all get galleys of the next Death Takes a Holiday book."

I'm halfway to the next table before Buck catches up with me. "What the hell was that about, Thea?"

"Just a little real-life investigative work, Buck. You should try it once in a while. Your Jock Banner relies all too often on brawn to solve his cases. What did you see, by the way, when you were out on your balcony?"

His face turns red and I'm afraid I've provoked him into an outburst—or a cardiac event—but then Pete, looking vague and distracted in his misbuttoned tweed blazer and crooked tie, drifts into view and attracts Buck's attention. "Why don't you ask Pete?" he says with an insinuating sneer. "Ask him what he was doing sneaking out of his room at five a.m. this morning." Then he deftly swivels toward the table where Shay has just seated herself, leaving me with Pete as my partner at the table with Bob, Barb, and Barb's book club, the Midwest Mavens. I'm about to reassure Pete not to pay attention to Buck's insinuation when I notice that his ears are bright pink, a clear sign that he's been caught at something he's embarrassed by.

"*Were* you sneaking out of your room this morning?" I whisper as we take our seats.

He pretends not to hear me, instead shuffling a stack of file cards, clearing his throat, and launching into a detailed history of the Battle of Monte Cassino even before the starting buzzer. Although his book is set during World War II, he begins with the 529 BCE founding of the Monte Cassino monastery. He's barely into the twentieth century and the fortification of the Winter Line meant to defend western Italy from the Allied troops when Bob clears his throat and interrupts him. I'm expecting one of Bob's gotcha moments, revealing a historical inaccuracy, but instead Bob, leaning forward with both curled fists braced on the table as if ready to defend the Winter Line himself, demands, "Do you know where the sentinel of fate with the fanged mouth spewing blood is?"

To my dismay, I realize that the question is directed at me. "How—?" I begin, wondering how he knows what the next clue is. But then I see Barb turn red and realize they must have seen the clue pinned to Nadine's robe.

"It's not in the iron beast," Bob continues. "Because there's no iron beast in the gardens or castle."

"No," I admit, "we made that up."

"You know, Thea," Pete begins, "I've always meant to tell you that there's no evidence that the iron maiden existed—"

"So Deb could have put it anywhere," Bob continues. "How convenient."

"Just what are you insinuating about Deb?" Pete, bristling so much that the lambswool fibers in his tweed jacket stand up on their own, demands.

"No one's insinuating anything about Deb," Barb says, turning to the Midwest Mavens. "We all loved Deb." The Mavens all nod eagerly, the loops of their eyeglass holders bobbing in unison as they repeat "We all loved Deb" like a flock of magpies. *Only it's not* flock—

"*We* think," Barb continues, "that she was killed because she'd figured out where the treasure is buried."

I sigh. "There is no treasure," I say, wishing that Fred and I had never come up with that particular plot point. *Isn't it a little corny?* Fred had suggested. I'm inclined to agree right now. "And I sincerely doubt that's why Deb was killed. It's unlikely that the poisoned drink was even meant for her—"

"Aha!" one of the Mavens crows. "You've made the same mistake that Pamela Lyall makes in *Triangle at Rhodes*, assuming that the drink that poisons Valentine Chantry was really meant for her husband, Tony, when in fact Valentine was always the intended victim."

Knowing better than to argue Agatha Christie with a Midwest Maven, I concede that such a theory is possible. "But if Deb was the intended victim, why were Kailee and Nadine killed?" I'm genuinely interested to hear how the Midwest Mavens will answer but it's Bob who jumps in.

"Because they were each getting too close to finding the treasure, of course! Didn't you notice that they were both killed at a location on the treasure hunt?"

"Sure, but that doesn't mean—"

"The killer doesn't want anyone to get to the treasure before they do," Bob continues, happily mansplaining Mystery 101 to me and the Mavens.

"But then, why did they leave the clue at the bell tower?" I ask. "If their goal is to find the treasure, why not steal the clue so they can follow the hunt on their own?"

Bob looks so angry at the question that I wouldn't be surprised to see steam issuing from his nostrils. But Barb responds calmly, "The killer took the clue in the well because they knew the next one would be in the bell tower, but they don't know where the one after the bell tower will be so they left it hoping we could help them figure it out."

"The killer needs our help finding the next clue," the Midwest Mavens chime in.

"Oh!" I say. "That makes a certain sense, I suppose. So . . . have you ladies figured out where the next clue is? What 'beast' are we supposed to find? There are so many!"

The Mavens exchange glances, the lenses of their reading glasses glinting like gold coins as if the treasure is already within their grasp.

Only there is no treasure, I remind myself.

After a moment of silent psychic consultation, Barb answers for all of them. "It must be a beast with a fanged mouth but there are so many! We're still looking. We've eliminated the cloisters, the gardens, and the ground floor." They all nod in unison and I imagine a flock—*only it's not* flock—of keen-eyed Magpie Mavens circling the castle, scouting out potential clues.

"We're searching in pairs, of course," one of the Mavens says, "to make sure we don't become the next victim. And we're carrying these—" She extracts a slim bright pink tube from her cardigan pocket, which I mistake for a lipstick before realizing it must be Mace.

"Here," Barb says, handing me a lime-green tube, "you've already been attacked once and we're afraid that you'll be the next victim."

"But why—" I begin, but then the buzzer sounds. I jump, my nerves stretched thin by lack of sleep (*not the Mavens' warning*, I tell myself). Joan is suddenly standing over me, tapping her watch, and pointing to the next table. I get up shakily and head toward a table where a group of women in their mid-forties are all wearing raven headdresses and badges that say *Riotous Ravens*. *An unkindness of ravens*, I recall at the same time that I remember the collective noun for magpies.

A mischief.

What sort of mischief are the Midwest Mavens inviting by

looking for the treasure, I wonder, glancing back at the sharp-eyed women, and what sort might they cause? I turn to Pete to ask him what he thinks but Pete has veered off course and is heading toward the door, trailing index cards as he goes like a molting pelican. Is he about to abandon me to the Riotous Ravens? And what's wrong with Pete that he'd forsake his precious index cards? I give the Ravens one regretful glance and then follow Pete out the door, calling his name as he hightails it toward the veranda. I catch up with him at the edge of the hedge maze.

"Pete!" I cry, grabbing him by an elbow patch. "Where are you going?"

He turns a tear-streaked face toward me. "It's all my fault!" he wails.

"What's your fault?" I ask, glancing around to see if we have an audience for what I'm suddenly afraid might be a murder confession. Fortunately, everybody seems to be inside at panels or speed dating.

"Deb's death—and Kailee's and Nadine's, too! That's why I was in the garden last night. I woke up and suddenly realized . . . Here, I'll show you . . . come with me!"

Pete lopes off into the hedge maze and I follow, feeling as if I'm in *Alice's Adventures in Wonderland*. Forget the medieval pelican; in his tweed jacket and waistcoat, Pete is a dead ringer for the White Rabbit. I wouldn't be surprised to see him pull out a pocket watch and announce that we're late. He's certainly going fast enough—but where to? He's taking a path through the hedge maze that's unfamiliar to me. The path twists and turns and grows narrower, the box hedges scratching my bare arms and tickling my nose with their acrid odor, until it finally spits us out into a gloomy square bounded by lichen-covered marble slabs.

"What is this place?" I ask, chafing my arms in the chill, dank air. It feels like we're at the bottom of a well. No one would hear me if I screamed. But I'm not really frightened of Pete, am I? Even if he is ranting as if he's the murderer.

"Deb said she thought it was either a medieval graveyard or a garbage heap where refuse was thrown," Pete says. "She brought me here on the first day I arrived to show me something. She was so excited! She said she'd unlocked the secret of the treasure. Look—" He crouches by one of the slabs and pulls away a heavy curtain of ivy. I kneel beside him, my curiosity getting the better of my suspicions, and peer at an ancient marble slab. At first I don't see anything, but then Pete runs his hands over the rough stone, tracing a pattern that is barely visible. There's an inscription, so old it's almost been erased by time and weather, but as Pete traces the letters I make out the initials *D.M.*

"*Dis manibus*," I say, my college Latin coming back to me.

"Exactly," Pete says, grinning, the sudden appearance of his white teeth jarring in the gloom. "'To the shades of the dead.'"

"A Roman inscription," I say, "but still used in Christian times on headstones. So this could have been a cemetery—"

"Deb thought the tombstone must have been taken from somewhere else and discarded here."

"But why would anyone discard a gravestone—" A thought

suddenly occurs to me. I lean past Pete and brush away the rest of the ivy, revealing another line of text, the words rimmed with soil. "*Hic iacet Bianca*—" I read aloud. "'Here lies Bianca.'" Could this be Bianca Rosa's tombstone? If so, it would be proof that Bianca Rosa really existed—and Deb found it! Was that what she wanted to tell me at the reception?

"Deb thought that someone wanted to erase Bianca Rosa's legacy and the story of the treasure."

"It wouldn't be the first time history has erased a strong woman's legacy," I say. It's a tempting theory. I feel myself lured by the same siren call that had led me to Castellarosa in my twenties—but then I come to my senses.

"Pete," I say, laying my hand on his, "this doesn't prove that Bianca Rosa existed or that the treasure is real."

"No? Look at this—" He brushes away more of the encroaching ivy to reveal three more words.

"*Thesaurum cordis mei*," I read aloud at the same time that Pete translates: "'Treasure of my heart.'"

CHAPTER EIGHTEEN

I remember picking up Fred's well-thumbed *Roget's Thesaurus,* which he'd carried with him everywhere, and asking him if he knew what the word *thesaurus* meant. When he shook his head, I told him. "Treasure."

"Don't you see?" Pete's plaintive voice cuts into the memory. "This proves that there really was a treasure. Somebody destroyed Bianca Rosa's tombstone to discredit Bianca Rosa and to keep people from searching for the treasure."

I stare at Pete, surprised that his usually pragmatic, precise historical mind has been so clouded. "It doesn't really prove that at all, Pete. First of all, it could have been a different Bianca. There's no second or last name here. And second, 'treasure of my heart' is a stock phrase of endearment. It doesn't have to refer to a physical treasure."

He shakes his head. "I said the same thing to Deb, but then she said—"

Instead of telling me what Deb said, Pete shocks me by bursting into tears. Loud, messy sobs that rack his body. At a loss for what to do, I sit down beside him and pat his rough, tweedy back, averting my eyes to give him some privacy in his grief. Looking around I notice that we're in a sunken depression surrounded by a jumble of ancient stones covered with moss and ivy. If this was a cemetery it was probably for unsanctified graves. Or it might have been a refuse pit, as Deb thought, a depository for broken stones discarded when the church took over the castle and turned it into a monastery. Only . . .

Why not use the stones? I've walked through enough medieval and Renaissance buildings in Italy to have seen scraps of ancient Roman masonry repurposed as building material. There are plenty of Roman slabs with Latin inscriptions in the monastery. Why were these thrown on the dust heap of history?

I brush away the ivy and look at the inscription again. *Hic iacet Bianca . . . thesaurum cordis mei . . .* Had someone not wanted Bianca Rosa to be remembered as a "treasure"?

"Don't you see," Pete says, "Deb found the treasure and someone killed her for it. I should have stopped her. I should have protected her." He takes out a handkerchief—an actual cloth handkerchief!—from his pocket and noisily blows his nose. "I should have told her how I felt! I thought I had time! But I always had to be so damn cautious! Weigh all the evidence, consider all my options, be *objective*. I pointed out all the same objections you have to Deb, which of course she knew. Debra was one of the smartest people I ever met. You know what she said to me?" His voice trembles and I'm afraid he's going to break down again, but he firms his jaw and balls his fists to gain control of himself.

"She said, *All of that may be true, Pete, but sometimes you just have to choose the story you want to live, and who else can write that story but you?* If I'd listened . . . if I'd taken her seriously . . . if I'd admitted even just to myself how much she meant to me, I'd have realized she was in danger and I'd have protected her."

I feel my own eyes smart with tears and squeeze Pete's hand to keep from crying. This is Pete's moment, not mine. "She was an extraordinary woman and you were a good friend to her, Pete. We won't let her story end like this. We're going to find out who killed her and we're going to bring them to justice."

"Then you'd better find them first," Pete says, squeezing my hand so hard I feel my bones grate against each other. "Because I won't wait for anyone's else's idea of justice before delivering mine."

PETE WALKS WITH me part of the way back but then tells me he wants to sit in the Memento Mori rose garden by himself for a little while. I leave him and make my way back to the hotel, passing a few treasure hunters on the way.

"Look, a unicorn!" a woman in Bermuda shorts cries out, diving into the shrubbery to investigate a marble statue.

"But unicorns don't have fangs!" her friend points out.

The Mavens already ruled out the cloisters, gardens, and first floor, I remind myself, passing a pair of bookstagrammers taking selfies next to a griffin statue. I'm itching to start my search upstairs but I remember that I'm supposed to talk to Aleister first about the manuscript contest. I check the chapel, but the publishing panel is over. Looking at the schedule posted in the lobby I see that there's a pitchfest going on in the dining room, which I recall that Aleister and Penelope had agreed to take part in it.

Sure enough, I find both my agent and editor ensconced at one of the rose-strewn tables, along with half a dozen other agents and editors listening to nervous writers pitching their book ideas. Penelope, wearing a face that can only be described as Resting Skeptic, is sitting across from a wildly gesticulating woman in a flowery purple caftan.

". . . it's *Gone Girl* meets *The Da Vinci Code*!" she shouts as I walk by. Penelope shoots me a *Save me!* look but I keep going to Aleister's table, where he is leaning back, long legs crossed, oxford shirt rolled up over tanned muscular forearms, a *deeply interested* look pasted on his handsome features. It startles me to realize that it's the same look he assumes when I tell him my next book idea. I'd always thought it was reserved just for me.

I wait patiently while a middle-aged woman stammers through a plot outline as convoluted as a Dickens novel. ". . . and then it turns out she's really the long-lost daughter of the woman who hired her . . . Did I mention she was adopted?"

"What a plot twist," Aleister deadpans, catching my eye. "Send me a synopsis and the first chapter, and I'll have a look at it."

"You will? Thank you!" she gushes, gathering up her scattered note cards and vacating her seat for me, which is, I notice as I sit, slightly damp and redolent of sweat and . . . *false hopes*, I think before I can stop myself. Aleister has never taken an unagented slush pile manuscript in his entire career. I'm not even sure why he's doing this pitchfest. Usually it's for agents and a few junior editors.

"Why are you doing this again?" I ask.

Aleister grimaces and leans forward, glancing left and right to check who's within earshot. "Joan roped me into it. She said editors are who writers really should be pitching to, and as long as I was here to celebrate your Poirot nomination and judge the discovery contest, I ought to represent my profession at the pitchfest."

"That sounds like Joan," I say, wincing as I imagine what she'll have to say about me ditching speed dating. "Have you heard any good pitches?"

He rolls his eyes. "That sweet-looking old lady over there in the embroidered cat sweater pitched me a book about a serial killer who makes quilts out of her victim's skins."

"Yikes," I say, "that's alarming. Um, and it reminds me . . . I wanted to ask if you'd seen anything of concern in the discovery contest entries."

"*Of concern?*" he repeats in that tone he uses to question my word choices. I can almost see the blue pencil in his head (I'm pretty sure it's still a blue pencil in his head even though he switched over to Track Changes more than a decade ago) scrawling *Avoid euphemisms!*

"I mean anything that would suggest an unstable person. Fred and I were thinking the murderer might be an aspiring writer who was jealous of the . . . competition, so to speak." I cringe at the unnecessary filter words I've tagged on, sure that Aleister would strike them out.

"Fred and you were thinking, eh? Good to know you two are on the case. I thought you'd had enough of solving mysteries with him."

Do I detect a hint of anger in his voice? Jealousy, even? After our brief fling in Germany, Aleister and I had met for lunch to make sure there weren't any hurt feelings. He'd assured me that he'd never let anything get in the way of our professional relationship. I had believed him. I even felt a little hurt that he valued me more as an author than as a love interest. Now I wonder if he had been entirely honest. Did he harbor resentment that I'd ended the relationship? Did he, I suddenly wonder with concern, think there was a chance of renewing that relationship now that Fred and I were officially dissolving our writing partnership and marriage?

"This is a real-life case," I say, "not a book. It rather ups the stakes."

"Of course. And yes, I've considered whether our murderer could be motivated by professional jealousy. You should see the death threats I've gotten over the years."

"Really?"

"Hell hath no fury like a writer rejected," he paraphrases. "But if you're asking if any of the discovery entries gave me cause to worry, how would I even judge? I just told you that kindly old grandmother is writing another Hannibal Lecter. We're in the murder biz, Thea, all the writers here are a little . . . *of concern*."

"Including me?" I ask playfully. "Do you think I'm capable of murder?"

He gives me a long, considering look as if he's taking my question seriously. As he does all my questions. One of the things I've really valued about Aleister over the years is how much careful thought he puts into all his responses, both editorial and personal. *Words are my business,* he once told me, *I never underestimate their power.*

"What I've always admired about you, Thea," he says finally, "is your ability to make difficult decisions and cut what has to be cut. That takes a certain ruthlessness. Does that make you capable of murder?" He smiles and lifts both hands, palms up to the ceiling as if asking the angels painted there to weigh in on my mortal soul.

So maybe not really okay with our breakup, I note.

Before I can respond to this rather startling assessment of my character, Aleister adds, "There *is* one manuscript that I think you may find concerning for other reasons. Here—" He picks up his iPad. "I'll send it to you."

My phone pings as he airdrops a document into my files. I look to see what he's sent me.

"*The Toxic Couple?*" I ask, repeating the title. "Why—"

"I'm afraid that the couple in the book have a suspicious number of similarities to you and Fred. If you're looking for someone with a grudge against you . . ." His voice trails off and he lifts his eyes over my head. It's an expression I'm all too familiar with from conferences and cocktail parties, signaling a shift of attention and the end of the conversation. As I get up, I see it's only another aspiring writer—no need to feel displaced—and yet, as I make my way out of the dining room I can't help feeling as if my relationship with Aleister, editorial and personal, has been irreparably altered.

I'M IN A hurry to get upstairs and open the manuscript on my laptop. *The Toxic Couple*! As much as I hate to admit it, I can see why the phrase might apply to me and Fred. I'm both dreading what I'll discover when I read the manuscript and desperately eager to find out what's in it. As I come up the stairs, though, I hear a loud argument that draws my attention.

"The cabinet is kept locked to prevent harm to the valuable objects inside." I recognize Sonia Wilson's voice, strained to the point of breaking.

Another voice, equally strained, rises as I approach the first landing. "We're just asking so that we can look inside that weird lion vase. You can stand here and watch us."

Zoe and Lindsay are standing on either side of a massive glass-fronted cabinet filled with china, vases, and bronze pitchers. Sonia is standing in front of the case, hands on hips, as if defending its contents from an invading horde.

"That *aquamanile*," she corrects, her voice rising into registers that makes the glass in the cabinet shiver, "is a twelfth-century relic brought back from the Crusades."

"The clue could be hidden inside that vase," Lindsay insists, ignoring the provenance and correct term for the object. I glance at the bronze ewer shaped like a griffin. As Sonia correctly stated, it's an aquamanile, a vessel that was used in church services to carry water for the priest to wash his hands. I suppose it could fit the description in the third clue of a creature *whose fanged mouth spits most terrible red streams*, although it seems like a stretch to me.

"Besides," Sonia says, "I don't even know where the key is.

And if I don't know then Deb Andersen could not have gotten inside to hide her clue."

That makes sense, but Lindsay and Zoe aren't buying it. Zoe removes a hairpin from her bun and brandishes it in front of Sonia. "I bet I can pick that lock. I used to break into my parents' liquor cabinet all the time."

"And damage a priceless fourteenth-century cabinet?" Sonia scoffs, looking ready to tackle Zoe if she takes another step toward the lock. Before they can come to blows, Greg appears and smoothly inserts himself between his wife and the guests.

"My wife is right," he says, giving Sonia his most uxorious smile. To my surprise, she visibly melts. Is this the secret to their marriage, I wonder, the magical words *My wife is right*? When was the last time I heard Fred say those words? As an added flourish, he draws a spindly old-fashioned key from his suit jacket pocket and hands it to Sonia. "This will be easier."

She smiles and, ignoring Zoe and Lindsay, unlocks the cabinet. A whiff of dust and ancient beeswax wafts out onto the landing as Sonia reaches inside and removes the heavy brass vessel with all the care of the officiating deacon who would have poured water from it onto the priest's hands during Mass. Seen up close, the object is unsettling. The griffin's tail is shaped like a scorpion's, with a tiny grinning face at its end. There's also something clasped in the beak as if the beast had just captured its prey. Zoe looks a bit cowed as she peeks into the dusty recess inside the griffin's belly.

"Be careful," Sonia purrs, "you never know what is hiding in dark places."

Zoe pales and looks nervously toward Lindsay, who rolls her eyes and sticks her hand into the belly of the beast. Her heavy rings and bracelet clang against the hollow walls, making a deep ringing sound that might be the rumbling of the hungry beast's belly. I think of the iron beast we invented in the book and wince at the thought that Lindsay will withdraw a bleeding stump from the ewer. Perhaps Lindsay is thinking the same thing because she withdraws her hand quickly as if afraid it might be snapped off. "Nothing in there," she mutters, cradling her hand against her chest. She gives me a resentful look, as if I had caused her an injury.

"See," Sonia says, turning to return the aquamanile to the cabinet.

"Wait," I say, surprising myself. "There's something stuck in its mouth." I push past Lindsay, who shoots me a dirty look, and bend down to look inside the beak-shaped spout. It looks like a small animal squirming in the griffin's beak. I move closer and something as black and shiny as tar slithers out of the beak and lands on my foot. I look down and watch in horror as a jet-black scorpion arches its tail and clicks its pincers at me. I step back, kicking my foot to dislodge the nasty little creature, and it skitters across the marble paving, sending Zoe yelping out of the way. Greg calmly lifts his foot and crushes it under his heel.

"You didn't have to kill it!" Lindsay shrieks. "Don't you know it's bad luck? Scorpions are symbols of protection."

Sonia rolls her eyes and then, turning to me, says, "That's what you get when you stick your nose where it doesn't belong."

CHAPTER NINETEEN

I leave Lindsay and Zoe quizzing Sonia and Greg about access to the rooftop and make my way up the next two flights of stairs, trying to shake off the feeling that scorpions are crawling all over my body. *Ew.* I remember finding the nasty creatures skittering around my washbasin and hiding in my slippers twenty years ago. When I screamed, Sister Beatrice told me they were harmless. *They've got little devil faces!* I had blubbered. She'd laughed and exclaimed, *Would that the devil was so easily spotted when he comes for us!*

That's the feeling that's crawling over me now—that the devil has come for me in a disguise I can't recognize. Something about the way Lindsay looked at me and the way Greg and Sonia looked at each other rubbed me the wrong way. What had I ever done to Lindsay? And why did I feel a stab of envy toward the Wilsons? Was I jealous that Greg and Sonia had the sort of marriage where whey looked at each other as if they were still in love?

I pause at the suite door, trying to remember the last time

Fred and I looked at each other like that, and an unexpected memory surfaces from our winter in San Miguel de Allende, a location so haunted by its aftermath that I want to tamp down the memory as soon as it rises. Even worse, the memory isn't from those first sun- and sex-drenched days; it's from the rooftop dinner with Jon Rooney and his entourage, when fueled by tequila and spite I'd driven Fred right into Siena's arms.

Jon had just asked me how I answered that worn chestnut of a question *Where do you get your ideas?* and I had come out with that silly quip about the bad behavior of my fellow human beings. Fred said I had been looking right at him when I said it so it was clear that I had meant *his* bad behavior. Only, hadn't I turned to him before I said it? Before I'd even thought of saying it? For just a moment Fred's eyes had caught mine and all the spite and silly resentment had fallen away and it was just him and me, locking eyes across a crowded room and knowing that nothing really mattered except us. Yes, that was the last time we had looked at each other like we really loved each other, the way I'd just seen Greg and Sonia look at each other. So why had I said that thing about bad behavior?

Siena.

My eyes had shifted past Fred's and there she had been, practically perched on Fred's shoulder, her long slender arm with its pretentious scorpion tattoo pressing against his, her eyes locked on mine, filled with pure spite. What had I done to her? I'd wondered. But then I'd realized: I'd taken Fred's attention away from her. Well, too bad, honey, he's mine, I'd thought, and then I'd said that thing about bad behavior, as if I needed anyone else's example, and Fred thought I meant him (which I did a little) and she got back at me by showing me that Fred wasn't really mine. She'd spent the rest of the night flattering Fred and asking him about his writing process until he'd told her about that other book he'd been working on—*a real book,* something literary, which he hadn't even told me about. Then while I was drinking shots with Jon Rooney he'd invited Siena down to *our* room to show it to her. Later he swore that it hadn't been about sex at all; it had all been about writing. As if sharing that part of him—and sharing our darkest moments—wasn't an even bigger betrayal.

Which is why I am reliving that moment. Not because of how Greg and Sonia looked at each other but because the scorpion had reminded me of Siena. And maybe because I needed to be reminded that no matter how friendly Fred was now, I couldn't really trust him.

I OPEN THE door, resolved to be on my guard with Fred. He's sitting at the desk, his laptop open in front of him, his Moleskine notebook propped open, a scattering of papers spread across the polished wood surface, shirt sleeves rolled up, and hair mussed as if he's been pulling at it. The scene is so reminiscent of a thousand writing sessions that I feel a pang sharper than a scorpion's sting.

He's not working on a Rick and Dora book, I remind myself as I take a seat on the opposite side of the desk (I can't help noticing he's left a chair and desk space for me to take my accustomed seat across from him). We're trying to find out who's killed Deb (and Kailee and Nadine). *Focus.* I open my laptop—a shield to deflect the power of any amorous gazes, but I needn't have bothered. Fred barely looks up at me, squinting instead at his computer screen. He needs reading glasses, I think, but is too vain to use them.

"I've been going through Deb's emails and I think she did have a theory about where the treasure was but she was so damn cagey about it. Listen—" He reads aloud, assuming a flat Midwest intonation so close to Deb's voice I feel a pang, as if she has entered the room. "*I'm having so much fun exploring the castle! It's like I'm inside* Death Takes the Castle. *I can see why you two were inspired to create Rick and Dora here. There's an indefinable aura of a great love steeped into these stones and a ghostly presence which I'm sure is guarding a treasure.*"

"Deb took her books seriously," I say. "She told me once that when she opened a book, she could feel herself physically falling into it like Alice down the rabbit hole."

"She certainly fell into something," Fred says. "Listen to this: *Today when I wandered through the cloisters, I could swear I spied a woman in a nun's habit slipping in and out of the shadowed colonnade. What was the name of that nun on whom you based Sister Benedetta?*

"Why did she want to know about Sister Beatrice?" I asked.

"I don't know. I gave her Beatrice's name but I said I didn't know where she was or even if she was still alive."

"Do you think Deb tried to find her?" I ask, recalling that Greg had said he thought the old nun had gone senile.

"She never said. Her next question was where we came up with the description of Bianca's tomb."

"Did you tell her we made it up?"

"I said we looked at so many tombs in so many crypts all across Tuscany that I caught a cold from the damp but that we never found Bianca's tomb in the crypts of Castellarosa. And she said—" He scrolls down his screen, squinting at the type until I'm tempted to show him how to enlarge it. But I restrain myself. It's not my business if he develops crow's-feet. *"I think I found it! Or at least a part of it."*

"She may have." I tell Fred about the fragment that Pete showed me.

"But that's not the tomb itself," he says.

"No, but she thought it was proof that the tomb existed."

"Maybe," he says, looking skeptical. "What do you think?"

I sigh. "I think that if I had known where our made-up treasure hunt would lead, I'd have suggested we go sightseeing in Florence instead."

"And forget about Rick and Dora?" he asks, sounding hurt.

"They certainly have caused a lot of trouble," I say, "and apparently not everyone is a fan. Listen to this—" I read the first lines of the manuscript Aleister sent me.

"The Kingsley-Banes were a famous writing couple renowned for their murder mystery series but oblivious to the little deaths they left in their wake like a blood trail."

"Ouch! What is that from?"

"A manuscript called *The Toxic Couple* submitted for the discovery contest. Aleister sent it to me."

"And Aleister thinks that it's based on *us*? We're not the only mystery-writing couple in the world."

I skim a little further and read: "*They liked to play a game called The Poisoned Chalice in which they pretended to poison innocent victims, much as they lured unsuspecting victims into their toxic orbit.*"

"Holy crap!" he cries, reaching for my laptop. "Let me see that—"

"I'll send it to you," I say, unwilling to give him access to my browsing history, which includes extensive cyberstalking of both him and Nadine.

My airdrop pings on his laptop and he settles in to download and peruse *The Toxic Couple*. "*Ted Kingsley-Bane fancied himself another Hemingway but really he was a Hemingwayesque manqué, having failed to achieve the prowess of the great writer while adopting his vices of women and drink.*"

"Wordy and pretentious," I decree. "Listen to this: *Rhea Kingsley-Bane called herself a feminist but she didn't care what women she walked over if they threatened her hold on her darling Ted.*"

"Who the hell wrote this?" Fred asks, scrolling back to the title page.

"The manuscripts are submitted anonymously to the judges; only the contest manager holds a key with the real identities of the contestants. Clearly, it's someone who loathes us. Maybe one of your scorned love interests?" I suggest.

"Why one of mine? You have your admirers—Speaking of which, it could be Aleister himself. Don't tell me he wasn't disappointed when you ended things . . . which you did, right? At least that's what you told me."

"Aleister couldn't bring himself to write this badly," I say, sidestepping the subject of my breakup with Aleister.

"How about Buck, then? He's always been sweet on you and he'd have no trouble writing badly."

"He wouldn't be this wordy and I'm pretty sure he doesn't know what the word *manqué* means. Besides, why would Buck enter the discovery contest?"

"To mess with us."

"I think this sounds like a woman," I say. "I'd have said Nadine, maybe, but she's—she *was*—a better writer. Is there anyone here who you were . . . er . . . *involved* with?"

"No!" he cries. "Despite what you think, there haven't been that many."

"I'm not sure you always realize the full power of your charm, Fred. There was that librarian in Scotland—Fiona, wasn't it?"

He blushes. "I was just being friendly—"

"And that bookseller in Denver who followed you around Bouchercon—"

"She said she wanted writing advice—"

"Ah, a would-be writer," I say. "This could be her—or there was that grad student in Boston who wanted to write her thesis on you—"

"On *us*," he points out.

"Yeah, no, she sent all her questions to you and practically sat in your lap when we did the reading at The Coop—oh, and there was our driver on the Midwest tour who wanted you to sit up front with her and was always suggesting I take a nap because I looked *knackered*—"

"Stop!" He raises his right hand, palm out. "You're making me sound like the Don Juan of the book circuit. I swear, I never meant to encourage any of those women."

Not even Siena? I think. But he looks so genuinely wounded I can't bring myself to say her name. "Maybe not," I concede, "but somehow, they kept flocking around. Fans and booksellers and aspiring writers—"

"I'm sorry," he says, cutting off my list. "That must have been shitty for you."

He's looking at me from across the desk, over the top of his laptop screen, our two laptops facing each other like we're in a game of Battleship. It's how we've sat a thousand times, writing our books, tossing ideas back and forth, working on a shared document, typing dialogue as fast as the lines came out of our mouths—so fast that at times I wasn't sure who was speaking, me or Fred or Rick or Dora. And I hadn't cared. I loved it. We were Katharine Hepburn and Spencer Tracy in *Woman of the Year* and Cary Grant and Rosalind Russell in *His Girl Friday*. We were as much a construct as Rick and Dora. And if that came with a string of girls googly-eyed over Fred . . . well, that was part of the mystique, to be the woman who got the guy all those girls wanted.

"It was my fault, too," I say. "You never wanted to do all those appearances and book tours and conferences. We could have stepped back from the public stuff."

"We were doing it for the books," he says.

"At the expense of our marriage," I say. I look down at the manuscript on my screen—at a line that jumps out at me as if it were typed in boldface caps: *"She stood by while he lured in the women because that was, after all, part of their brand*. It makes me sound like I was your enabler."

He winces. "That's not true—"

"Maybe not, but at least one person saw us that way. And it sounds like she wants to punish both of us. We have to find out who this is." I look back at the header on the file page. It reads *Discovery Ms. #112*. "The contest manager has a key that links the manuscript numbers to the writers' real identities. I'll ask Aleister—"

"Deb had the list," Fred says.

"Crap. Someone else must have access."

"It will be on her laptop," Fred says.

"Which is in Joan's room."

"We'd better get to it before—"

"The murderer does," I finish for him, our lines spilling out as quickly and smoothly as Rick and Dora's always did.

We close our laptops at the same time, and yet, as we get to our feet, I still feel as if we're acting out a scene in one of our books. Only this is a mystery plot we have no control over. I remember suddenly my suggestion to Fred that we send Rick and Dora out in a blaze of glory. I can only hope now that I hadn't been indulging in a little obvious foreshadowing.

CHAPTER TWENTY

On our way out I text Joan to ask if she has Deb's laptop.

It's still in our room, she texts back immediately (God bless, Joan, she's never far from her phone). *Why?*

I'll explain IRL. Can you meet us there?

Us?

Me and Fred.

The ellipses do their little dance and I imagine Joan delivering her customary warnings, but if she began to, she erased them. All that appears is her room number, which is one floor down, almost exactly below our suite and right above Buck's room. Deb must have had a fit when she smelled his cigar on their balcony.

As we make our way down, we pass treasure hunters traipsing up and down the wide stairs. The domed stairwell echoes with their shouts to one another as they spot exotic birds and animals carved into the banisters, woven into tapestries, and painted on stained-glass windows. Their discordant cries sound like an invading army has breached the walls and set loose a pack of hunting dogs. I think of the quiet that ruled the convent for centuries, now shredded, and Fred and I are the ones who flung open the gates and let the beast inside. How Sister Beatrice would have hated this!

We run into Joan on the second landing heading to her room, key in hand. "I could barely make it up here," she mutters. "I was stopped so many times by treasure hunters demanding if I knew the solution and did I think poor Deb was killed to protect the secret of the treasure."

"Where'd they get that idea?" I ask, skipping to keep up with Joan's fast pace.

"Oh, that's the newest theory floating around. Haven't you seen the posts?" She stops long enough to open her phone and scroll through a WhatsApp thread full of conjecture and salacious rumors.

Was Deb Andersen murdered by satanists? Is the treasure of Castellarosa the lost treasure of the Knights Templar? Are the recent murders at Castellarosa orchestrated by the Illuminati?

"Have they all lost their minds?" Fred demands as we reach Joan's room.

"I don't know," Joan says, turning to face us instead of opening the door. "You tell me. Why do you two want to see Deb's laptop? You're the sixth person to ask me this morning. Do you think the location of the treasure is on it?"

"That's not why—" I begin at the same time Fred asks, "Is it?"

Joan rounds on him and bares her teeth in a snarl. "You helped Deb put this wretched treasure hunt together, so you would know better than I do. Did she say she'd found it?"

"She hinted that she was close to finding Bianca's tomb, but no, she never said she'd found it. But she definitely believed it existed and that it was where the treasure was."

"And I suppose you encouraged her in that belief."

"What? No!" Fred draws himself up to his full six feet two inches and looks down on Joan, but somehow the effect is not to diminish Joan but to make Fred look unhinged.

"We didn't come about the treasure," I say to keep the two from coming to blows. "We need to see the contestant key for the discovery contest."

"The discovery contest?" Joan echoes, frowning. But then her face lights up. "Ah, you want to find out who your little fan is."

"*Our little fan*?" Fred and I both repeat.

"That's what Deb called her. She said there was an entry by someone who clearly had a beef with you two. Didn't she tell you about it?"

Fred shakes his head but I remember Deb starting to tell me something at the cocktail party before Greg led her off. "She said there was something she wanted to tell me. I thought it was about the treasure hunt but maybe it was about this manuscript. Did she say anything else about it? Did she mention who wrote it?"

Joan shakes her head as she lets us into the room. There are two double beds, one made up crisply, the other rumpled, sheets twisted, a pink knit nightgown puddled in the folds of the duvet. On the foot of the made bed, a matching Vera Bradley tote and suitcase sit on a luggage rack, expectant as the pet dogs that adorn medieval sarcophagi. Deb's luggage, no doubt.

Where will it go now, I wonder, and who will inherit Deb's hand-knit cardigans and her comfortable orthopedic shoes?

"Didn't the police want her things?" I ask, to keep myself from tearing up.

Joan sniffs. "They rummaged around but I packed it all back up after. I'll ship it back to her niece in Duluth. But this—" She reaches into the night table drawer and extracts a floral quilted iPad case in the same Vera Bradley print as the luggage. "I kept to myself."

"Joan!" I exclaim, honestly shocked. "You withheld evidence from the police?"

She shrugs. "I didn't like the idea of that supercilious man reading Deb's private files. Besides, he had her phone. He could see her emails and texts and anything that mattered to their investigation. They didn't need anything here."

I open my mouth to ask how she could know that but a sharp glance from Fred makes me shut it. *Not important right now,* the look says. *Let's get into the iPad first.*

"Do you know her password?" Fred asks as I slide the iPad out of its case.

Joan smiles. "Agatha91590. Agatha Christie's birth date."

I type in the password and the screen opens up to last Saturday's *New York Times* crossword puzzle, completed according to the timer on top in twenty-nine minutes. The hardest puzzle of the week. I'd abandoned it halfway done on the plane. I close the browser window and scan the neat array of file folders.

"There—" Fred says, leaning over my shoulder to point to one that is labeled "Discovery Contest."

It's almost disappointingly easy. Deb loved a good mystery; wouldn't she want us to have to decode arcane references? But she was also an organized woman who lent her skills to a dozen clubs, charities, and associations, ensuring they all ran smoothly so that the rest of us could go about our business without worrying about how the gears were oiled. I click on the folder and a list of files appears: "Announcements," "Rules," "Entries," and "Key." As I click on the last, I picture the big heavy iron key that Rick and Dora find near the end of *Death Takes the Castle* that opens the crypt. I'm almost disappointed when a neatly typed numbered list appears instead of a magical portal.

I scroll down until I come to #112. "*The Toxic Couple,*" I read aloud. And then my voice fails me.

"Well, look at that," Joan says. "Lindsay Monahan, the little vixen!"

"But how?" I ask. "And why? What have we ever done to her? Do we even know her?" I turn to Fred. He's staring at the name as if the letters might rearrange themselves.

"I don't think so. I haven't talked to her much here."

"She came right up to me at the reception—"

I bet you don't remember me. She'd said it like a dare. I thought at the time she was trying to catch me out for forgetting such a loyal fan, but maybe she wanted to make sure I *didn't* remember her. When I picture Lindsay, I see the black bangs, horn-rimmed glasses, and round face like a cartoon drawing.

"Her hair's dyed and she wears those heavy glasses," I say to Fred. "It's like a disguise. She could have looked quite different when you last saw her. Could she be Fiona?"

"Fiona was taller and had freckles," Fred says, with a perfect recall that makes me wonder if it was true that nothing had happened between them.

"What about that grad student in Boston?"

"Do you think she's one of Fred's conquests?" Joan interjects.

Fred sputters an objection to Joan's choice of words but I tell her, "Maybe. Someone Fred flirted with who's got a grudge. *The Toxic Couple* presents both of us in an unfavorable light."

"Hm," Joan says, "Lindsay *is* a rather hostile young woman. She asked me at a panel today if I thought cozies reinforced the patriarchy by emphasizing traditional feminine occupations."

"That's extremely reductive," I say, while guiltily searching through my mind for a cozy heroine with a less traditional hobby or profession, until Fred breaks into my mental inventory.

"Why don't we go find her and ask who she really is and what her beef with Rick and Dora is?"

"I saw her and her friend Zoe on the first-floor landing half an hour ago searching through a china cabinet for the next clue," I say, shuddering at the memory of the black scorpion skittering across the floor and Lindsay shrieking while Greg crushed it under his heel. She had sounded half hysterical, going on about how scorpions were symbols of protection—

An image appears in my mind of a scorpion, only it's not the live one that came out of the ewer. "Oh my God," I say, "I know who Lindsay is and—"

I look down at Deb's laptop and notice a folder marked "Treasure Hunt" and open it. A map of the castle appears with

X's marking where all the clues have appeared—the rose garden, the maze, the cloisters well, and, on top of the tower, a gargoyle. "I know where she is."

I PRACTICALLY SPRINT up the stairs, with Fred and even Stair-Master Joan trying to keep up with me. "Are you going to tell me who she is?" Fred calls after me.

"I want to see if I'm right first," I call back. Because if I'm wrong, I think, I'll sound like a crazy, jealous wife.

When I reach the third floor, I try the door to the rooftop but find that it's locked. When I left Lindsay, she was quizzing Sonia and Greg about access to the roof. Greg had been saying something about the roof being closed due to construction. *There are loose titles and rainspouts,* he'd explained. *It's not safe.*

But that wouldn't have deterred Lindsay, especially when she heard the word *rainspout*. Any Goth Librarian worthy of the name would know that where there were rainspouts there were gargoyles, the grotesque statues that medieval architects constructed to funnel water away from a building and serve as protective symbols. They were less popular in Italy than France, where they originated (and flourished on cathedrals like Notre Dame), but Castellarosa on the Via Francigena had many French influences, including a quartet of gargoyles on the tower battlements. Sister Beatrice had said it was too dangerous to go up onto the roof but Fred and I had snuck up there one day and I remember the gaping mouths stained red from the rusty pipes inside—just like the *terrible red streams* in the clue.

"Should I go down and get a key from Greg and Sonia?" Joan asks.

"It will take too long," I say, pacing the hall. "I know there's another way onto the tower roof."

Even though Sister Beatrice had said it was too dangerous to go up to the tower, I'd seen her one day closing a window, her habit smelling of smoke, and I'd guessed that she went up to the roof to sneak cigarettes. I stop at a large casement window and lean across the window seat to lift the glass. As I do, I notice a footprint in the dust that looks very much as if it were made with a Doc Marten boot.

"This way," I say, scrambling up onto the window seat and stepping out the tall window onto a narrow ledge. I can hear Joan shrieking behind me but the sound is soon eclipsed by the shriek of the wind rattling the rickety iron frame of an old fire escape clinging to the wall of the tower. I grasp the rusted railing and haul myself up the ladder toward the tower roof, cringing at the creak and sway of the metal.

Lindsay got up it, I tell myself, although it occurs to me halfway up that I don't really know that. She could have gotten as far as the window seat and decided the fire escape was a deathtrap. I look down and see Fred holding the bottom of the ladder, trying to keep it steady for me, a look of sheer terror on his face. He's yelling something at me but his words are lost in the howl of the wind. He's probably telling me to come down but the idea of backing down this rattling ladder is more terrifying than going up—so up I go, not stopping until I clear the edge of the crenellated ramparts. I feel like a knight storming the castle wall and half expect to be met with flaming arrows and scalding oil as I clamber over the stone wall.

Instead, I spot Lindsay's bright red dress flapping in the wind as she leans over one of the gargoyles on the opposite side of the roof. Not leaning over, I see as I approach; she's leaning into the gargoyle's mouth. It looks as if her entire right arm and shoulder have been swallowed by the stone beast. As if she's being eaten alive.

I walk gingerly across the roof, trying not to make a sound. I don't want to startle her. She's so close to the edge she might fall. When I hear someone behind me, I look back and see Fred and Joan reach the roof and I pat the air to indicate that they should tread softly. When I'm about six feet away, though, I step on a loose clay tile that cracks with the sharp retort of a firearm. Lindsay wrenches her neck around to stare at me, her arm still buried in the gargoyle's mouth. Is she stuck? I wonder. Her face is so contorted she looks as if she's turning into one of the leering stone monsters.

"You!" she croaks, her voice as raspy as the creak of old metal. "Haven't you stolen enough already? You can't take this from me, too!"

"What have I taken from you?" I ask. "You're the one who took my life for your book."

She snorts. "Only after you ruined mine." Her eyes shift over my shoulder where she must see Fred.

"What are you talking about?" Fred asks. "Do I know you?"

It's exactly the wrong thing to say. Lindsay's eyes widen and she straightens up, drawing her arm out of the gargoyle's mouth, her sleeve pushed up past her elbow. She's holding up the next clue, brandishing it at Fred and me as if it contains damning evidence of our sins.

"You can't have it! I'll take it to the grave if I have to!"

Fred gasps, but it's not her threat he's reacting to, it's the ink-black scorpion writhing up her arm as if it crawled out of the gargoyle's mouth. *"Siena?"* Fred asks, so dumbfounded I almost feel sorry for him.

She smirks. "Oh, *now* you remember me. You were happy enough to forget all about me once you left San Miguel."

I glance back at my husband. "Fred? What did you do?"

"Nothing!" he cries. "That's the whole point! Nothing happened! We got drunk on too much tequila and we were talking about writing and she said she wanted to see the book I was working on—"

"You said you wanted to read *my* book," Lindsay says, pounding her fist on her chest. "And then all you did was talk about your book. But you promised you'd read my manuscript. I left it with you."

"You did?" Fred asks, looking genuinely puzzled, which just makes Lindsay angrier.

"I found it in the garbage in one of the housecleaner's trolleys."

"I don't remember—"

"I threw it in the garbage," I say. "I'm sorry, Lindsay. I was so angry—"

"I threw mine out as well," Fred says.

"You did?" I ask, realizing that I'd never even asked him about what happened to that book.

"You see!" Lindsay cries. "You're doing it again. You two only care about each other. You don't care who gets hurt around you."

I turn to Lindsay and see that her face is wet with tears and stained red with the rust from the gargoyle's mouth. "I'm sorry, Lindsay. You're right. I was upset and jealous when I found you in our room and I realized that Fred had shared that book with you, but I didn't mean to hurt you—"

"You had me fired!" she wails, brandishing Deb's clue at me.

"What?" I ask, genuinely confused. "What do you mean?"

"Don't play dumb with me. Jon Rooney fired me. He said you complained to him about me."

"I never—"

But then I remember. I was at the front desk the morning I found Fred with Siena in our room, trying to get a different room, and Jon Rooney appeared. *Why do you need a different room? What's Freddie gotten up to now?*

And I, hungover, betrayed, and bitterly jealous, said, *You should be asking what your assistant Siena got up to.*

"I didn't ask him to fire you," I say. "But I shouldn't have said anything. I'm truly sorry—" I take another step forward and she takes one back.

"You *will* be sorry," she says, waving the envelope in my face, "when I find the treasure you never found because you were too blind to see it, just as you were blind to everything—"

"Stop!" someone shouts behind me. Before I can stop him, Greg Wilson races past me toward Lindsay. He must have heard the commotion and come up to the roof to warn us that the edge was not stable. The great stone gargoyle is rocking on its feet, as if it's woken from its centuries-long slumber. As it tips, its weight takes a chunk of stone with it and Lindsay stumbles. Greg rushes toward her, reaching to catch her, but he's too late. The last I see of Lindsay is the scorpion on her arm twisting in the air as if it's trying to save itself.

CHAPTER TWENTY-ONE

I rush forward but Fred puts his arm out to stop me. "It's too late," he says, his voice heavy with despair.

Greg turns, his face ashen. "I told her the tower was not safe. You heard me—" He looks to me for confirmation but it's Joan who impatiently reassures him.

"Yes, yes, it's posted all over the hotel. You needn't worry about a lawsuit."

Greg's face turns from gray to red and I can see him preparing a retort—one I have no interest in hearing. "I'm going down to see her," I say, starting toward the fire escape. Luckily, I'm saved from having to retrace my steps down the rickety ladder. Muttering about the folly of setting foot on that *deathtrap,* Greg ushers us through the tower door and down a narrow flight of stone steps to the fourth floor. Without another word to us or a backward glance, he hurries on ahead, barking into his cell phone as he goes. We follow down the now-deserted stairs. Where has everyone gone? Had they heard so quickly of Lindsay's fall?

I find the answer in the olive grove, where everyone has gathered. The whole Goth Librarian contingent, garbed in black drapery like mourners in a play, surround Lindsay's body. I see Detective Bardi is trying in vain to clear the spectators.

"We should talk to Bardi and tell him what happened," I say to Fred, who has remained close by my side, mute and pale.

"Too late," Fred says, the same words he said on the tower, as if he's stuck in that moment. But then he points at Bardi and I see that Greg has gotten to him first. The hotelier is waving his hands and pointing up to the tower. The detective listens with growing impatience and ends by leveling his gaze at me.

"Uh-oh," I say. Whatever Greg has told him it wasn't favorable to us. "We'd better get over there."

I start walking toward the detective and Fred follows me. I consider sending him away—who knows what he'll say in his current state of shock—but that would look odd and we're already almost there, the crowd parting for us as if they all know we're the central players in this drama. Why do I keep thinking we're in a play? Is it the Goth Librarians' drapey black garb that makes them look like the Weird Sisters of *Macbeth*? Or the ominous clouds amassed in the east, so like a painted backdrop? Or maybe it's because it would be so much easier to believe this isn't real. When I get close enough to see Lindsay's broken body, the circle of blood haloing her head, her lifeless white face staring sightlessly at the sky, I know it's all too real, down to the ink-black scorpion on her arm. I follow its curving tail to her outstretched fingers, splayed open as if she were grasping at the last minute for a lifeline—

Her empty outstretched fingers.

"Signora," Detective Bardi says, "once again you are present at the scene of death. Mr. Wilson tells me you were arguing with the victim on the tower before she fell. Can you tell me what your disagreement was about?"

She turned out to be the woman who ended my marriage, I almost say. Luckily the words don't make it to my lips. My eyes are glued to that black scorpion as if I'm afraid it will come to life to sting me—Lindsay's last retribution after death.

"We found out she'd written a book about us," Fred says. I'm surprised at how calm he sounds. I was afraid he wouldn't be able to cope but now I'm the one who's struck mute at the sight of Lindsay's body. *Because something isn't right.* "A very angry book," Fred goes on. "We wanted to talk to her about it. But neither of us got anywhere near her. It was when he"—he looks toward Greg—"ran at her that she fell."

Greg clucks his tongue. "The poor girl had been forced out to the very edge of the roof, which I warned them all was unstable and dangerous. When I saw her falling, I rushed forward to save her."

"No one forced her to the edge of the roof," Fred says. "She went up there to find the next clue in the treasure hunt. She had her hand in the gargoyle's mouth."

"That's right," Joan says, coming to stand beside me. "I'm afraid that's what this has been about all along. She said as much before she died. She held up the clue and said that when she found the treasure she would show everyone that she was better than Fred and Thea. I'm afraid this happens sometimes with would-be writers. They become so jealous of successful writers and embittered by their own failures they become unhinged, as this poor girl clearly was. She must have been so obsessed with solving the treasure hunt that she killed anyone who got in her way."

"That's not true!" Zoe cries. "Lindsay wasn't unhinged and she would never hurt Kailee!"

"How well did you really know her?" Joan asks. "Did you know, for instance, that Lindsay wasn't her real name?"

"Is this all true, signora?" Bardi asks me. "Had you known this woman before? Did you know she had a vendetta against you and your husband?"

"We'd only just figured it out," Fred says for me when I fail to answer.

"And how did you know she'd be on the tower?" Bardi asks.

"We figured out where the next clue was," Fred says.

That's it, I think, that's what's wrong—

"I see," Bardi says. "And you say she had found the clue before she fell? So then—" He holds his arms up as if to embrace the scene before us. "Where is it?"

"It's gone," I say. I scan the olive grove once more but there's no sign of the envelope. "Lindsay was holding the clue when she fell but now it's gone."

DETECTIVE BARDI INSTRUCTS his officers to clear the olive grove of spectators and search the surrounding area for the envelope bearing the clue. Then he barks at me and Fred not to leave the hotel or speak to anyone until he's dealt with us.

Dismissed, we skulk off like schoolchildren given detention. As we pass through the lobby, I can feel everyone's eyes on us. Did everyone hear Greg Wilson's accusation that we forced Lindsay over the edge of the roof? I notice Zoe whispering with a group of Goth Librarians, who steal glances at us as we walk by. Good God, what will we do if the librarians turn on us? The Death Takes a Holiday series will perish without their support.

Joan must be thinking the same thing because when she catches up with us at the foot of the stairs she says, loudly enough to be overheard, "Don't you two worry, it will all be sorted out in the end and everyone will realize that you had nothing to do with poor Lindsay's death."

I'm not sure if that's helpful or not, but I'm glad for her support. She walks up with us to the second landing and asks me if I still need Deb's iPad. I start to say no, but then realize that Joan is trying to signal that she'd like to talk to me alone. I tell Fred that I'll meet him back in the suite and follow her to her room. As soon as Fred's out of earshot she hisses, "Do you want me to stay with you? Are you sure you feel safe with Fred?"

"What? Yes . . . why? Do you know something?"

"It's just that I find it a little suspicious that he didn't recognize Lindsay when they'd been . . . *intimate*."

I blush. "I didn't recognize her either," I say. "She looked totally different. And you saw him on the roof—he didn't do anything to her—"

"Didn't he? Did you see her face when he pretended not to recognize her?"

I stare at Joan. I guess I can't blame her for not trusting Fred after I told her the whole San Miguel story, but right now her suspicions aren't helpful. "I'm not worried about Fred," I say, perhaps a little too coldly. She holds my gaze for another moment and then briskly opens her door and grabs Deb's iPad. "Here," she says. "Maybe you can make more sense of this situation than I can. You were always better at the complicated plots. I'm just a little ole cozy writer, after all."

"Joan—" I begin, but a veil comes down over her face, shutting me out as effectively as the door she closes in my face.

AS SOON AS I come into the suite, I ask Fred, "Did you really not recognize Siena?"

"No!" he cries. "I barely remembered her. I drank so much tequila that night and in the morning after you . . . found us . . ." He turns bright pink. "I could barely look at her and I told her that she had to leave."

"That mustn't have been very nice for her, to have her literary idol toss her out on her ass the next morning. Did you at least try to talk to her later?"

"No! I was trying to talk to you—to explain—"

"How you ended up with a girl in your bed?"

"We were reading each other's books!" he said. "And we must have passed out. I swear, I don't remember much after you started flirting with Jon Rooney."

"After *you* abandoned me to the wives' table," I counter. "And I wasn't flirting. I'm not the one who ended up in bed with someone else—"

"But apparently you did go to Jon the next morning to tell him what happened."

"I didn't go to him; I met him at the front desk when I was trying to get another room. He asked me what happened—"

"And you couldn't wait to tell him how I had fucked up and now you were a free agent. Did he suggest he could help make things even when he offered to share his room with you?"

"No, he did not, and if he had I wouldn't have taken him up on it. And I didn't share his room; he gave me an empty adjoining room with its own door, which I kept locked—"

"And did you ask him to fire Siena?"

"No! I had no idea he did that!"

Would I have minded if I'd known? I wonder. Suddenly the fight drains out of me. We've had this argument a dozen times before—*You did this! But only because you did that first!*—that it feels like it's carved a deep groove inside my brain. "But then," I say, sinking onto the couch, "I didn't tell him *not* to fire Siena and I didn't bother to check what happened to her after I left San Miguel."

"Me neither," Fred says, sinking down beside me and lowering his head into his hands as if it's become unbearably heavy. "I ignored her text messages and spent the week holed up writing *Death Takes a Siesta*. It was the only thing I could think of doing to make things up to you. I deleted her contact info and blocked her so I could tell you I hadn't had any contact with her, and I tried very hard to scrape the memory of that night—what little I had of it—out of my brain. No wonder I didn't recognize her."

"No wonder she hated us," I say. "We *are* toxic."

"But to write that book—" he says.

"It's what I would have done. What better revenge than to make the people who have hurt you into villains."

He smiles ruefully. "Like killing off our exes in *Death Takes the Castle*?" he asks, lifting one eyebrow.

"Or making that nasty reviewer the villain in *Death Takes the Cake*," I say, wincing. "I guess we've done the same thing. But we never killed anyone in real life."

"We don't know for sure she did either," he says. "She wrote the book because she was angry at us, but why would she kill Deb, Kailee, and Nadine?"

"Murder isn't rational," I say. "She said that when she found the treasure everyone would see how blind we'd been. Maybe she thought that was how she'd get her revenge but Deb and Kailee and Nadine got in her way. They each died looking for the treasure hunt clues."

"As did Lindsay," Fred adds. "I don't know. Something doesn't fit."

"Maybe it's in here," I say, opening my laptop, where the manuscript of *The Toxic Couple* is still on the screen.

He shudders. "I don't know if I can read that right now; it feels a little too close to the bone."

"I'll read it. You look through Deb's files," I say, handing him Deb's iPad. "Look over her notes for the treasure hunt. You worked on it with her—you might notice something I wouldn't."

He nods and powers up the iPad. Once again, I feel us slipping back into our familiar roles. I was always the one who wrote the outlines and mapped out the research, divvying up our assignments, making sure Fred didn't hare off on wild-goose chases or down rabbit holes. Just as Rhea does in *The Toxic Couple,* I see. *Ted was the creative one but he was undisciplined,* Lindsay had written, *and so Rhea kept a tight rein on him, both in the study and in the bedroom. Who could wonder that he slipped his harness when her back was turned?*

I wince at the unflattering depiction and remind myself that she didn't really know us. She had observed me through one dinner and spent one night with Fred—a drunk Fred, who was angry at that careless remark I'd made at dinner . . . And she'd read Fred's book, which was a thinly veiled version of our marriage in its worst days. That's where she got this unflattering picture of me.

I look up at my husband, whose tousled hair and studious frown make him look like a schoolboy doing an all-nighter during finals week, and consider asking him, but he'll just tell me he doesn't remember. That he's forgotten that night. Which means, I remind myself, that all his protestations that *nothing happened* are meaningless. How does he know nothing happened if he doesn't remember?

I go back to my reading, looking, I have to admit, not just for a clue to why Lindsay would kill to find the treasure, but also to decide if we were really the monsters Lindsay thought we were. As we work, the room grows dimmer and a cool damp breeze floats in through the open windows. I look outside and see that the clouds that had been hovering on the horizon this morning have advanced on Castellarosa and it has begun to rain. The voices of the officers searching for the missing clue in the olive grove are replaced by the steady beat of the rain. Joan texts me that they haven't found the missing clue and that the dinner tonight has been canceled.

At least she's still talking to me.

What are people saying? I text back.

The gray ellipses beat a pattern in time with the rain for so long I think Joan may have been swallowed up in the encroaching fog. I picture usually blunt Joan drafting one message after another and then erasing each one as it's judged too harsh even for her. Finally, she types: *You don't want to know.*

I log into the conference WhatsApp group and scroll through the comments.

What do Fred and Thea have to hide?

Why were they on the roof with Lindsay?

Should the Morgan-Lanes be disqualified from the Poirot contest? (this from Buck, the rat)

What did Lindsay Monahan's book reveal about the Morgan-Lanes that they would kill to hide?

"Holy crap," I say, looking up at Fred. "Someone's leaked Lindsay's manuscript."

He nods. "I saw," he says calmly. "I was thinking we ought to order room service rather than going down to the dining room tonight."

He says it the way he would when the writing was going well and we decided to work through dinner—not as though we have become pariahs in our own community. He orders for us and I go on reading, conscious now that everyone at the conference is reading along with me. When the food comes, I let Fred take the tray from the waiter and lock the door behind him. I feel like we're under siege up here in the castello's tower suite. The rain is coming down so hard it sounds like the footsteps of an advancing army; the thunder like cannons bombarding the castle walls.

As we eat the hand-rolled *pici* in a rich spicy *aglione* sauce and drink the Montepulciano from a neighboring vineyard, Fred tells me what he's found out from Deb's notes—or rather, what he hasn't found out.

"She wrote down all the clues except for the last one in the gargoyle. All she wrote was, *Ask Thea about the last clue*."

"Did she mean the last clue in *Death Takes the Castle*?"

"I think so. Most of the questions she asked me were about details from the book. She said she wanted to include Easter eggs from the book in the treasure hunt, but when she asked me about the last clue, I told her I couldn't remember what we'd been thinking and that she should ask you. Did she?"

"Ask me? No . . ." I pause, thinking. "At the reception she said she had something to ask me, but then Greg came to escort her onto the stage—" *What had she said, exactly*? "Do you have your copy of *Death Takes the Castle*?" I ask.

"Sure," he says, rooting through his satchel and pulling out *Death Takes the Castle*. I flip to about three-quarters through to the scene just before Rick and Dora descend into the crypts. They have been searching the castle for the lost treasure of the Knights Templar, brought from the Holy Land by Bianca Rosa's knight. Just as they despair of ever discovering it—and the villain is closing in—they find an inscription in a fragment of marble embedded above the entrance to the crypt that reads:

Love is blind
As the creatures who live beneath the earth
And cannot see what it cannot find
Or know before it's lost what was its worth.

"Deb said she wasn't sure what this one meant," Fred says.

"I don't blame her," I say. "I can't quite remember myself. It was a line from the original poem and I thought it might have been an error of transcription. I mean, *duh*, of course you can't see what you can't find."

"Rick and Dora figure it out," Fred says.

"Only because the inscription is literally over the entrance to the crypt," I say.

"Maybe Deb wanted to ask you where the inscription was."

"Only in the twelfth-century poem," I say. "I looked all over the castle for it in vain because of course it never existed. The story of Bianca Rosa and her noble knight is a fairy tale."

"But what about the inscription Deb found in the garden?"

"A coincidence," I say firmly. "Deb might have thought she'd found the treasure of Castellarosa but it was a fiction we created—one that caused more damage than it was worth." I toss the book across the desk, scattering papers and rattling empty teacups. "This is useless," I say. "We're not going to figure out why Lindsay did what she did because it doesn't make any sense. It's not like in a novel where the villain explains their motives and it all adds up. And we're not going to find the next clue because there isn't one. If Deb was going to ask me about the clue at the reception, she must not have planted it yet. Deb's treasure hunt is a dead end. Everyone that's died for it has died for nothing."

CHAPTER TWENTY-TWO

After dinner we switch reading assignments. Fred starts in on *The Toxic Couple* with a scowl pasted on his face that turns eventually into an abashed look of horror. Like a man watching his dearest illusions about himself turned inside out and shredded. I think it will be easier to read Deb's notes but it's not. It's clear in every entry how much she loved *Death Takes the Castle*. I remember in the review in her newsletter she wrote that reading the book had brought her back to the joy of first discovering Nancy Drew and Agatha Christie, Mary Stewart and Elizabeth Peters; that you were on an adventure along with characters you loved, exploring an old castle, looking for treasure but finding love instead. *Because that's the real treasure of Castellarosa,* she'd written, *love—and perhaps most of all the love of books*.

Fred hadn't understood why I was so excited about her review. He was still hoping for a full page in *The New York Times* and comparisons to Hemingway (or at least Raymond Chandler). He'd read Agatha Christie, of course (and together we watched the David Suchet *Poirot* episodes so many times we could lip-sync the lines), but I don't think he'd ever heard of Mary Stewart or Elizabeth Peters and he hadn't grown up on Nancy Drew like I had. Nor did he understand why a review by a Midwestern retired librarian was so important. But I did. I saw how influential she was in the mystery world and guessed right away that having her as an ally would pave our way in that world.

Had I used Deb, I wonder now, opportunistically leveraging her influence to advance our career?

Maybe in the beginning, I have to admit, but I'd come to love her. And now she had died while following the steps of this silly treasure hunt we'd made up twenty years ago. The map on the iPad screen blurs. When I close my eyes, I find that the garden paths and castle corridors and cloister walks and underground crypts (the last completely fictitious because the only crypt we'd found was small and plain and didn't have a sarcophagus for Bianca Rosa) have been imprinted on the inside of my eyelids.

"You have to get some sleep," Fred says, removing the iPad from my grip and taking my hands in his. I let him pull me to my feet and lead me into the bedroom—a motion as imprinted in the nerve endings and pathways of my brain as that treasure map. For a moment I think he is going to take me all the way to bed, that he will pull me down to the mounds of pillows and crisp white duvet, his arms encircling me, his mouth finding mine, our bodies meeting, fitting together as if we'd both been traveling two paths that had always been headed toward one another. As if all the maps led here.

Does he feel it, too?

He stops by the side of the bed and I think I feel him pulling me toward him—

Will I go?

I'll never know. He drops my hand, steps back, tells me to get some sleep, and retraces his steps out the door, closing it behind him with a firm click. I'm left standing by the side of the bed as if it's the edge of an antique map where ancient cartographers penned *Here be dragons*. As lost as those explorers standing at the place where all the maps end.

I FOLLOW DEB'S treasure map into my dreams, where it is laid out over the Tuscan hills like a blanket of fog. I am hovering over it, able to see everything at once—the winding castle corridors and secret passageways, the garden mazes and cloister walks—as I circle downward toward the heart of the castle, burrowing into the crypts like a blind mole—

Love is blind
As the creatures who live beneath the earth
And cannot see what it cannot find—

Of course no one can find anything down here. It's dark as the grave but somehow as I wander the underground passages, the limestone walls and arched vaults emerge out of the darkness and I see that this underground city is populated by stone figures. Medieval knights and ladies lie on stone biers, hands pressed together in prayer, faces placid in death, a loyal lion or dog crouched at their feet. I wander from one pair of statues to another, searching—but for what I don't know. I only know that if I don't find it I'll be trapped down here forever, so I look into each stone face with an attention so urgent I wonder it doesn't wake the dead—

And then it does. A pair of stone eyelids fly open, revealing the black void beneath them. As I rear back in horror, I hear the creak of stone and armor. All the sleeping knights and ladies in the crypt are stirring and rising, shuffling toward me. I run, searching each stone face for the one I'm looking for, wakening a stone army of the undead hungry for what I can give them—life.

It's not real, I want to yell at them. The life I give them is a cruel imitation. Still, I search each face until I reach a dead end—a stone crypt with two statues lying at its center. I know this place; it's just as I described it in *Death Takes the Castle.* A rosebush springs from each of the figure's hands and climbs upward to the vaulted roof, the flowers pale as death, the thorns barbed and sharp. I have to wend my way through the thicket of rosebushes, the thorns tearing at my clothes and flesh, so that by the time I reach the sarcophagus I am dripping with blood—

Which is what they want, I realize, as my blood splatters on the dog crouched at the woman's feet and it stretches to life and bares its fangs, hungry for more. It's what they all want, and as the thorns ensnare me, snug as a hunter's net, the stone hosts close in for the kill. Still, I struggle to look into the faces of Bianca Rosa and her knight, determined to see what I cannot find, to know before it's lost. But when I look down at the stone faces it's not Bianca Rosa and her knight I see; it's my own face I look into, and Fred's, who opens his eyes and says my name—

"Thea?"

His voice is so real and urgent it wakes me up. I open my eyes and make out a figure hovering over me, limned in light like a halo, like a medieval painting of an angel. My body feels heavy as stone and I remember my dream. I am lying dead in the crypt waiting for Prince Charming to kiss me awake—

Or the host of hungry zombie knights to devour me.

"Thea?"

The angel leans closer and shakes me.

"Wake up!"

It's Fred. My knight errant come to waken me from my stony sleep.

"I've figured out what comes next in Deb's treasure hunt," he says. Of course, I realize, he knows that the only way to wake me from this enchanted sleep is not with a kiss but with a plot twist.

HE'S ALSO MADE coffee in the little Moka pot in the kitchenette—thick, sludgy espresso strong enough to wake the dead, which is what he looks like, pale and jittery as if he hasn't slept at all. When he drags me into the living room, I see what's kept him up. He's pushed all the furniture to the sides of the room and laid note cards down all over the floor, each weighted down by books and coffee cups and assorted bric-a-brac.

"What the hell, Fred? This looks like Carrie's apartment wall in *Homeland* when she's had a psychotic break."

"Yeah, but she always figures out the puzzle, doesn't she?" he says, tapping his forefinger against his temple as if that's the pertinent point and not his alarming mental state.

I should have seen the signs earlier. There was always a point in writing the books when Fred went off the rails. Although I would carefully outline each book in advance, Fred preferred a more "organic" approach. *If we know everything that's going to happen, where's the fun? And if we're not having fun, how can we expect our readers to?*

It depends, I would retort, *on what your idea of fun is.* Dismantling my meticulously crafted plot, unraveling its carefully woven threads until we were left with a pile of tangled yarn, made me feel as if the neurons and synapses in my brain had been turned inside out and scrambled.

And yet.

Fred had a knack for pulling on the one loose thread of my construction—a dubious alibi, a chance remark of a suspect, a coincidence that wasn't—and sending the plot careening in a wholly different and unexpected direction. *Wouldn't it be funny if she were the killer?* he would ask, naming a minor character who'd been idling behind the scenes. *No one will have seen it coming.*

Because it makes no sense, I'd retort.

And then he would proceed to demonstrate not only how the minor character could have committed the crime but why she was the perfect one to have done so.

But, I would plead even as I began to see he was right, *we'll have to rewrite the whole book and we'll blow our deadline and miss our pub date!*

We'll be a little late and Aleister will have to crash the book out to make the pub date, but it will be a better book.

And I would have to admit he was right. I'd warn Aleister that we might be late and go to work seeding the new culprit into the earlier chapters—and find that there really wasn't that much to do after all. The innocent minor character whom I'd never pegged for the killer had been lurking behind the scenes all along, giving themselves away in subtle clues that the reader would never notice at first but later recognize as the most brilliant foreshadowing.

See, Fred would say when the book was done, not too late and far better, *subconsciously you knew all along who did it*.

It was one thing, though, to scramble a book plot and risk missing a deadline; it was another to play guessing games when a murderer was afoot. I look down at the floor, hoping for some sense of order, and see the same kind of Florentine notecards Deb had used for her clues, each one covered with Fred's handwriting in red ink, dotting the marble mosaic. He's holding another card in his left hand and his fountain pen in his right, his hands and shirt sleeves spattered with red ink.

"Where did you get those cards?"

"Deb gave me a set of them as a thank-you present for helping her with the treasure hunt. I wrote the clues down on them and placed them where we found them."

I look down, confused for a moment. What does he mean *where we found them*? But then I see. The marble pattern in the floor is a map of the monastery and its grounds. This room, I remember, was once the private quarters of the abbess, and before that it would have belonged to the duke, who ruled the castle and the surrounding farmlands. Perhaps he had commissioned the marble floor map so he could look down on his domain. The old marble is faded but I can still make out the monastery with its cloisters and chapel and towers and the surrounding rose gardens and olive groves and cypress avenue leading up to the bell tower. Fred has placed numbered cards where clues have been found so far or where the missing clues should have been found:

#1 Rose Garden
#2 Cloister Well
#3 Bell Tower
#4 Gargoyle Tower

He's holding a card marked #5 with the last clue over the poison garden. "Why the poison garden?" I ask.

"Look," he says, kneeling down and tapping the floor, "it marks the location of the old crypt." He taps the floor again and I trace the pattern with my finger. The inlaid pattern of jasper, malachite, carnelian, and onyx has faded over time so it's hard to see what he's talking about, but then I make out a shape below the garden, as if revealing a crypt beneath. The shape looks like a recumbent knight in armor with a woman by his side. It looks so much like the one in my dreams that I shiver. "Is that—"

"A sarcophagus. The poison garden is located in the ruins of the old chapel and beneath the chapel—"

"A crypt," I say, finishing, his sentence. "And if the crypt is real, then the treasure may be as well."

WE TAKE THE secret passageway down to the library to avoid running into anyone in the hallways, using our phone flashlights to light the way. When we reach the library, Fred crosses quickly to the French doors that lead out into the garden, but I pause for a moment, remembering arguing with Nadine when I was in here last. I'm ashamed now of how I acted with her after overhearing what she said on the phone—

"Fred," I say, catching up with him. "When I was in the library before, I overheard Nadine saying that she didn't think I'd cause any trouble. What did she mean? What wasn't I going to cause trouble *about*?"

Fred turns to me, his face blanched by moonlight. "She was talking to a British publisher who wants to buy my new book, but they were worried about the do-not-compete clause in our contract. They were concerned you might use it to keep me from publishing my new book. That's why I was looking at our contract."

"You thought I would stand in the way of you doing what you always wanted?" I ask, appalled.

"You didn't want me to publish my first book back when we wrote *Death Takes the Castle*, remember? You said the publisher would consider it a conflict."

I open my mouth to object—had I really told Fred he couldn't publish the novel he'd been working on for years?—but before I can, he says, "It doesn't matter now. What matters is stopping this killer and I think we'll find them with the treasure. Come on."

For someone who hasn't slept he sounds eager and energized, a boy on an adventure—just like twenty years ago. I didn't force him into looking for the treasure then, I think, or force him into writing *Death Takes the Castle.* But had I really told him he couldn't publish his own novel? And was that why he didn't show me the novel he wrote in San Miguel and showed it to a stranger instead? Is that the plot twist in our story—that I have been the villain all along?

The rain has stopped and the sky has cleared, revealing a moon bright enough outside that we don't need our flashlights. As we hurry across the sodden lawn toward the garden, I glance around to see if there are any late-night stragglers about. Now that the rain has stopped, it's a lovely warm night, perfect for sipping wine under a pergola or taking a moonlit stroll through the rose gardens, but the veranda and lawn are abandoned. I suppose that four murders might make even a hardy crew of mystery buffs think twice about roaming the grounds alone after dark.

When we walk between the giant cypress trees guarding the entrance to the gardens, the moonlight vanishes. It is dark as death in here beneath the funereal trees. Will we even be able to find our way through the maze to the poison garden? As if hearing my thoughts, Fred says, "You found it the first day. Lead on."

"I think that was just lucky," I say.

"Don't think too much about it," he says, "just follow your instincts."

It's what he would say when we were stuck in a book, when I was sure we had written ourselves into a corner (usually because Fred had proposed some outlandish plot twist) and that we'd have to scrap the book and start all over again. *We'll find a way out,* he would say, *we always do.*

I close my eyes for a moment and picture the garden with the ruined chapel at its center and its labyrinth path laid out in old Roman stones. *The labyrinth radiates out through the garden and castle,* Sister Beatrice had said. Did that mean, I wonder, that the hedge maze followed the same pattern? I had walked the labyrinth at the center almost every day when I was here twenty years ago, so often that I could do it with my eyes closed. So that's what I do now. Keeping my eyes closed, I walk forward, trailing my fingertips along the edges of the damp yew hedge, scattering raindrops in my wake, Fred so close behind me I can feel his breath on the back of my neck. I don't stop until I feel rough sandstone beneath my fingertips. Then I open my eyes and see the walls of the old chapel glowing pink in the moonlight.

"You did it!" Fred crows. "You found it!"

We follow the old chapel wall to the old oak door and enter the poison garden. For a moment the garden looks so different from how it had in the daytime that I think we have come to the wrong place, that the maze—and my *instincts*—have led us to Death itself. The lunar landscape is awash in white, unearthly blooms, so pale they might have grown beneath the ground. Pendulous alabaster trumpets hang from every wall and bright white stars stud the darkness. The air is sickeningly sweet.

"I guess it makes sense that it would be a night garden," Fred says, his voice less certain than his words.

But he's right. The garden has been transformed by its night-blooming flowers. As we step foot on the labyrinth path, I recognize moonflowers and night-blooming jasmine, but not the half dozen other strange pale blooms that creep and climb over every surface. Fred walks behind me, not daring to step off the path this time. Who knows what these flowers would do to you if you trod on them? Some of them look as if they might have teeth.

I keep my eyes on my feet to make sure I stay on the path and read the Latin inscriptions as we go. *Mors vincit omnia*, "Death conquers all." *Mors certa, vita incerta*, "Death is certain, life isn't." *Memento mori*, "Remember you must die."

Why are they all about death? I had asked Sister Beatrice.

They're all gravestones, she had replied, *taken from the old Roman cemetery.*

At the center of the labyrinth Atropos waits for us with her thread and her scissors. *Mors semper hic nobiscum*, reads the inscription at her feet. "Death is always here with us."

I look down at the inscription—and notice something. I kneel down and touch the word *hic*. *Here*. I dig my fingers into the deep carved letters and pull. The slab shifts, grating stone against stone. Fred is suddenly by my side, helping me move the loose slab. He points his flashlight down, revealing a flight of stone steps. I feel a puff of air waft against my face that smells like death and decay. We've found the crypt.

CHAPTER TWENTY-THREE

I can't believe the entrance to the crypt was here all along," I say. "Do you think Sister Beatrice knew?"

"I wouldn't put it past her," Fred says. "She was a cagey old bird."

"But why wouldn't she tell us?" I wail, sounding like a child who's been lied to by their parents.

"Maybe she thought we should have found it ourselves . . . and now we have." He doesn't sound happy. Uplit by his flashlight, his face looks ghastly, like those of the stone zombie knights of my nightmare.

"We still don't know if the treasure is down there," I say.

I aim my flashlight down the stairs but the beam is swallowed up before it reaches the ground. How deep could it be? There are subterranean crypts below medieval churches that go two or three levels down into Roman and pre-Roman ruins. The thought of descending far below the earth makes my skin crawl. It's the one adventure I never felt any enthusiasm for. When we wrote a book set in Paris, I nixed researching a scene in the catacombs and I refused to consider a spelunking book.

"I'll go," Fred offers, remembering my phobia. "You can stay here and I'll tell you what I find."

"And let you find the treasure on your own?" I scoff, trying to sound skeptical rather than terrified. "No way. Rick and Dora always go together. Lead on."

The entrance is so small Fred has to dangle his legs over the side and scoot down on his butt for the first few steps, but once his head has cleared the roof he stands up and turns to face me. He already looks small and far away. I feel like Orpheus glancing back at Eurydice and watching her plummet down to Hades. This is how it will feel if he dies before you, I think. The idea of losing him scares me worse than the idea of going underground. I swing my legs over the edge and follow my husband into the underworld.

Thankfully the narrow stairs open up at the bottom to a wide vaulted space of stone arches supported by columns. I shine my flashlight up at the column capitals and a dozen human skulls grin back at me.

"Macabre," Fred says, "but fitting, I suppose. Look over here. I think there's a sarcophagus in this alcove."

I turn away from the hollow eyes of the skulls—*carved,* I think, not real skulls, although the early Christians weren't averse to stacking up real skulls in their catacombs—and follow Fred to an alcove into which a stone sarcophagus has been fitted. A knight in medieval armor reclines on top of it, his hands crossed over the hilt of his sword, a lion crouched at his feet.

A bronze plaque on the wall above identifies him as Duke Raimondo Urbano, who died in 1020.

"This is from before the convent was founded," I say, glad of the scholarly distraction to keep me from thinking of being underground with all these dead bodies.

"He's way too early to be Bianca's knight," Fred says, dismissing Duke Urbano. "Come on, there are more tombs through here."

I follow Fred through an arch into another vault. There are alcoves on either side with sarcophagi in each one, some with a single figure lying on top of a marble plinth, some with a couple. The men are all wearing armor with lions at their feet, the women are in medieval dresses and pointy hats with dogs crouched at theirs. The dates progress from the eleventh century through the twelfth, but none of them are Bianca Rosa and her beloved.

"This is pointless," I say, after we have peered into a dozen stone faces. "If the story is true that Bianca and her lover were buried alive underground there wouldn't be a sarcophagus for either of them—just a pile of bones."

"Then we're looking for a pile of bones," Fred says.

We've come to the end of the long arcade of tombs. I shine my flashlight on the alcove and find a long rectangular bronze plaque instead of a sarcophagus. The Latin inscription on it has been corroded by centuries of dripping water and mold so I can barely read it. I make out several *deo*s and *sancto*s and the ever-familiar *mors*.

"Death, death, death," Fred says, coming to stand beside me.

"We get it. We're all going to die. Do you ever wonder whether, if we had met at a cheerier spot, we might have written in a different genre?"

"What, like if we had met at a Sandals in the Caribbean we'd have written rom-coms?"

"Exactly," he says, grinning, "or if we'd met at a quaint New England inn we'd have written Hallmark Christmas movies."

I snort, the sound discordant in this place of death. "Would you have preferred that?"

He shakes his head. "No, if we had to go genre, I'm glad it was mystery—hey, does that look like a handle to you?"

He's trained his flashlight on a skull face deeply inset into the bronze plaque, its eye sockets sunk deep into the wall. When I trace my hand over it, I find that my fingers fit neatly into the eye sockets. When I push, the metal groans as if I've hurt it but doesn't budge.

"Here, let me try." Fred pushes my hand aside and fits his into the sockets. The moan turns into a shriek as he pulls and I fear we are awakening a monster. My eyes fall on another word—*cave*—"beware." Beware of what? I wonder as a gap appears between the plaque and the wall.

"It's not a plaque," I say at the same time that Fred says, "It's a door." A door that opens to another flight of stairs spiraling down even farther below the ground. These stairs are cruder and the walls rougher, as if they were dug out of the rock with bare hands. An odor of decay and sulfur wafts up along with a roar like the sound you hear when you press a conch shell to your ear. Because the stairs are shaped like a shell? I wonder.

But then I remember that the sound you hear in a shell is just an amplification of ambient noise. This sound contains sighs and whispers, as if it had caught the last gasps of the dead.

"You can wait here," Fred offers gallantly.

It's a tempting offer. My whole body recoils from entering this subterranean corkscrew. But looking back down the long arcade of the dead I decide I'd rather go with Fred into the underworld than stay up here with the unknown dead.

"We might as well," I say, "since we've come this far."

It's what Dora says when they're about to do something very stupid. Fred smiles grimly at the reference and starts down the stairs, but I stop him. "Let me go first," I say. "I got us into this in the first place." Fred looks surprised as I start down the stairs ahead of him. It's not bravery, though, it's an aversion to having all those stone knights and ladies at my back.

The stairs twist into the earth for so long I begin to wonder if this isn't some medieval torture device like the iron maiden or Saint Catherine's Wheel. I imagine the walls tightening around us, squeezing us in a deathly embrace. I'm half blind with panic by the time the spiral stairs spit us out into a low domed room. There are no arches and vaulted arcades here, only one lone bier with two carved figures lying atop, as if it is waiting to receive our bodies.

"What do you think these two did to deserve the bargain-basement burial?" Fred's tone is light and jocular but I can tell he's putting on a show, pretending the sight of the tomb isn't unnerving. He's never minded underground explorations. In college, he told me, he explored the tunnels beneath his

Upstate New York campus and went spelunking in the nearby ice caves. It's not being underground that has him on edge or even the claustrophobic space. It must be the tomb itself—a great monolithic slab of dark stone that rises out of the dirt floor like a prehistoric rock formation. As if it had grown here.

I approach the sarcophagus gingerly, as if I'm afraid the lid will fly open and Dracula's hand will snake out to grab me. There are two figures on top just as on the sarcophagi above us, but when I get close enough to look down on them, I see these figures are nothing like the stiff effigies lying in state above. A man and a woman lie as though on a bed, but instead of stiffly laid out on their backs, they face each other, arms embracing. A thin blanket is draped over them, so deftly carved that the shape of their bare limbs is at once veiled and revealed. Their knees touch, their feet tangle together. The man's hand rests on the woman's breast, the woman's cradles the man's cheek. Their eyes hold each other's gaze.

I hear Fred breathing beside me, rendered as speechless as I am, as if we are both afraid to disturb the couple. Then I feel his arm encircle my shoulders and lean into him, grateful for his warmth. *We are still alive,* I hear myself think, *we still have time*. And then, before I can ask myself *time for what?* I say, "It looks Etruscan. There's one like it at the Boston Museum of Fine Arts."

"I find it hard to believe that there's anything *like* this," Fred says, his voice full of awe.

"This one is a remarkable specimen," I say crisply, reverting to full academic mode. "The carving is especially fine, the expressions on their faces almost modern. Many scholars believe Etruscan women enjoyed equal rights with men—"

I babble on about the Etruscans. Although it wasn't my academic specialty, I had toured the necropolises at Cerveteri and Chianciano before coming to Castellarosa. I'd even wondered if the author of the anonymous love poem might have seen some Etruscan artifacts and been influenced by their culture, especially the equality between men and women evident in their grave sculptures. "I had a theory that Bianca Rosa might have been influenced by Etruscan artifacts," I conclude. "But Fraser said that was unlikely."

"I've always thought your dissertation adviser sounded like an asshole," Fred says, "and here's the proof you were right."

I shine my flashlight on him to see if he's laughing at me, but his face is as washed clean of irony as I've ever seen it. Instead he's gazing at the sarcophagus with the solemnity of a mourner at a grave, as if he had known its ancient inhabitants intimately. *What was your secret?* I want to ask them. *How did you keep your love alive for over two millennia when I failed before two decades?* I look closer and notice that the woman is wearing something around her neck. I bend over her to see what it is and make out a cross. "Oh!" I exclaim, surprised. "They're not Etruscan."

"No," Fred says, moving his flashlight over to the side of the sarcophagus. "Look at this."

On an Etruscan sarcophagus the sides might be carved with a wedding procession, but this sculpted relief illustrates a knight's journey to a castle on a hill that looks very much like Castellarosa. There is a meeting in a rose garden, a stolen kiss, an expulsion by a robed and crowned figure, then a sea journey on a ship across an ocean to a land of minarets and domes. Then there's a battle, in the midst of which the knight discovers a chest brimming with treasure.

"It's the story from Bianca Rosa's poem!" I cry, my voice echoing in the domed space like an alarm. "My God, Fred, do you know what this means? My thesis was right—" I start to laugh but stop quickly. The sound is jarring in this place of death. The echoes linger and reverberate above us like drumbeats.

"Yes," Fred says, "you were right. And so was Deb. The treasure was real."

"Maybe," I say, "but who knows where it ended up."

"It ended up right here," Fred says, rapping his knuckles against the bottom of the sarcophagus. Again, the vault snatches at the sound and sends back a volley of echoes, this time like the footsteps of an advancing army. I hurry to Fred's side to make him stop it—and see what he's knocking on. Sitting at the foot of the sarcophagus is not a dog or a lion. There's a chest, just like the one carved in marble on the side of the sarcophagus, only this one isn't carved out of stone. It's crafted of wood and leather, decayed but still miraculously whole, and studded with brass nails and jewels.

"Is it . . . ? Do you think it's still . . . ?"

"Full?" Fred asks, reading my mind. "Let's find out."

He starts to lift the lid. I reach out to stop him, afraid—of what I don't know. A booby trap? A nest of scorpions and vipers? A genie's curse? Treasure is never what you think it is; it always comes with a price.

But Fred's too fast. He opens the lid, ancient hinges screeching like a banshee's wail, centuries-old leather and wood crumbling under his touch. I aim the flashlight inside. When the beam hits the contents it sends up a spray of prisms that flutter across the domed ceiling like escaped butterflies, making the crypt into a magic snow globe.

"Gold," Fred says, his voice full of awe.

"Bianca Rosa's treasure," I say and think, Maybe just this once there won't be a price to pay for this gift.

"Correction," an officious voice pronounces. "*Our* treasure."

I look up and see Greg Wilson standing at the entrance to the stairway. He's holding a gun pointed at Fred. "Thank you for finding it for us," he says. "Now kindly step aside."

CHAPTER TWENTY-FOUR

"You can put the gun down," Fred says, holding his hands up and stepping between me and the hotelier. "We weren't planning on taking it."

"No?" Greg asks, still aiming the gun at us. "And what were you planning on doing with it?"

"Isn't it obvious?" Sonia steps out from behind her husband and shines a heavy flashlight directly into my eyes, forcing me to look away. "They will use it to publicize their next book. *Mystery writers solve real-life mystery*. It would sell lots of copies, wouldn't it?"

"It would be great publicity for the hotel," Fred says. "You'll be booked solid for years."

"That's what your friend *Deb* said to me as I escorted her to the stage," Greg says.

The way he pronounces Deb's name—his voice thick with disdain, as if he's making fun of her Midwestern accent and floral cardigans and sensible shoes—makes my skin crawl. I also don't like Sonia's use of the conditional tense—they *would* use it; it *would* sell lots of copies—as if our future existence is in doubt.

"And what did you say back to her?" I ask, stepping forward so I'm next to Fred. He shoots me a warning look but it's too late.

"I told her that I didn't believe in the treasure, to which she replied that I would then be very surprised when it was discovered because she was sure she had figured out where it was. She even suggested that I should be ready to alert the Ministry of Culture to oversee the preservation and removal of the artifact. *Imagine,* she said to me, *if it's a trove of crusader gold how valuable it will be!*"

"Is that it?" Sonia asks, aiming her flashlight at the chest and stepping toward it to get a better look.

As she draws near, I sense Fred tensing and angling his body so he'll be closer to her. *Does he plan to jump her?* But Greg must see this, too, because he holds his wife back. "Careful, my dear, I'm afraid our guests are already quite protective of the treasure. I wouldn't be surprised if they thought it belonged to them."

"Of course not—" I begin, outraged that they would think we thought anyone owned such a cultural treasure, but Fred interrupts.

"We could share it," he says. "No one need know we found it. We certainly won't tell anyone, will we, Thea?"

I gape at him. What's he talking about? He knows I'd never go along with looting a cultural artifact. Does he think I'm that money-grubbing?

"How generous of you," Greg says, "but it's a little late for making deals. We've already invested too much in finding the treasure. Now step aside—" He takes a step closer to us, waving his gun menacingly. "Go sit against the wall."

I have no intention of obeying but Fred takes my hand, steers me around the sarcophagus, and then pulls me down onto the floor. His hand, I notice, is as cold as the stone at my back. As soon as we're seated, Sonia rushes to the chest and aims her flashlight into the interior, setting off a kaleidoscope of gold sparkles that light up her face.

"Look at all this gold!" she croons, reaching her hand into the chest and lifting up a handful of it that she then lets spill through her fingers. "It must be worth millions!"

"We can play with it later, darling," Greg says. "Put it in here—" He tosses her a bag, one of the conference tote bags, I notice, with its silk-screen Poirot and *MurderCon* printed in dripping red letters. Which is when it hits me.

"You killed Deb!"

Fred squeezes my hand and I realize what he's been trying to warn me about. He wants us to pretend that we don't know what they've done so they won't have to kill us, but as I look from Sonia, her face sallow and avaricious in the gold light as she pours the coins into the tote bag, to Greg, whose eyes are as cold as the stone of the sarcophagus, I can see that these two have no intention of leaving us here alive.

"We didn't mean to," Greg says. "We only wanted to dope her up a little so we could get her to tell us where the treasure was before she set the mob on the hunt. But I'm afraid my wife miscalculated the dose—"

"I did nothing of the kind," Sonia replies testily without taking her eyes off the gold pouring through her fingers into the canvas bag. "She must have had an allergic reaction."

"You put belladonna in her drink!" I cry, remembering now that Sonia was sitting next to Deb on the dais. The drink wasn't poisoned when I passed it to Deb, I realize, but the thought brings no comfort.

"Just a couple of berries," Sonia says. "The medieval herbalist guide we sell in the gift shop said it wouldn't be lethal. She must have had an allergic reaction. It wasn't my fault. And then that loud, bossy woman wouldn't let me have her laptop."

"I think she means Joan," Fred says dryly.

"So we had to follow the treasure hunt just like everybody else," Sonia complains.

"Because you couldn't figure it out yourselves," Fred says, clearly no longer trying to pretend we don't know what they've done. Has he given up on getting us out of here alive? Or maybe he's just succumbed to curiosity. *It's bad enough,* he once commented when we were watching an episode of *Poirot, that the villain just caves and confesses all, but why does everyone just sit there giving them a chance to pull out a gun on them?*

To give themselves time to plot their escape, I'd said. Is that what Fred is doing? And if so, what kind of plot is he hatching? Although he's still sitting, he's shifted his weight and angled his body forward as if preparing to spring to his feet. I follow his lead and do the same. Both Sonia and Greg are too entranced by the gold to notice.

"That's why you followed Kailee to the well," Fred continues. "But why kill her?"

Sonia sighs. "That was an accident, too. The stupid girl wouldn't let go of the clue. She made such a fuss I had to push her away and she lost her balance and fell into the well."

I realize that she's left out that she must have had to remove the cover to the well first, but I don't point that out. Instead, I say, "You took the clue. Why didn't you just go to the bell tower and get the next clue?"

Greg looks embarrassed, but Sonia just looks annoyed. "Because we couldn't make heads or tails of it! You people—you're so proud of your little puzzles, as if they make you smarter than everybody else."

"I had to search your room hoping for some clue," Greg admits.

"That was you?" I cry. "You tried to kill me!"

"You attacked me!" He sounds like he wants an apology. "I barely got out of there alive."

"Then how did you figure out that the next clue was in the bell tower?" I ask.

"When I was leaving your room, I saw Nadine St. George heading out the east gate. I followed her to the bell tower and watched her find the clue—"

"And then you killed her," Fred says.

"She left us no choice," Sonia answers. "She was so proud of herself for figuring out where the clue was, all because she realized they were placed in the order of murders in your book, which made us realize we didn't need her help to find the next clue."

"You bastard!" Fred begins to rise but I put my hand on his arm to hold him back.

"But then you left the clue pinned to her cloak," I say, more to distract Fred than because I want to hear any more of their craven justifications.

"Well, yes," Sonia concedes. "We realized that the next murder in your book wasn't in a real place so we needed one of your lot to lead us there. Which that Goth drama queen did—"

"Was pushing Lindsay off the roof an accident, too?" Fred asks.

Greg shrugs. "Truthfully, that woman had been getting on my nerves. All of you have, quite honestly, with all your complaints and petty demands for almond milk and gluten-free bread—in Italy of all places!"

"And hypoallergenic pillows and unscented toiletries," Sonia chimes in, shaking her head at the many whims of her entitled guests. "For a bunch of people who write about murder you're awfully fragile."

"I rather think we'll be retiring from the hotel business," Greg says, smiling fondly at his wife.

"Couldn't you have done that without murdering four people?" I ask, hoping that Fred and I won't soon be added to the tally.

"After sinking all our capital into this money pit?" Greg scoffs, as if this were a reasonable explanation for murder.

"We're up to our eyebrows in debt," Sonia says, holding up a gold coin and looking at it lovingly. "This is our way out."

"Do you think you can just cash in twelfth-century gold coins at the local bank?" I demand.

Greg and Sonia exchange a pleased look. "We've made a

number of connections in the underground art market," Greg says.

I remember the missing altar painting from the chapel. "You've been selling off art from the convent walls!"

"Why not?" Sonia asks, shrugging. "We paid for this place. Whatever is here belongs to us. Of course, that old nun gave us a hard time. She sent the Ministry of Culture to reclaim the paintings because she said they belonged to the *people*."

Fred and I exchange a glance. "Sister Beatrice?" I ask.

"Yes, the old shrew, such a bother." Sonia clucks her tongue. "But she did give us the idea that there might be more valuable objects on the premises. Your friend Deb got in touch with her and she came here spouting nonsense about the treasure and how your book had all the answers—so then we had to read your book."

He makes it sound like a chore.

"So, you see, everything that's happened really started with you two." He smiles at us as if concluding an interview or book club talk. Then he turns to his wife. "Have you got it all? We don't want to have to come back once we seal this place up."

My stomach turns at the words *seal up*. I've managed to avoid thinking about how far underground we are while listening to Greg and Sonia's self-serving speeches, but now the reality of what awaits us sinks in. "What are you going to do with us?" I ask.

"Why, nothing," Greg replies with a horrible grin. "We'll simply leave you to your"—he flutters his hand around the domed space, which feels as if it's gotten smaller in the last few minutes—"research. Perhaps you'll entertain yourselves by writing a new novel while you're here and in a few hundred years historians will find it along with your bones and you'll become part of the lore of Castellarosa."

"Do you think that's a good idea?" Sonia whispers to her husband as if we won't hear her in this cramped and airless space. For a moment I think she's become our unlikely ally, but then she continues, "Just to leave them . . . *alive*? What if they get out?"

"Like their fictional counterparts?" He scoffs. "That kind of thing only happens in books."

"But shouldn't we make sure?" She looks pointedly at the gun in Greg's hand. I feel Fred tense beside me, his weight shifting onto the balls of his feet. He's getting ready to rush Greg if Sonia wins her argument.

Which will force Greg's hand and make him shoot Fred.

"The noise might be noticed," he hisses back at his wife. "And bring someone down here."

"Out here in the middle of the garden?" Sonia scoffs. "Two stories below the ground? No one would hear it."

But she doesn't know that for sure. A gunshot might be the only way we don't end up trapped down here.

Fred is halfway to his feet, but so am I and I'm closer to Greg. I lunge forward, laser-focused on the gun in his hand. I feel like I'm flying. I feel like my alter ego, Dora. This is just the kind of thing she would do. Every time I wrote her doing something daring and foolhardy, I had wondered if I'd be brave enough to act like her in real life—and here I am! Flying through the air toward a loaded gun just as if I'd written the scene—

And then, midair, buoyed by adrenaline and exhilaration, I recall how those scenes always played out, and from the corner of my eye I spy Fred, hurtling past me, putting himself in between me and that gun.

Just like Rick would do.

The gun fires, the sound so loud in the tiny chamber that I feel it in my gut like a blow. I'm falling, hitting the ground, wind knocked out of me, something hot and wet seeping down my ribs. Fred is on top of me, mouth moving, but I can't hear a word he's saying. My ears are ringing with the echoes of the gun. *Have I been shot?*

I look over Fred's shoulder and see Greg and Sonia silently mouthing something and then they turn and vanish. I try to push Fred away, to tell him to follow them, that we can't let them get up the stairs and lock us in here, but when I shake his shoulder, my hand comes away bloody. I'm not the one who's bleeding, I realize.

"You've been shot," I say, only I can't hear my own words over the percussive echo that rings through the crypt like church bells ringing a death knell. For a second I think it's another shot—that Greg has come down the stairs to finish us off—but then I realize it's the sound of the metal door at the top of the stairs slamming shut, sealing us into this crypt, buried alive just like Bianca Rosa and her beloved knight.

CHAPTER TWENTY-FIVE

Quick," Fred says, his voice cutting through the ringing in my ears. "Run up the stairs and see if you can open the door."

"But you're hurt," I say, easing his weight off me and crouching beside him. It's too dark to see anything. The only light comes from one of our phones lying a few feet away, its flashlight a dim beacon. I crawl toward it and then shine it on Fred. He looks awful, slumped against the sarcophagus, his face gray as the stone, his once-white shirt stained a lurid red.

"Where were you hit?" I ask, running my hands over his chest and fumbling with his buttons. He cries out as I peel away the sodden cloth.

"I think it's just my shoulder," he says, as if that's an expendable part of his anatomy. But he's right. I make out torn flesh in his right shoulder. At least the bullet didn't hit his heart or lungs, but there's so much blood. If I can't stop it, he'll bleed to death. I strip my outer shirt off and press it to the wound. He cries out in pain.

"Sorry," I say, "but they always say to apply pressure to the wound."

"Why don't I take over that part and you go up and check the door." He pushes my hand away and presses the already soaked cloth with his left hand, wincing. I don't want to leave him. I don't want to go up those stairs alone. I don't want to confirm that we're trapped in here.

"I don't know where the other phone is," I say. "And I don't want to leave you in the dark."

Fred looks at me and nods, as if acknowledging all my unspoken fears. "It's okay," he says. "Take the phone. I don't mind the dark."

I still don't want to leave him but if I can't get him out of here, he's going to bleed to death. I take the phone and press the hand he's holding over the wound. "Keep pressure on that," I say sternly, meaning, *Don't die on me.*

The stairs feel even tighter going up them—and longer—as if the burial chamber has sunk deeper into the ground since we entered it.

Because we're closer to death?

I shoo the thought away and climb faster—so fast I slam into the closed door at the top. It doesn't budge. But of course it wouldn't; it opens in, not out. I take a step back and scan the flashlight across every inch of the heavy metal door, looking for a recessed handle like the one on the outside, but there's nothing. The surface on this side is smooth and unadorned metal.

Odd, I think, the Etruscans wouldn't have made a door like this; it must be from the Middle Ages when the tomb was discovered. But why would anyone have made a door like this to a tomb? Who were they trying to keep out?

Unless it was to keep someone—or some *thing—in.*

I realize I'm shivering in only my T-shirt, the cold of the tomb seeping into my exposed skin. I imagine the cold sinking deeper and deeper into my body. I imagine never being warm again.

I grit my teeth to keep them from chattering and examine the edge of the door, looking for a gap wide enough to dig my fingertips into and pull the door open. Surely over all these centuries the doorframe has shifted, allowing a gap. But although I'm able to dig my fingers in between the door and the jamb, I can't get enough purchase to pull. All I get for my troubles are broken nails. When I pull my hands back, I see that they're bloody—

When they found her buried beneath the ground, she'd torn out all her fingernails trying to claw her way out of her living tomb.

Where the hell did that gem come from? I wonder. Then I realize it came from a scene in *Death Takes the Castle* when Rick and Dora find the body of a nun who had been buried alive in a crypt. I wrote it.

Serves you right, I tell myself, turning from the immovable door and heading back down the stairs, *to suffer one of the horrible fates you dreamt up for your fictional characters.* Sonia had been right when she said that we had started all of this, only Fred didn't deserve the blame. I was the one who had dreamt up the story of *Death Takes the Castle,* desperate for a diversion from my failed dissertation and as a ploy to spend more time with handsome and charming Fred Morgan. If only I had left him to write his literary novel. No one ever got buried alive in an Etruscan tomb in a literary novel.

When I get back to the tomb, I point my flashlight to where I left Fred—and find that he's gone.

"Fred?" I cry, my voice echoing in the vaulted empty space as if I am the only one here.

"Down here," he calls back.

I follow his voice around the sarcophagus and find him crouched on the other side. Instead of applying pressure to his wound he's running his left hand over the relief along the side of the sarcophagus.

"What are you doing?" I demand, crouching down beside him. "You have to keep pressure on that." He allows me to push him back against the wall and press my sodden shirt compress to his shoulder.

"I wanted to know what was on this side. I thought it might give us some answers . . . Any luck with the door?"

"No. Maybe if I can find something to wedge into the gap . . ." I strafe the room with my flashlight but there's nothing here but the sarcophagus and the now-empty treasure chest. Maybe if I break the chest apart, I can use a wooden plank to pry the door open. "Keep pressing this," I tell him as I get up and walk to the foot of the sarcophagus. I seize the chest in both hands and crack it against the stone lid of the sarcophagus, picturing Greg and Sonia's smug faces. It explodes with a satisfying crack—and then dissolves into a pile of useless pulp. Something metal clangs to the floor.

"What was that?" Fred asks, starting to crawl toward the sound.

"Stay put," I bark, aiming my flashlight on the floor. Something glints in its beam. I stoop to pick up a gold coin. "Look. Sonia missed one." I hand Fred the coin and sit back down beside him, checking that he's still applying pressure to his wound.

"Great. If we had two you could use them to cover my eyes as fare to the Ferryman."

"Shut up," I say. "You're not going to die. Someone will come for us. Someone will figure out that the clue leads to the poison garden and they'll find the entrance to the tomb."

"Sure," Fred says, sounding unconvinced. "In the middle of the night, in the middle of the gardens . . ." His voice drifts off. I shine the flashlight in his face and he blinks, struggling to keep his eyes open.

"Hey, no napping. I'll go crazy sitting here with no one to talk to."

"Is that why you roped me into being your writing partner twenty years ago? You needed a Watson to your Holmes?"

I snort. "You're much more like Hastings, with your love of fast cars and eye for beautiful women."

"Ouch," he says, clutching his chest as if I've inflicted a new wound. "Kick a man when he's down. Hastings isn't exactly the brightest bulb in the pack, but I suppose you're right about the cars and the beautiful women. I picked you, didn't I?"

"Did you?" I ask. "I always thought I picked you."

"I fell in love with you the first time I laid eyes on you," he says, all kidding gone from his voice. "You were in the chapel, kneeling on the floor, making a rubbing of a twelfth-century inscription and presenting a very fetching view of your bottom."

"What are you talking about? We met in the taverna."

He shakes his head. "Nah, I saw you days before that and plotted to run into you in the taverna. You were so absorbed in your research I figured the only way to get your attention was to pose with a notebook in my hands like a monk in the scriptorium."

"But you were really writing your novel—"

"Barely. I hadn't written a word for months. And then you came along with this incredible story of medieval heroines and crusading knights."

"I was just repeating a legend—"

"One that turns out to be true. Look at the sarcophagus—" He gestures weakly with his left hand, which I notice is trembling. I move closer, pressing my body against his and putting my arm around his shoulders so I can clasp his injured shoulder to staunch the bleeding. Then, with my free hand I point the flashlight at the sarcophagus. The carved figures spring to life under the beam. A knight, no longer in armor or mounted on a steed, but still wearing the cross of the Templars and using his sword as a crutch, walks along a path. He's hunched under the weight of a heavy chest strapped to his back and wears a long beard. He's looking up to a castle on a hill.

"It looks like the knight returning to Castellarosa," I say, "but he's old, as if he's been gone a long time." I track the beam to the next scene and narrate it to Fred, whose eyes are drooping. "When he gets to the castle it's full of nuns. He lays his treasure down in front of an old nun—she has a rose embroidered on her habit. I think *she's* Bianca Rosa."

"So she wasn't dead," Fred says in a voice so faint I can barely hear it. "He makes it back in time."

"Just," I say. "After he lays his treasure down, he collapses. The next scene shows Bianca Rosa tending to his sickbed."

"Just like you taking care of me."

"You wish," I say, jostling him. "You're going to be fine after this. You won't need me to wait on you."

"It's my right arm, Thea. I'll need you to write for me. Just as you always have. What happens next? Does she nurse him back to health?"

I've scanned the rest of the relief but I don't answer right away. I consider lying, making up a story. After all, that's what I've always done. It's what I'm good at. But I don't want my last words to Fred—and let's face it, these could be our last words to each other—to be lies.

"No," I say, "she doesn't. "The next scene is his funeral and his burial here along with the treasure chest and his sword, which she lays over his body. Only—" I move the flashlight closer to the sarcophagus, because its beam has become fainter. Don't die on me, I think, not sure if I mean the flashlight or Fred. I can barely make out the next scenes. "It looks like she takes the coins out of the chest. The next scenes show her buying paper and ink. More nuns come to the convent and work in—Fred! It looks like a scriptorium. I was right! There's was a scriptorium here. Bianca Rosa funded it with the gold from the knight's treasure."

Fred doesn't say anything right away and I'm afraid he's lost consciousness, but then his voice comes weakly as if from far away. "Then what's this?" He holds up the gold coin in his palm.

I take the coin from him and hold it under the dying beam of the flashlight. Is it my imagination or is its sheen a little tarnished? I scrape it against the stone of the sarcophagus—and the gold flakes off. "It's not solid gold," I say. "It's some other metal gilded with gold leaf. All this time, the treasure was false."

"That was never the treasure," Fred says, his voice a barely audible whisper.

"What do you mean?" I ask. When he doesn't answer I shine the flashlight at him. His eyes are closed, his face as white as marble and as lifeless.

"Fred!" I shake him, squeezing his wounded shoulder, not caring if I hurt him, but the motion shakes the last life out of the phone battery and we're plunged into darkness. "Fred?" I cry again, but he only slumps against me.

I wrap my arms around him and give in to the tears. This can't be the end of our story, I think helplessly; it's a terrible ending! I would never write it this way. Our readers would *hate* it! After all we've been through together, even the bad parts, I see now that I never gave up entirely that we would someday find a way back together and not in a maudlin, dying-together kind of way. Dora would never put up with that! Dora, as I'd written her, would never give up on Rick.

But then, maybe the problem lay in our foundational myth—Bianca Rosa, who was only reunited with her damned knight to have to bury him with his sword—

A Knight Templar's sword made of tempered steel.

I gently ease Fred down to the ground, feeling the tickle of breath as I lean over him. *Dum spiro, spero,* I think: "While there's breath, there's hope."

I get up and lay my hands on the edge of the sarcophagus. The lid must weigh a hundred pounds. I'll never be able to move it. I push against it anyway, digging my heels into the dirt. Nothing happens. I move a few feet away from Fred and brace my feet and shove with all my might, every muscle in my body straining against the unforgiving stone as though it were Death itself—that grinning trickster we put in our books as if we could placate him by making him our hero.

Please, I pray, *I don't need the books or the readers or the money. That was never the treasure. The treasure is Fred. It's us. It's our love. None of the rest of it matters.*

A coarse laugh greets my prayer. Death laughing at my supplications. The sound grows and I feel myself sliding. Falling. The sound is stone grating on stone. The sarcophagus lid is moving. I make one more gigantic heave until my muscles and sinews give out, strained to the breaking point, and I collapse over the lid, as if into the arms of the couple who lie there. I let myself take three breaths in their arms and then I feel around the edge. I find I've opened a narrow gap, enough to squeeze my hand into the sarcophagus. I find dust and brittle bones. I reach farther, my entire arm swallowed up by the open mouth of the grave, fingers reaching . . . until they graze cold metal.

The sword.

My hand scrabbles against it and pushes it farther away. I

draw my arm back and brace myself one more time against the edge of the lid. I place my feet against the wall until I'm suspended between the wall and the sarcophagus and push against the lid with every atom of my body. It moves . . . enough that the balance tips and the lid crashes to the ground and I fall headfirst into the stone casket, coughing on grave dust and bonemeal. I scrabble to find the sword and cut myself on its blade, still miraculously sharp after all these centuries. The pain revives me. I find the hilt and lift it from the dust and then use it to balance myself as I stand up and clamber out of the coffin.

For a second, I imagine how I must look, covered in grave dust, rising from an ancient sarcophagus with a sword in my hand like an avenging angel. Joan of Arc ready to do battle. I crouch beside Fred and feel for a pulse. It's weak, but still there. "Hold on," I tell him. "I'll be right back."

I grope my way to the stairs, the sword held in front of me so it clangs into the metal door so hard it makes my ears ring and my arm throb. I feel for the gap between door and jamb, insert the tip of the sword as far as it will go, and use it as a lever, praying the ancient metal doesn't cleave in two. Instead, it's the old wooden jamb that splinters and the door creaks open on its ancient hinges—

Into bright light.

Perhaps this has all been a hallucination and I am dying.

But then a voice comes from behind the light—"Praise God, I've found you!"—and I fall into the waiting arms of Sister Beatrice.

CHAPTER TWENTY-SIX

You poor child, you're covered in blood." Sister Beatrice clucks over me, holding me at arm's length. She's wearing a headlamp clamped over her wimple, making her look like a combination of a haloed saint and R2-D2 from *Star Wars*. Is she really here, I wonder, or am I hallucinating?

"It's not mine; it's Fred's," I say, grabbing her hand to reassure myself that she's real. What in the world is she doing here? But questions and explanations will have to wait. I pull her down the stairs. "Quick, we have to stop the bleeding and get him help."

Sister Beatrice goes straight to Fred and leans over him, her headlamp casting them both in a pool of light like a Renaissance painting of the Annunciation. The illusion fades as she extracts a first aid kit from her canvas knapsack and efficiently cleans and bandages Fred's shoulder.

"Is he going to be all right?" I ask.

"He's lost a lot of blood and his pulse is faint," she tells me, never one to mince words. "We have to get him to a hospital."

She looks around the room, the first glance she's spared since setting to work on Fred. "You found Bianca's tomb. I knew it was somewhere beneath the garden but I was never sure where."

"Is that what you came back for?"

She turns her headlamp on me, blasting me with light. "I came because your friend Deb contacted me with some questions about the lost treasure. I came here to meet with her and I realized as soon as I got here that the Wilsons had been selling off some of the old artifacts. In addition, the owners of the agriturismo I stayed in told me that the Wilsons had unpaid bills and debts to local businesses. I went to Florence to talk to an old friend in the art market to confirm my suspicions. I just got back last night and heard about poor Deb's death and I came right here—and saw the Wilsons heading out into the maze in the middle of the night and figured they were up to something. I thought I might find a hidden cache of stolen art, but instead I heard a shot and saw them coming out of the poison garden so I came down here to see if anyone had been hurt—and I was right!"

She aims the beam down on Fred and then takes out of her kit a small ChapStick-size tube and wafts it under Fred's nose. He moans and blinks open his eyes, staring first at the haloed nun crouched above him and then at me, his eyes widening at my appearance under my coating of grave dust.

"Are we dead?" he asks me.

"Not yet," I tell him "Sister Beatrice has come to our rescue."

"Only after your wife burst out of the crypt with a crusader's sword," Sister Beatrice tells him. "Can you stand up, young man? We can help you but we can't carry you."

Fred glances from the nun back to me, his eyes drifting to the sword lying by my side. "I guess I'd better before you two go full Valkyrie on me."

He groans, apologizing to Sister Beatrice each time he curses, as we help him to his feet. I hand him the sword to use as a walking stick. It must remind him of the carving of the old knight using his sword as a cane and he glances back at the now open sarcophagus with its lid lying by its side.

"Don't . . . tell . . . me," he pants as we make our slow and laborious way to the stairs. "After . . . I passed out, the mummified remains of Bianca Rosa and her knight burst out of their tombs . . . to pursue the looters of their treasure."

"I'm afraid I'm the one who pushed open the lid. I had to get the sword to wedge open the door." I look down, expecting to find the lid broken in two, but it is miraculously intact.

"What else could you do?" Sister Beatrice says. "I suppose the Wilsons took the treasure."

"They took the coins," I say, "but they'll be disappointed in them. It looks like they're not solid gold."

I show her the coin we'd found. She waves it aside. "Of course," she says impatiently. "I long ago guessed that Bianca used the coins to fund her scriptorium. But the chest? Did they take that?"

We've reached the stairs and I'm much more interested in getting Fred up them and to a hospital than discussing long-lost treasure. "They left it, but I'm afraid I wrecked that, too." I point at the pile of pulp and splinters lying at the foot of the sarcophagus. To my annoyance, Sister Beatrice leaves Fred's side to go investigate. She waves impatiently at me. "We can't fit three abreast anyway; start up the stairs with Fred. I'll be right there."

She's right. We can't even fit two across. I make Fred, using the sword as a crutch, go first and I stay at his back, supporting his weight as best I can while giving him not-so-gentle nudges upward.

"I feel like Orpheus . . . leading Eurydice out of hell," he gasps.

"Sure, you get to be the hero," I grouse. "I just moved a five-hundred-pound plinth, rescued a thousand-year-old sword, and found a nun with a medical kit, but I'm just the helpless damsel."

"Orpheus isn't much of a hero," Fred says. "He loses the girl. Promise me you're not going to vanish before we get out of here."

"I'm not going anywhere," I tell him. "And certainly not back down there. I may never go into a basement or subway again."

When we reach the door, I'm relieved to find it's still ajar. He pauses on the threshold and examines the splintered doorjamb. "It looks like you hewed it with a hatchet." He's leaning heavily on the sword's hilt, like the hoary knight on the sarcophagus. My heart catches in my throat at the sight of his face, which has aged years, as if we have been trapped underground for decades and not hours. I can see the old man that he will become—*if* we can get him to the hospital. *Where's Sister Beatrice?*

I turn to find the nun right behind me. "It looks like you took a hatchet to the chest as well," she says.

I notice that the knapsack strapped to her back is bulging and wonder what she's found of value in all that pulp, but before I can ask her, she strides ahead, leading the way out of the crypt. She keeps up a steady monologue like a tour guide as she goes.

"This must have been the crypt of the original tenth-century chapel. After it was destroyed and the castle became a monastery, the new chapel was built within the walls and the gardens were grown over the old crypt. Bianca Rosa knew about it, though, and she selected it for her knight's burial and eventually her own."

"But why hide the knight's tomb?" I ask, trying to keep up with her while struggling to keep Fred upright. "And her own?"

"Because she'd become the abbess," Sister Beatrice shouts back at us. "And had a reputation to maintain and a monastery to run. She couldn't give the Church any reason to take away her position and burying her lover in the chapel might have done just that. Nor would she have wanted to give up control of the gold. The Church would have taken it—a nun couldn't possess personal wealth, after all—and allocated it to other monasteries. She wanted it to finance her scriptorium."

"But why did she have fake gold coins made?" I ask.

"Maybe it was to have something to give the bishops if they ever learned about the treasure."

"And the story that Bianca Rosa was buried alive with her knight?" I ask as we climb the steps out of the upper crypt.

"A foundational myth," Sister Beatrice says, looking back at us from the top of the stairs. "A brilliant public relations stunt to cement the reputation of the monastery."

"That's quite a story," I say, helping Fred up the steps.

"Yeah . . . a great backstory," Fred says, "but what about *our* present story. Greg and Sonia might be halfway to Rome by now. We can't let them get away with killing Deb and Nadine and . . ."

"Kailee and Lindsay." I finish naming the dead for him when he runs out of breath. We've come out of the crypt, into the poison garden, its pale fleshy blooms flushed pink with the light of dawn. I feel like we've risen from the dead. I turn toward the warm glow—and realize that something is wrong. The glow in the sky isn't the sun rising.

"The bastards," Fred swears. "They've set Castellarosa on fire."

SISTER BEATRICE CHARGES ahead of us. I can feel Fred's impatience to go faster, but he's too weak. We limp along, his weight on my arm heavier and heavier as we go, in silence. Saving our breath . . . or not wanting to speculate on who else we may have lost. As we get closer, I smell the smoke. It's so thick in the air that I can't make out the shape of the castle until we come out of the hedge maze and then what I see is pure chaos. The lawn below the veranda is crowded with hotel guests in robes and nightgowns and pajamas. I spot Zoe in a Hello Kitty romper, her eyes a racoon mask of smudged mascara. A woman in a quilted bathrobe, whom I belatedly recognize as Sue from Pittsburgh, has her arm around her. Buck wanders by in boxer shorts and a Philadelphia Eagles T-shirt, dictating notes into his phone, and Pete, in a plaid flannel robe and CPAP mask dangling from his neck, is sitting on a lawn chair writing in his notebook.

What ghouls we writers are, I think, but then I spot Joan handing out water bottles and Shay, in an elegant silk kimono with a stethoscope around her neck, checking people for smoke inhalation. I head toward her, figuring that she's the best equipped to help Fred. Her eyes widen as she sees Fred and takes in his bloody shoulder and chalk-white face.

"What the hell happened to you?" she demands, helping me get Fred into a chair and immediately checking his pulse and strapping a blood pressure cuff around his arm.

"Greg Wilson shot him," I say. "And locked us underground in a tomb. Sister Beatrice bandaged him but he's lost a lot of blood."

"No kidding, his blood pressure is dangerously low. We need to get him to a hospital stat. And who the hell is Sister Beatrice?"

I look around for the nun but she's vanished into the crowd and smoke. *Had I imagined her?* I turn to Fred for confirmation but his eyes are closed. "Never mind," I say. "I need someone to drive us to a hospital—" Before I can finish my sentence the blat of a siren interrupts us and I see a police car driving across the lawn. It stops in front of us and Detective Bardi gets out.

"A nun just ordered me to take you to the hospital," he barks, looking surprised and unaccustomedly abashed at himself for following a nun's orders. "As if I don't have enough to do catching whoever lit this fire."

"It was Greg and Sonia Wilson," I tell him as Shay helps me drag Fred into the back seat of the police car. "And they'll be halfway to Florence or Rome by now. You can chase them as soon as you drop us at the nearest hospital."

He looks like he's ready to put up an argument but Shay nails him with an icy stare. "This man will die if you don't get him to a hospital right away."

Detective Bardi throws up his hands, no match for doctors and nuns, and gets into the driver's seat while I get in the passenger side. I glance back at the castle as we pull away. There's a line of volunteers, led by Joan and Barb, spraying water on the facade with garden hoses. "Did everyone get out?" I ask.

"We think so," Bardi says. "Your friends organized a phone chain to make sure everyone was accounted for. You and your husband and the Wilsons were the only ones who weren't. I have to admit they were pretty damned organized about it."

I smile to myself. *Of course they were.*

As if to make up for his lapse into praise he barks at me, "You'd better tell me the whole story."

I don't mind. Telling stories is what I do best.

AS HE RACES down the mountain, taking the hairpin turns like a race car driver, I tell Detective Bardi everything that the Wilsons told us in the crypt—how Sonia poisoned Deb's drink to get her to tell them where the treasure was, and then, when she died, how they became obsessed with finding the treasure to save their failing hotel even if it meant killing Kailee, Nadine, and Lindsay.

"All for some gold coins," he mutters. "Greedy Americans."

"Not all Americans are like that," I tell him. "But yes, plenty are and as it turns out the gold isn't even real."

I take out the gold coin from my pocket and hold it up in the light. The sun catches it, sending prisms dancing around the car. "Gilt," I say, scratching at the thin veneer on the coin. Bardi glances at the fake but dazzling coin for a dangerous second as he takes a tight curve—and then slams on the brakes just in time before plummeting off the mountain. We skid to a stop inches from a gully that has opened up in the road. The bridge is gone, washed out in last night's rain. My heart, still thudding from the abrupt stop, sinks at the sight of it. How will we get Fred to the hospital now?

I look back at him as Bardi, cursing under his breath, gets out of the car. Fred, his face gray, is breathing in shallow gasps. I look back through the windshield at Bardi, who's standing at the edge of the gulley looking down. I get out of the car and scan the road—or what's left of it. The old stone arch of the aqueduct, built by the Romans, is intact, a narrow causeway spanning the void. Too narrow for a car but if we could get Fred across it, we could still get a lift to the hospital.

I join Detective Bardi to tell him my plan, such as it is, and then I see what he's looking at. Thirty or so feet below us, caught in the cataract of the swollen stream, is a red sports car that I recognize as the Porsche parked behind the hotel that belonged to the Wilsons. It's twisted around a tree like a swizzle stick and cantilevered above a sheer drop to the valley below. From here it looks like a child's toy, discarded and stamped on. It's hard to believe anyone is in it, but then I spy a spill of blond hair and a flash of a white hand. The sound of sirens draws my eyes away.

An ambulance comes around the curve and brakes just before the washed-out bridge. Two paramedics jump out and wave their arms at us. Bardi shouts something in Italian at them and a spirited consultation ensues in shouts and hand gestures, which results in the two paramedics making their way across the aqueduct with a stretcher.

"They'll take you and your husband to the hospital, where you'll stay put until I interview you both," he says sternly. But then, still looking down at the wreck of steel and flesh below us, his face and tone soften as he mutters something in Italian under his breath. Before I can ask him what he means he begins climbing down into the gully toward the wreck. Why? I wonder. They must surely be dead. Watching his black-clad form wading his way across the shallow stream puts me in mind of a pilgrim making his way on the Via Francigena. The water is so bright around him that the dazzle of it seems to swallow him up. I shade my eyes from its harsh glitter and then realize why it's so bright. The stream is full of the gilded coins. They must have spilled out in the crash as the car plummeted down the ravine. It must have looked to Greg and Sonia like a shower of gold in their last moments. Suddenly the words Bardi said take shape in my head. Not Italian, but Latin. *Belua fera est avaritia.*

Greed is a savage beast.

CHAPTER TWENTY-SEVEN

The hospital is in a small town in the valley about fifteen kilometers from Castellarosa. I remember visiting it once twenty years ago when we took the train to Florence. The hospital is small and I worry they won't take good enough care of Fred but the paramedics assure me it is more than adequate for what he needs—blood and fluids—and to go any farther will put Fred at risk. When his heartbeat flatlines two kilometers away from the hospital and it takes a defibrillator to revive him, I quit worrying about finding somewhere bigger and better.

Although small, the hospital is clean and staffed with competent and caring professionals. A surgeon removes the bullet from Fred's shoulder and stitches him up, stabilizing his shoulder, which was shattered by the bullet. When he shows me the X-ray I'm amazed that Fred had been able to function at all with that much damage.

"You must have been in excruciating pain!" I say accusingly when he regains consciousness.

He tries to shrug it off, but the motion awakens the pain in his shoulder and he grimaces instead. "I was in shock," he says, and then, smiling crookedly, "Besides, would Rick have moaned and groaned over a mere *flesh* wound?"

"Rick is a fictional character who can't die until we say so," I lecture.

"I thought that was the idea," he says, no longer smiling. "To kill off Rick after he makes a grand heroic gesture. Wasn't taking a bullet good enough?"

"No," I snap. "You were right—it's too corny. That scene needs work."

He lifts his bandaged arm a fraction, causing another wince. "You'll have to do the writing for me," he says. "How's your shorthand?"

I start to tell him he can damn well hunt and peck with his good arm before he turns me into his goddamned secretary, but his eyelids begin to sink and I tell him instead to rest up so he can get back to work. Then I go to the waiting room and sob for half an hour over how close I came to losing him.

Since it's clear he's going to be in the hospital for a while, I rent a room at an agriturismo on the edge of town next to an olive grove, the same one where Sister Beatrice had been staying. Joan visits and sniffs at the drab decor and tells me I should have Fred airlifted to a major hospital in Milan, where at least I could stay in the Four Seasons.

"After this experience I'm only staying at name-brand hotels where the proprietors aren't homicidal maniacs. None of this would have happened at a Marriott! I knew the Wilsons were shady when they stinted on the pillows and hangers."

Joan had been right that the Wilsons had been cutting corners because they were in financial distress. When Detective Bardi stops by the hospital, he tells us that the Wilsons were up to their eyeballs in debt and hadn't paid their bills at the local vendors and contractors for months. "The possibility of finding a cache of crusader's gold must have seemed like the answer to all their problems."

"They could have just waited for the treasure to be found," Fred says. "The publicity would have sold out the hotel for years."

"Maybe," Bardi agrees with a shrug, "or closed it down while the Ministry of Culture investigated the site and dug up the grounds."

"Is that what they're doing?" I ask, dismayed at the thought of the ancient hedge maze, poison garden, and heirloom rosebushes uprooted.

"Not yet, but the Ministry of Culture has seized the property and it will be determining if it should be declared *of essential cultural significance* and what the best handling of its use will be in the future. The Wilsons would have been aware that was a possibility. And besides—" He shrugs again, putting his whole body into the gesture and adding open palms lifted to the sky as if weighing the Wilsons' fate in his hands. "*Chi troppo vuole, nulla stringe.*"

Before I can parse a translation, Fred provides one. "'Those who want too much, end up with nothing.'" He grins, proud of his Italian, and I try to return the smile, but all I can think of is how close I came to losing everything.

ALTHOUGH I'VE BECOME fond of my room overlooking the olive grove and the goats that wander the property freely, and have no need of a Four Seasons, I do wonder if we shouldn't consult a more prestigious orthopedic surgeon for the additional surgeries Fred will need on his shattered shoulder. I mention this to him when his doctor signs off on him leaving the hospital, but he tells me he likes the surgeon here, with whom he's established a camaraderie based on a mutual love of soccer, Brunello wines, and Italian cars. "Besides," he adds, "we need to stay here to finish the book."

"Book? What book?"

"*Death Takes a Bow*, obviously," he says, rolling his eyes. "I've been looking over your original outline—" He produces the pages I gave him on the plane that he'd marked up in red a million years ago. How did he get them? I wonder. Then I remember that Joan had brought our suitcases from the hotel when the fire department had allowed guests to collect their personal belongings. My clothes had smelled of smoke and I'd noticed that my portfolio was missing. She must have mistakenly put it in Fred's suitcase. "And I have some notes."

"But I thought you didn't want to end the series? And there's the book you started in Scotland, the one you showed Nadine, and . . ." I trail off, thinking of all that's happened since I wrote the outline of *Death Takes a Bow*. All the deaths. "I thought after everything that's happened the last thing you'd want to write about was murder."

"Are you kidding?" he asks incredulously. "After finally getting to meet some real-life murderers? Not that I don't think we can improve on their methods. As I said, I have notes."

Copious notes, as it turns out, all dictated into his iPhone and garbled by the voice-recognition software. And so, when we've settled into the agriturismo—the owners have given us the run of the whole barn as long as we're willing to share with the goats—we begin work on *Death Takes a Bow*. Slowly at first, since only one of us can write or type and we disagree on almost everything.

"Too brutal," I deem one method of extermination I'd originally suggested. "We can't kill her, she's too nice," I complain of one intended victim.

"You've gone soft," Fred tells me. "They aren't real people; they're characters."

"Then what's the point?" I ask. "If we don't care about them, they won't seem real to our readers."

"If you don't let anything bad happen to them, the readers won't get past the first chapter."

We bicker over cappuccinos and home-baked cornetti in the morning and hand-rolled pici and glasses of the local red wine at night while from the kitchen come shouts and the clash of banging pans. Our young hosts, Valentina and Gianni, routinely shout at each other in Italian while they cook, sounding as if they're trying to kill each other, but they always emerge smiling, their faces serene and rosy as they carry in plates of steaming pasta and fresh-baked bread. Fred and I don't stop arguing, but every disagreement leads to words on the page, the scenes taking shape and falling into place like tiles in a mosaic. The writing feels familiar but different. The story takes on a bit of gravitas from being the last story and because of what Rick and Dora have been through together. The mysteries they've solved and the deaths they've seen have taken a toll on them. Just as they have on us.

One evening, sipping wine under the pergola and watching the shadows lengthen beneath the olive trees as the sky turns rose gold, Fred asks, "Do you think they stay together?"

I know he's talking about Rick and Dora, but also not *just* about Rick and Dora. Afraid to answer, I ask a question instead. "Why wouldn't they? After all they've been through together—"

"Exactly because of all they've been through together," Fred says. "Every time they look at each other they'll be reminded of all the horrors they've seen—all the death."

For a moment I think about a day in San Miguel. Fred and I had wandered into a little church, exploring it for material for the book. I'd been inspecting a painting and realized Fred had wandered off, no doubt to read in one the pews, I figured, because he was often bored by churches. But when I looked for him, I'd found him in a small side chapel dominated by a painting of the Madonna and Child. There was a book spread out beside the votive candles in which people could write prayers for those they'd lost. Looking down, I'd recognized Fred's handwriting.

For Beatrice, he'd written, the name we'd chosen for our child if she'd been a girl. If she had lived.

When I turned around, Fred had gone. Why hadn't I gone after him? Why hadn't I ever told him that I'd seen what he'd written?

Because it hurt too much and I couldn't bear to see that same hurt in his eyes.

"But then, who else would understand what they've seen and done?" I say now. "And what they've lost."

"I wouldn't blame Dora for having had enough of Rick and all his ridiculous stunts," he says.

"Like saving her life?"

"Like putting her life in danger in the first place."

I have no answer to that one. But that night, instead of parting at the doors to our separate rooms, I take Fred's hand and lead him to mine.

WE FINISH THE penultimate chapter in the first week of December, just in time for Fred's second round of surgery. "Let's leave the last chapter until after that," Fred suggests.

In the past, I was always the one who wanted to wait to write the last chapter—the epilogue—until we'd reread and edited the whole manuscript, to remind ourselves of what needed tying up. Fred would be in favor of just ending where the action ended. *I hate tying everything up with a bow,* he'd complain, *it's too neat.*

World order has to be restored, I would counter.

As if that's ever possible, he'd contest.

This time it feels like a delaying tactic. When we're done with the book and the surgery there will be no reason to stay in Italy. It will be time to go back to New York. But where in New York? To our separate homes in Rhinebeck and the city? We may be sharing a bedroom but we haven't talked once about our future.

The surgery goes well but Fred comes back looking pale and drawn. Valentina frets over him, making him special bone broths and restorative herbal teas. I offer to read aloud to him and he chooses *Curtain: Poirot's Last Case,* a book I've always found unbearably sad—the wheelchair-bound Poirot haunting the emptied halls of Styles, the scene of his first case with his *bon ami* Hastings. The melancholy description of the grand old English country house turned into a shabby hotel reminds me of Castellarosa and I wonder what it's like now since the fire.

"I was thinking I'd go up to Castellarosa," I tell Fred a few days before Christmas. "Do you want to come?"

I expect that he'll say no, but instead he nods gravely as if acceding to a grim but necessary duty. We rent a car and drive through the valley, past frostbitten grapevines and rust-colored hills. Heavy clouds obscure the tops of the hills and scraps of fog blow across the steep road. It feels like the mountain doesn't want us to come back. The bridge where the Wilsons plunged to their deaths has been repaired but only one lane is in service. *Periculosa!* A sign warns.

"No duh," Fred remarks as I inch across the narrow causeway, keeping my eyes off the treacherous cataract below.

The fog continues to play peekaboo with the road the rest of the way up and then descends like a stage curtain over the castle on the last approach. "Like that scene in *Rebecca* when the drive to Manderley keeps twisting and hiding the house," I say, hoping to lighten the mood with a literary reference.

"More like Brigadoon," Fred mutters. "Maybe the whole place has sunk into a wormhole and we'll go with it."

I consider turning back but there's no place to turn around on the narrow mountain road. Finally, the massive stone walls of the Porta Rosa loom out of the fog. I park the car in the lay-by, noticing an ancient Citroën and a battered pickup truck. "Someone's here," I point out to Fred.

"Looks like a repairman," he says, ducking his head to look into the Citroën, where a St. Christopher medal hangs from the rearview mirror, "and a nun."

Sister Beatrice had emailed to tell me she was working with the Ministry of Culture on a report that would decide the fate of the property, but I didn't expect to find her here so close to Christmas. As we walk slowly up the stone steps, Fred pausing every few feet to rest, a light snow begins to fall, a rarity in Tuscany but not unheard-of. The snow intensifies the silence, which feels like a blanket muffling the very stone. I wonder if this is how the knight felt on his return to Castellarosa, not knowing what he would find there—the castle destroyed, his beloved dead or married or become a nun, as turned out to be the case.

The bare stone facade that appears out of the fog might be the blasted mansion of Thornfield Hall or Manderley, destroyed by fire. But at least it still stands. Thanks to the efforts of the conference guests only part of the castle burned down. The rest stands as it has for over a thousand years. The one glaring detail that brings me back to the present is the bright yellow sign warning of danger and prohibiting entry to all but essential staff and workers. The sign has the seal of the Ministry of Culture and the emblem of a local university.

The caution stops me but not Fred, who takes my hand and leads me across the ancient stone lintel into the dark empty entrance hall. Denuded of tapestries and furniture, the castle has been restored to its medieval core. It's as if the fire has burned away all the modern trappings and stripped it down to its essential self. As we stand there on the threshold, I glance over at Fred. His face is leaner since the surgery and months of painful rehab and he holds himself differently. Gone is the ease with which he used to stride into a room, replaced by an awareness of his own mortality. He, too, has been stripped of something over these last few months—his old habitual confidence, the belief in his own invincibility. I think of the knight, broken by war and his long journey, coming face-to-face with his beloved. What did they see in each other's faces after all those years apart? Was there some fragment of their past selves they still recognized? When Fred glances back at me, I wonder what he sees. What have these months taken away from me? I listen for an answer in my own head and hear instead the echo of voices in the lofty hall. For a moment I imagine they are the echoes of the past, the knight and Bianca Rosa greeting each other after their long separation.

"Well, there you are at last. I thought I was going to have to send out a search party to find you." Not Bianca Rosa greeting her long-lost lover, but Joan, storming into the hall like a crusader herself, armored in a quilted vest, Lycra leggings, and sheepskin boots.

"What are you doing here?" I ask. "I thought you went back to Texas."

"I did—and wish I were there now instead of this drafty old castle, but someone has to manage Deb's bequest and Pete was going to blow it all on candle wax and paper and glue. Come on—it's too damned cold in here; we've set up camp in the library."

"Pete's here?" Fred asks, as we follow Joan down the hall.

"Of course—and before you complain that he hasn't been to visit it's because I told him to leave you two alone while you were finishing your book. Have you finished it, then?"

"All but the last chapter," I tell Joan.

She catches my eye as we pause outside the library. "Winding things up is always the hardest part," she says. "Divvying up rewards and costs and figuring out who gets a happy ending." I have a feeling she's not just talking about book endings.

"Or even what constitutes a happy ending," I say. "Fred hates endings that tie everything up in a neat bow."

Joan raises an eyebrow, refraining from comment, and holds the door open—to a scene that might have come out of a medieval book of hours. A long oak table is set at the end of the room beneath a row of mullioned windows. The pale wintry light coming through the old glass limns everything with an otherworldly aura—the book open on the table, the face of the old nun bending over it, the slight, balding man beside her. *Nun and Scribe*, it might be called. Sister Beatrice raises her face, her round glasses winking in the wintry sunlight, and smiles.

"Ah, you've finished, then."

Has everybody been waiting for us to finish the book?

Before I can explain again that we still have the last chapter to write, Sister Beatrice spreads her hands open above the tome upon the table. "Come see what you have found."

As I approach the table, I notice there's a space heater warming the room and a tray set up on the windowsill with an electric kettle and tea things. The room has the air of an expedition encampment and I feel a pang of envy at the tight-knit group gathered around the table.

"Found?" I repeat. "I don't remember finding a book." But then, staring at the mottled pages on the table I recall the lump of pulp lying at the bottom of the chest I destroyed. "It was in the chest," I say, sinking down into the chair Pete draws out for me.

"Yes," Sister Beatrice says. "You found the *real* treasure."

SISTER BEATRICE STARTS to give us the summary but Joan breaks in with the elevator pitch. "It's *The Da Vinci Code* meets *The Notebook*."

Pete makes a face and Joan sighs. "Okay, it's *Abelard and Héloïse* meets some other boring historical book nobody's ever heard of," she amends.

"It's Bianca Rosa's story of how she met Rossino—"

"That was the knight's name?" I ask.

"It's the name she gives him," Pete says. "She calls him her red rose."

"And so the story in the poem is true?" I ask.

"Sort of," Sister Beatrice says. "They met here at the castle of Bianca's father and fell in love. He was a knight bound in service to fight in the Crusades. She swore to him that she would wait for him to come back. When her father tried to force her to marry, she said she would take a vow of celibacy instead. She refused to eat or drink until he allowed her to take the veil and he, rather than lose his daughter, gave not just his permission but this castle as her dowry."

"And she became a nun?"

"Yes," Sister Beatrice says, "and eventually an abbess who dreamed of creating a scriptorium to copy the books brought back from the Crusades. When her knight returned with a treasure in gold she kept it secret from the Church and used it to found a scriptorium."

"Not as good a story as being buried alive or betraying her father," Joan grouses.

"Better for her, though," Pete says.

"And better for the young women she sheltered here," Sister Beatrice adds. "And for the books they copied and produced. She brought master scribes and illuminators and bookbinders to Castellarosa and began a scriptorium—the only one run by nuns in Italy."

"Why did no one ever know about this?" I ask, remembering how my adviser had scoffed at the idea of a twelfth-century scriptorium run by nuns.

"We think that after her death the Church shut down the scriptorium and effaced her memory," Pete says.

"They took the fruits of her labor for themselves and vanquished her memory lest other women look to her as a model," Sister Beatrice says. "As she suspected they would, which is why she had this—the true story of her life—buried with her. *The treasure of my heart,* she wrote, *is the story of our love and what it inspired.*" I remember the words on the gravestone Deb found: *Hic iacet Bianca . . . thesaurum cordis mei.* It hadn't been a gravestone at all, but a marker pointing to the tomb—and to her book. *Here lies the treasure of my heart.*

"Here—" Sister Beatrice turns the book toward me and points to the last lines, a coda centered on the page. It takes me a moment to decipher the ancient script. The capital letter is a chalice intertwined with rose vines, one white and one red. But then, as if rearranged by a spell, the words spill into my head as if directly from the mouth of the woman who penned them a thousand years ago. Fred, who has come to sit beside me, lets out a long breath when he has finished reading them. I look up and meet Sister Beatrice's faded blue eyes.

"Why is the book still here?" I ask. "And not in a lab somewhere at a university or a museum?"

"Because this is where it belongs," she says simply, "and where it should be read. The Ministry of Culture has taken over the building and we have proposed that Castellarosa be made into a center for early women's writing."

"We?" I echo.

"Deb bequeathed her life savings to fund a foundation for women's writing," Joan says.

"With a proviso for scholarships for women scholars."

"She named Pete and me co-trustees." Joan grimaces but it turns into a fond smile as she looks at Pete. "So, we're stuck with each other."

"For a worthy cause," Pete says, returning her smile with doubled warmth.

"Wait," Fred says, "how much money did Deb have?

"A lot!" Joan says. "There was oil on the family farm and she invested wisely. But you're the real expert," Joan adds. "We wanted to ask you to write the story of Bianca Rosa and her book—"

"But we thought we should wait until you finished your last Death Takes a Holiday book. Have you—"

"All but the last chapter," Fred and I say in unison.

"Well, what are you waiting for?" Joan asks.

We talk and drink tea and plan and strategize for another hour, and then, seeing that Fred is getting tired, I suggest a brief walk in the garden before our drive home. Although there's not much to see in the gardens this time of year, no one points that out or offers to accompany us.

The snow has stopped and the sky has brightened to a polished bronze sheen as we walk slowly up the cypress alley toward the bell tower. We walk in silence to the crag overlooking the valley. The wind is sharp here and smells like woodsmoke and pine.

"What do you think?" Fred says finally. "Do you want to stay and work on the Bianca Rosa book?"

"I'm hardly a scholar—" I begin, turning to him. And then I realize that's not what he's asking. "That depends."

"On?"

"On where you'll be. Can you write your novel here? I'm not the only one who left something undone. "

I hold up my hands to take in the sweep of hilltop and valley, of olive groves and ancient stone battlements, the quiet that hangs in the air like a hawk coasting on currents. But he doesn't look away from me when he gives me his answer.

I am the vessel,
Your words fill me and I spill them out to the wind,
And lo, behold—mirabile dictu!—
I am still full,
Overflowing with wonder.

"De Amore Rosae"
Bianca Rosa de Castellarosa

ACKNOWLEDGMENTS

Thanks, as always, to my fabulous agent, Robin Rue, and her assistant, Beth Miller, and everyone at Writers House for their ongoing support and encouragement. Thank you to my wonderful editor, Tessa James, and to all the people at William Morrow whose hard work brings books into the world.

I was lucky enough to have a real-life Castellarosa in which to write this. Enormous thanks to Jennie Lee for having the vision to create the Essere Residency in Tuscany and giving me the opportunity to write there. Thank you to Valentina Grossi and the whole Grossi family for sharing their home and hospitality. And thank you to all the residents of Essere Fall 2024 for putting up with my murder plots and inspiring me with your dedication to your craft: Cynthia Manick, Eden and Jeff Poynter, Ellen Caldwell, Fe Vasquez, Hathaway Barry, Hope Houston, Jeanne Ferron, Linda and Michael Sattel, Lynne Budny, Melana Bontrager, Naomi Nye, Princess Mhoon, Raven Miller, Robin and Michael Wellner, Samantha Melvin, Suzanne Dubus, and Tracy and Tom Corvo, with special thanks to Kala

Kaspar, Holiday Dmitri, and Melissa Grace Young for indulging me in my quest to see an abbey, and to Maria Deeley and Rebecca Henriquez Lazouras for being the best Castello flatmates ever.

Thank you once again to Nathaniel Bellows, Gary Feinberg, Nancy Johnson, Andrea Massar, Wendy Gold Rossi, Scott Silverman, and Ethel Wesdorp for reading early drafts and giving me your invaluable feedback.

Thank you to my college Latin professor, Robert Pounder, who provided me with the Latin translation of Thea's writing motto, *Ita scribendo atque vivendo*.

The idea for this book came to me on a train from Naples to Ascea Marina where my husband, Lee Slonimsky, was to receive a prize for the Italian translation of his collection of poetry, *Pythagoras in Love*. As we gently disagreed on the itinerary of our previous research trips to Italy, we both simultaneously asked each other, "Have we ever taken a trip that wasn't about writing?" To which I think Fred and Thea would have replied, "Why would we ever?" Thank you, Lee, for always being the best partner, in writing as in life.

ABOUT THE AUTHOR

CAROL GOODMAN's rich and prolific career includes novels such as *The Widow's House* and *The Night Visitors,* winners of the 2018 and 2020 Mary Higgins Clark Awards. Her books have been translated into sixteen languages. She lives in the Hudson Valley, New York.